"We could kiss right now, Grace.

"I could even take you home and we could make love," Levi went on.

Yes. Grace's rational mind had shut off and she knew it. What was more, she didn't care....

But he was still standing back from her.

"We could do it for old times' sake and it might be kind of nice—it might even be fantastic."

It *would* be fantastic. She knew it would....

"Levi." She tried not to sound as though she was pleading.

He placed an arm around her shoulder—a gesture almost brotherly in nature. She leaned against him, as close to collapse as she'd ever felt in her life.

Levi Shanahan was her ex-lover—and it appeared he was determined to stay that way.

Dear Reader,

When I told my daughters that Superromance was going to
publish *Jessie's Father,* my eight-year-old chanted,
"Mommy's going to be published! Mommy's going to be
published!" My ten-year-old was quick to correct her:
"Mommy's not getting published. Her book is!"

And here it is.

Jessie's Father was a delight to write, although the research
was a little onerous. Since the hero owns and manages a
gourmet coffeehouse, Jolt O' Java, I felt compelled to spend
hours at my own neighborhood coffeehouse, Bean Scene,
absorbing the atmosphere and sipping lattes. Oh, well, you
know what they say about dirty jobs...

I hope you enjoy Grace and Levi's story. And may I
recommend a large moccachino with sprinkles on top to go
with it?

C.J. Carmichael

JESSIE'S FATHER
C.J. Carmichael

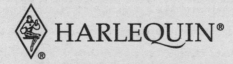

HARLEQUIN®

TORONTO • NEW YORK • LONDON
AMSTERDAM • PARIS • SYDNEY • HAMBURG
STOCKHOLM • ATHENS • TOKYO • MILAN • MADRID
PRAGUE • WARSAW • BUDAPEST • AUCKLAND

ISBN 0-373-70851-3

JESSIE'S FATHER

Copyright © 1999 by Carla Daum.

Visit us at www.romance.net

Printed in U.S.A.

I'd like to thank my fellow writers at the
Alberta Romance Writers' Association for the support and
encouragement they've given me over the years,
in particular Andrea, Terri and Marlene.

CHAPTER ONE

"ARE YOU IN POSITION?"

"Yes." Fourteen-year-old undercover agent, Jess Shanahan, breathed the reply into her father's cell phone, which she'd snuck out of his car last night after he'd gone to bed. He rarely used it, but still she felt nervous. It would be just her luck for him to blow a gasket or something on the Burrard Bridge today and need the phone. When he found out what had happened to it, he'd blow another gasket. She definitely wasn't supposed to be here, especially not now, right in the middle of Mr. Abbot's algebra review.

"Have you filled the watering can?" Neil, her sixteen-year-old boyfriend, asked.

Jess nodded, then realized he couldn't see her. "Yeah. It's awfully heavy. What time is it?"

"Five minutes to. Look, Jess, I better go. I'll talk to you after school, okay?"

"Thanks, Neil."

"Good luck."

Jess turned off the power and slipped the phone into the front pocket of her shirt. She'd been planning this for weeks, ever since her father's box of keepsakes had so conveniently fallen off the highest shelf of his closet while she was vacuuming. The stash of old love letters had landed at the top of the heap, held together by a plain rubber band. She'd felt a bit squeamish reading them—this was her dad, for Pete's sake! But she'd skimmed through enough of them to know he and this woman had been in love and to find out the woman's name. Grace Hamilton. Once Jess had that, getting the home address was a cinch. At the time, she'd thought it was all proving too effortless. She'd been right.

Having Grace's home address was great, but the problem was, Grace didn't appear to spend any time there. So Jess had had to find out where she worked. The name of the company and the head-office address were easy to locate. The biggest problem was Grace's executive assistant, a woman named Jackie O'Connor, who screened every phone call, letter and potential visitor before passing on any messages to Grace. It had taken a few days of quiet observation to find a small hole in Jackie's screening process: the executive assistant always took a bathroom break at ten o'clock. Made sense, Jess thought. Jackie seemed to be the oat-bran-and-prune-juice type.

At this moment, peering out the small glass window at the top of the fire-escape door, Jess couldn't believe the time had finally come for action. Her stomach ached the way it had two months ago when she had to give an impromptu speech before the entire class. She had the same panicky feeling now, but just as in class, she had no alternative. So she waited in the stair-well, her attention fixed on the dark wooden doors that led to the headquarters of Body and Soul, Inc. Brass lettering displayed the company's name on the wall next to the doors, along with the company logo: styl-ized figures of a male and a female body standing back to back.

Jess checked the display on her Indiglo watch—

9:58. She glanced down at her jeans and plaid shirt, the watering can in her hand. As far as she could tell, she looked just like the other employees who worked for Branch Manager, the outside firm that took care of the office building's plants. Her research had been thorough. Her disguise was foolproof. Nothing could go wrong; she knew it. Yet as the seconds ticked by, the pounding of her heart grew louder, faster; her palms were sweaty. She gripped the plastic handle of the watering can. She had to be ready to move at an instant's notice.

A minute passed. Then another. The pounding in her chest seemed to move up to her throat. And then, right on schedule, one of the doors opened and an older woman, dressed in a serious gray suit with matching gray hair pulled up in a bun, stepped out. Jackie O'Connor. Jess held her breath as the woman headed briskly toward the washrooms.

She had to move now. Slipping out from the stairwell, she walked through the door Jackie had just come out of. Her legs felt funny—stiff yet wobbly—but she moved quickly toward the chairs where visitors were supposed to wait for their appointments. A pretty, red-haired girl at the reception desk was working the phones and didn't even notice her.

A fig tree stood behind the chairs. Jess brushed aside the dull brown moss that lay around the plant's base. There was something funny about this soil. Looking up, she saw the bright, artificial sheen of the leaves. Tentatively, she brushed her fingers against one. Silk! She was about to water a fake plant!

Lowering her watering can with a shaking arm, Jess glanced at the receptionist to find out if she'd noticed. Seeing only the back of the woman's red curls, Jess was cautiously relieved. She couldn't afford to make mistakes like this. Head held high, but careful to avoid eye contact, Jess took the corridor to the left of the waiting area hoping her face wasn't as flushed as it felt. How could she have been so dumb?

A man about her father's age, dressed in a suit and carrying a stack of papers, brushed by her, then pushed through a second set of double doors—the entrance to the executive wing. He let the doors close behind him, practically in her face. Switching the watering can to her other hand, Jess followed in time to see him slip through a final set of double doors at the end of the short hall.

Jess paused. There was a definite change in this part of the office: the carpet was thicker and the furniture appeared to be more expensive. Her gaze fell on another plant in the executive assistant's office area. Jess stuck a finger into the pot and was reassured when it came out covered in dry dirt. After dumping half her supply of water into the pot, she began moving down the hall. Brass plates conveniently identified the occupants of the offices. She paused again when she came to the corner office at the end of the hall. Black lettering engraved into the brass said Grace Hamilton. Not giving herself a chance to chicken out, she burst through the door—and found the office empty.

How could this be? She and Neil had seen Grace drive into the building parking area at eight that morning and her car was still sitting in its stall. Jess patted the phone in her front pocket, wanting to call Neil, but she didn't have time. Jackie O'Connor would return from her bathroom break any second.

Did Jess turn back now? She couldn't. She'd put in so much hard work, so many hours of planning. She headed toward the double doors she'd seen the man walk through earlier.

The conference room. Grace had to be in there. Did Jess dare interrupt? She didn't have any choice. Trying to ignore her queasy stomach, her sweaty palms and the wild pounding of her heart, Jess filled her lungs with air and reached for the shining brass doorknob.

GRACE HAMILTON, PRESIDENT of Body and Soul, Inc., looked away from the debt/equity ratio she'd just written on the white board and frowned as the door to the conference room slowly opened. She'd told Jackie absolutely no interruptions today. With rumors of a hostile takeover bid hanging over the company, Grace had to convince the other members of the board that bold, decisive action was necessary.

Ten years ago, Body and Soul had been in the germination stage. Grace had been fascinated with the way Eastern medicines and philosophies were gaining popularity in the West. Was it too bizarre to think they might have an impact on the world of beauty and fashion? Might cosmetics actually have health, even spiritual, benefits for the women who used them?

She'd done her research both into the products and the market possibilities. After she'd found a company in the Okanagan that could manufacture the types of soaps, creams, oils and cosmetics she wanted to sell— most of them derived from organically grown plants and herbs—she'd opened her first store.

The concept had taken root immediately. Publicity was boosted when she convinced two Hollywood stars working on location in the city to stop in for a complimentary stress-relief makeover. A local TV crew was on hand, and the footage was scooped by *Entertainment Tonight.*

Since then she hadn't looked back.

Today, Body and Soul was a public corporation with thirty-six employees at head office and sixteen franchise operations scattered throughout British Columbia and Alberta.

And Jarvis Enterprises was presently buying up shares like mad, trying to accumulate a majority interest that would allow them to take over the company that had been growing like wild. Yet she hadn't built Body and Soul so that one of Canada's major retail conglomerates could swallow it whole. No way.

The question was, how to fight it? Some members of the board felt a defensive strategy was best. Grace disagreed. She wanted Body and Soul to be proactive, to continue with their ambitious expansion plans. Of course, that required borrowing funds. She could understand why that strategy made some people nervous. So far, the company had been extremely fortunate in being able to fund its growth through phenomenal sales figures, with no need to go into debt.

At this point, it was time to reach for something higher. And it was her job to convince the board Body and Soul was more than ready to tackle the lucrative market in central Canada. Nothing short of a bomb threat in the building was going to stop her from achieving that goal.

But now, into the suddenly hushed room, stepped a young woman dressed in work clothes and lugging a plastic watering can. Why had Jackie allowed the plant people in here, today of all days?

''Could you please come back later?''

Grace had spoken in a voice loud enough to carry

firmly to the back of the room, but to her astonishment, the stranger didn't pull away in apology. Instead, the young woman closed the door deliberately behind her. Her long, strawberry-blond hair swung around her shoulders as she turned to face them, and Grace saw with surprise that she was only a teenager, maybe just thirteen or fourteen. The girl's flared jeans dragged on the floor as she took a tentative step forward, her chin cocked determinedly.

"I'm not here to water the plants."

In concert, the six men and one other woman seated around the oval mahogany table glanced up from their papers. After examining the earnest face of the interloper, they looked to Grace as if asking what she intended to do about this situation. Grace, as president and chairperson, was standing at the head of the table in front of a chart demonstrating key indicators of the company's financial health. She leaned forward to the control panel by her chair and was just about to press the button to summon her executive assistant—how the hell had this person made it past Jackie?—when the girl spoke again.

"Excuse me, I know I'm interrupting…"

Eyes, outlined in thick black liner, scanned the faces of the seated board members, then stopped at Grace.

"Yes?" Grace prodded the stranger impatiently, her finger poised just a hairbreadth above the button, her mind still buzzing with the facts she was hoping to use to convince the other board members they could fight the impending takeover attempt. And win, because Grace Hamilton wasn't prepared to accept any other outcome.

"I was wondering if I could talk privately with you for a moment."

Was this kid for real? "I'm sorry, but I'm very busy."

"Maybe after the meeting?"

"After this meeting, I have another, then another. My day is booked." Grace walked out from behind the table and gently applied pressure to the girl's shoulder to lead her back toward the door. "Talk to my assistant. Book an appointment."

The girl stopped abruptly, and Grace was forced to drop her hand. She was aware of the twitter around her as the other members of the board reacted to this highly unusual interruption to their meeting. She had to get this intruder out of here.

Planting her hands on her hips, Grace didn't try to hide her annoyance this time. "Yes?"

The teenager's chin went up an inch. "I can't wait to book an appointment."

The impertinence. She didn't even back down when Grace fixed her with her iciest stare. "Why not?"

"Because I've been looking for you for a long time."

"Whatever for?"

"Because you're my mother."

My mother. Could she have heard correctly? Grace reached out to the back of a smooth leather chair as a gasp bit into the silence of the room. From the corner of her eye, she noticed Douglas Eberhart, her vice president of finance, turn to her and smirk.

"Very interesting, Grace," he said. "Which one of your old bosses was the father?"

Grace glared at him until he finally dropped his gaze.

"Just kidding, of course," he mumbled.

Grace felt a pain in the palm of her hand, then realized she was holding her marker so tightly she was in danger of snapping it in two. Deliberately, she set it down on the table in front of her. She'd made a terrible mistake with Douglas, but unfortunately she couldn't do anything about that now.

"I don't know what your agenda is young lady," she said, "but I do know I'm not your mother. I'm not married and I've certainly never had a child." She took a deep, reviving breath, wondering if maybe Douglas had paid the girl to disrupt her meeting. She wouldn't put it past him, not after the way he'd been behaving recently.

"Before you interrupted, we were discussing some very important business, so I'm going to have to ask you to leave. Now." This time, Grace used both hands to firmly indicate the direction in which she should walk.

But the stubborn teen wasn't moving. "My name is Jess. And I'm not leaving. I'm right. I know I am." She dug her feet into the heavy wool pile and crossed her arms over her chest.

Grace sighed, running a hand through smooth, shoulder-length hair, the color of—well, an awfully similar color to that of the young troublemaker currently causing her such grief. She could sense her fellow board members' reactions to this situation. Curiosity, annoyance, impatience. But despite Douglas's rude comment, she didn't think any of them were taking this seriously. Certainly not Roberta, who had the only truly sympathetic expression among them.

"Well, I'm afraid…" Grace stopped. She didn't want to carry on this battle of wills in front of an audience. "I know we were just getting to the meat of the presentation," she said, addressing the board members. "But perhaps we'd better have a short break for coffee while I handle this. I'll ask Jackie to bring in refreshments."

She and Jess left the room, and her astonished assistant raised her eyebrows as they passed, letting Grace know that the scamp had somehow snuck past her.

"Could you take the coffee and muffins into the meeting room, Jackie? We're breaking a little earlier than expected."

Then she marched the troublemaking teen along the corridor to her office and closed the door behind them.

"Now, young lady, you'd better have a good excuse for bursting into my meeting. The very future of my company might be at stake, so I warn you, I'm not in the mood to put up with any nonsense."

Jess, who'd been drawn to the window and the spectacular view of Vancouver's inner harbor, turned to face her. The black liner around the girl's eyes drew attention to her pale complexion, as well as her youth and vulnerability. For a moment, Grace almost felt sorry for her, then thought of the ground she'd lost in that morning's meeting and grew cross once more.

"I told you why I came here. I tried to phone you, but that—that woman would never put me through."

Grace allowed a slight smile. "That's her job." She leaned against the glass surface of her neoclassical desk. "By the way, shouldn't you be in school?"

Jess was now examining a painting on the wall.

Grace tried again. "What makes you think I'm your mother?"

A hint of trepidation crept into the girl's expression. "I read the love letters. Between you and Dad."

Love letters. Grace blinked as the memory of a

smell hit her—the paper-dust aroma of the old library where she had once studied. She saw herself sitting in one of the cubicles that lined the walls, surrounding the stacks of hard-backed books. Trying to concentrate on the legality of an oral contract, she'd heard a tapping in front of her, then a piece of paper had fallen on top of the open page of her business-law text. Oh, Lord... Grace pressed her fingers to the center of her forehead and warned herself to remain calm.

"How old are you, Jess?"

"Fourteen."

Of course. "And your father? What's his name?"

Prepared as she was, it was still a shock to hear Jess say, "Levi Shanahan."

Grace took the name like a slap to the cheek, her face flinching ever so slightly at the impact. She didn't think of Levi very much these days, but occasionally she'd wondered what it would be like to see him again. In those scenarios, however, there was no teenage daughter. In fact, Grace had never even considered that he might be married. Familial encumbrances did not suit the Levi Shanahan she had known.

Imagining running into Levi as he was walking down a street was one of the few flights of fancy she permitted herself. He would be tanned, just returned from a sailing jaunt in the South Pacific. He would stop dead, staring at her. "Grace Hamilton. I never would have believed it." His eyes would draw her toward him the way they always had. Then the two of them would walk for hours, talking, laughing. They would end up at his sailboat, make love down below...or, better yet, take off into the setting sun and make love out in the harbor under the indulgent gaze of the stars.

"Your name was in the letters," Jess said. "You'd done one of those cross-out things—you know, where you draw a line through all the letters that are the same in your name and your boyfriend's name—"

"Okay, okay."

Lord, it was hard to believe she had ever been that young, or that foolish. And to think this scamp had read every word. Grace was too old to let something like that embarrass her, but still...

"I knew your father. I even went out with him for a while before I graduated with a degree in business. But I'm not your mother."

Some of the animation died from Jess's face but none of her determination. Grace watched her struggle for composure and felt an unfamiliar tugging at her heart. There was something sad, almost tragic, about a child searching to find her mother. And it didn't make any sense. Surely Levi had to know who her mother was. So why not tell her? And where was the woman anyway? Had she died? Here again, why wouldn't Levi have told her?

"Isn't this something you should be talking to your father about?"

"Yeah, right." Jess turned to stare out the window once more, only this time she seemed quite unaware of the spectacular scenery.

"You mean he won't tell you about your mother?"

"Just that we're better off without her."

"Come on. He must have said more than that."

Jess sighed and faced Grace again. "He told me she left when I was only a few days old, that she wasn't ready for the responsibility."

Jess's nonchalant recitation of the facts made the

story that much more bleak. Surely it hadn't happened that way. This couldn't be true....

Grace began to notice the way Jess was looking around, looking at *her*.

"You must have lots of money if you're the president of this company and have such a big, fancy office."

"Getting here took a lot of hard work," Grace said, then felt annoyed that she'd allowed herself to become defensive. The simplicity and elegance of her office epitomized the principle upon which she had built Body and Soul—that beauty was both physical and spiritual in nature and just as you need to condition your hair, you need to condition your mind; hence the marriage of beauty products with the spiritual benefits of aromatherapy, massage and relaxation techniques.

"You couldn't have done it if you'd had a baby to look after, could you?"

"Oh, Lord." She should have seen that one coming. "Look here, young lady—"

"Don't call me that! I told you my name is Jess."

"Okay. Jess." The kid had spunk; no doubt about that. How many girls her age would have the audacity to interrupt a board meeting the way Jess had? "Let me be perfectly frank with you." She waited until Jess was looking her straight in the eye. "Having a baby isn't the sort of event a woman is likely to forget. And I assure you that I've never so much as missed a period, let alone experienced a labor contraction."

It was like throwing cotton balls against a glass window, for all the impact her words had on the girl. Jess just smiled at her sympathetically.

"It's okay that you skipped out. I've had a good

life. My dad is great—he really is. I just want a chance to get to know you.''

"Save me the big reconciliation speech, Jess. I'm not your mother.'' The flash of hurt on Jess's face made Grace feel guilty for her harsh words. She wasn't handling this very well and she knew it. Damn, of all the days... "Look, Jess,'' she began, then stopped. What could she add to convince this girl she was wrong? Obviously, she'd already made up her mind. She wasn't prepared to listen to anything Grace had to say.

Part of her was tempted to call security and send the kid on her way. Then she could recover lost ground with the board, finish the meeting. But how could she throw her out knowing Jess believed she, Grace, was her mother? Talk about rejection. The teenage years were tough enough without dealing with something like that. After all, the girl had come here expecting a teary-eyed reunion with her long-lost mother, and instead she was getting the corporate brush-off from a consummate businesswoman.

"I read the letters,'' Jess reiterated. "I know how much you loved my dad. And I know why you left, too. I know how important it was for you to have a career and make a success of yourself.''

Grace felt something inside her shrink at the thought of this susceptible girl reading her revealing, heartfelt letters. She pushed aside the uncomfortable feeling of having been exposed, reminding herself that Jess's feelings had to come first.

"You need to talk to your father about this. Obviously, he must have become involved with another woman shortly after his affair with me ended.'' But how could he have? Illogically, Grace felt betrayed.

To have taken another woman to his bed so quickly—maybe she hadn't meant as much to him as she'd thought.

And yet he *had* saved the letters.

"I've already told you my father won't talk to me about it." Tears, so far held at bay, now glistened on Jess's long eyelashes.

Grace melted at Jess's vulnerability. "Jess, I didn't desert you so that I could concentrate on my career. I couldn't have done that because I'm not your mother. I've never had a child."

Jess's face took on a pinched expression. "I don't expect you to ask me to live with you or to take care of me or anything. I just thought maybe we could spend a little time together. You know, get to know each other."

Grace resisted the urge to scream, *I'm not your mother!* Instead, she tried a more gentle approach. "You seem like a great kid, Jess, and if there was the slightest chance I could be your mother, I'd be happy to spend time with you. However—"

"We have the same hair color," Jess pointed out quickly. "And the same eyes."

Gray-blue. Yes, Grace had noticed. She let out a long, shaky breath. Of all the unfortunate coincidences...

"And you were in love with my father."

Grace sank to the edge of the desk. Levi Shanahan. It all came back to him. "Yes. I loved him," she admitted.

"He was crazy about you. He saved all your letters. That has to mean something."

Did it? She'd thrown hers out long ago. No sense romanticizing something that never would have lasted anyway. They'd known right from the start they were too different for their affair to have any permanence. She was going to set the business world on fire. He was going to explore the far corners of the earth. But he, it appeared, had allowed his dream to be derailed. Grace still couldn't believe it. Levi Shanahan the father of a fourteen-year-old girl.

"You must have broken his heart."

The corner of Grace's mouth curled as she remembered the casual way he nodded when she told him a week before graduation about the job she'd accepted. Of course, he already had a one-year open-ended airline ticket around the world, so what did he care? Was there a woman alive who could break Levi Shanahan's heart? She strongly doubted it.

Across the room from her, Jess paced, her head downcast, her hands clenched. Guilt, unreasonable guilt, prevented Grace from getting Jackie to send the kid home in a cab. She just couldn't do that to her. It was obvious Jess didn't believe her. She thought that Grace was her mother but just didn't want to admit it.

Was she going to have to give the kid her medical records to convince her she'd never had a baby?

Just then, the office door opened and Douglas appeared. He looked polished and urbane in his expensive wool suit and trendy Ralph Lauren glasses. But Grace had learned the hard way that appearances were deceptive.

Douglas had joined her team in the early years, taking care of the accounting and financing ends of the business. From the start, they'd worked together beautifully. He'd understood her vision and shared her enthusiasm for the future of her company. Together they'd worked long hours, evenings and weekends with very few moments of discord.

When had he changed? Upon reflection, Grace realized it must have happened gradually, but she'd first noticed it when they'd found out about the takeover attempt two weeks ago. She'd been shocked when his reaction was to run his hand over his smoothly shaven chin and suggest that maybe the takeover was exactly what the company needed.

"Who better than Jarvis Enterprises to provide the kind of leadership we'll need for a cross-Canada expansion?" he'd asked.

Why, Grace Hamilton, of course.

Douglas's lack of faith in her abilities had stung. For the first time, she wondered if she'd made a mistake in sharing her authority with this man.

Did Douglas really believe she wasn't capable of managing this company into the future? Or was his opinion blinded by self-interest, motivated by jealousy of some sort?

She wasn't about to deny they'd worked as a team to bring the Body and Soul enterprise to its current success, but the company had been her idea, and she'd done all the groundwork. She was its undisputed leader. Did Douglas resent that? Did he have a problem with the fact that Grace's name and face had dominated the many articles in the *Globe and Mail,* that she'd been the one included in a survey of up-and-coming business leaders in *Maclean's* magazine? Or that Grace had made the cover of *Vancouver* magazine and been named Entrepreneur of the Year?

She'd done her best to share the glory as well as the financial success of the business. She'd always given credit to others and instituted a profit-sharing plan with generous share options for all her employees. But perhaps that wasn't enough for Douglas.

"There certainly is a resemblance," Douglas said, looking from Grace to Jess, then back again.

He was encouraging the kid and he knew it. Inwardly, Grace seethed, but she struggled not to show it. He smirked, the aggressive intimacy in his eyes reminding her of her biggest mistake of all.

"This is a private conversation, Douglas. Did you have some reason for interrupting?" Her formality infuriated him as she'd known it would.

"Excuse me," he said, sarcasm edging each word, "but people are starting to get a little impatient. We do have work to do, you know."

Grace set her teeth, praying for the self-control not to sink to his level. "I know. I'm sorry this is taking so long." He had no idea *how* sorry. "But I'm afraid you're going to have to adjourn the meeting. Get Jackie to reschedule it for early next week."

"Yes, Boss." He gave a mock subservient nod, then backed out into the corridor, leaving the door open.

With a frustrated sigh, Grace closed the door and turned once more to the girl who had managed to upset her day so thoroughly. The board meeting was blown; if Grace wasn't careful, she would miss the staff marketing meeting at one. So much for thinking Douglas had planned this whole thing. She was beginning to wish he had.

"How did you get here, Jess?"

Slim shoulders shrugged. "Bus."

"Where do you live?"

"Kitsilano. My dad has a coffee shop and we live in the apartment above it."

Grace stared at the car key she'd pulled from her

purse. Levi running a coffee shop? Maybe she and Jess were talking about different Levi Shanahans.

But what about the love letters? No, it had to be him, and he was the only one who could sort out this mess. She would take Jess home; trendy Kitsilano wasn't far from downtown, just over the Burrard Bridge. And once Levi told his daughter that Grace wasn't her mother, she would finally have to accept the truth.

Great plan. Even if it meant seeing the only man she'd ever been completely head over heels about. She pressed the cool metal of her car key into the palm of her hand hard enough to make it hurt and reminded herself that at least he had no way of knowing she'd never felt that way about another man since.

"Come on," Grace said, picking up her briefcase briskly. "I'll take you home. We'll talk to your father and straighten this whole thing out."

"What about your meetings?"

"If I hurry, I'll make the next one."

Still Jess hesitated. "I'm supposed to be at school."

No kidding. "And I'm supposed to be convincing my board of directors to stand by me in our struggle against a hostile takeover attempt. Now, are you coming, or do I have to call Jackie in here to make you?"

"Okay." Jess picked up her watering can. "I'm coming."

CHAPTER TWO

"I'LL HAVE A LATTE, skinny, with an almond shot, and Leanne will have a cappuccino, please."

The order came from Greta, a tall, thin woman who worked with Leanne at the consignment clothing store across the street from Levi Shanahan's Jolt O' Java.

Levi nodded and reached for the medium-size take-out cups. "How's business?"

"Picking up. We got some great new Alfred Sung suits that are flying out the door. Of course, now that the cherry trees are beginning to bloom, people feel like updating their spring wardrobes."

"Chocolate sprinkles on the latte?" The two women always ordered the same thing, but it never hurt to be sure.

"You bet."

He rang up the order, then waited patiently as Greta dug her coffee card out of her purse.

"Two more lattes and the next one's on us," he said, stamping her card.

"Thanks, Levi."

She smiled and dropped a quarter in the small ceramic bank shaped like a cup of frothing cappuccino, which Jess had gotten him for Christmas last year.

"Sure thing." He wiped the counter clean, then took the next order. He had three competent staff on the morning shift; all he had to do was keep an eye on things. But he enjoyed dealing with the customers. So many of them were regulars.

Funny, how things turned out. As a kid, he'd been determined to see the world, meet all sorts of interesting people. To live a simple, unencumbered life.

Never in his wildest imaginings had he pictured himself working behind the counter of a coffee shop at thirty-five, the single father of a fourteen-year-old girl, owner of a string of real-estate properties that had more than tripled in value since he'd bought them.

Well, sometimes life didn't turn out the way you planned. And the truly crazy part was, if he had the choice, he knew he wouldn't want it any other way. Having a child of his own was more exciting than any adventure he could have dreamed up for himself. And he was willing to bet you met just as many interesting people when you stood behind a coffee-shop counter all day as you did traveling constantly.

People like the new mother coming in the door right now. Meg was an aspiring young actor trying to come to grips with the way parenthood was changing her life. She had her five-week-old baby in a fabric sling that she wore over one shoulder. He wished he'd had one of those things when Jess was little. Meg claimed the only thing between her and insanity was his double mocha creams. He could definitely relate. Those early days with Jess—though magical in retrospect—had been among the most challenging of his life.

"Had a rough night?" Meg usually made it in by ten; it was almost lunchtime now.

"You said it. I better get a bagel with my coffee." The young mother threw her purse on the counter, then tried to shuffle out money and her coffee card with her one free hand. "Jennie was up at two, then four, then six. She finally settled when Ian went to work, and I managed to get a few uninterrupted hours of sleep. Days like this I could really use a double espresso.''

Levi nodded. ''I can imagine.'' Since she was nursing, however, she always ordered decaffeinated. He took her large mug to a sunny corner table and helped her settle into her chair. ''The bagel will be out in a minute.''

''Thanks, Levi.''

Inching a corner of the sling away from the baby's face, he took a quick peek. ''Cute little thing, isn't she?''

Meg smiled. ''Especially when she's sleeping.''

Funny how just seeing a baby could plant a smile on your face. Levi went to the back room to check on stock. He thought about Jess at that age. The hardest thing had been the lack of sleep. But once they'd gotten over that hump, raising Jess had been a lot easier than he ever would have thought. Until she'd reached her twelfth birthday…

It was adolescence, he knew, and while he'd been expecting some sort of change in his little buddy, he hadn't expected as much as he got.

Would it be this hard if she had a mother?

Now there was a question he'd never have an answer to.

Levi reached up to peer behind some dusty boxes. He heard the sound of the door open again, then his daughter asking the guys at the front where to find him. Odd. It wasn't time for lunch, and Jess never came home to eat anyway.

Prepared to deal with some sort of emergency, Levi hastened out of the back room and stopped short at the sight of a tall, slender woman looking right at him. He noticed the linen suit, the silk blouse. The long legs shimmering in silky hose and ending with patent-leather pumps the color of the suit. Then he saw the shoulder-length golden hair, the intelligent gray-blue eyes. Eyes that had always tried to hide so much. And usually succeeded.

Surprise numbed his mind for a second. Then he blinked and held out his hand. "Grace Hamilton. It's been a few years."

"You remembered."

As if she thought he wouldn't. Her hand felt smooth and cool, the way her voice sounded, like polished glass. "Entrepreneur of the Year," he said, amused at the hint of color that showed high on her cheeks.

That she'd been successful anyone could tell at a glance, but of course he'd already known as much. He'd read about her company in the newspapers and magazines. It had been all too easy for him to mark the progression of her career. Her company, Body and Soul, was listed on the Toronto Stock Exchange. It had been well received by the financial markets, was even part of his own stock portfolio. As president and chair of the board, she had to be sitting pretty. Completely out of his league.

"It hasn't been that long, Grace. And you've hardly changed. Except maybe become thinner." And sharper? There was an edge, at any rate, not apparent fifteen years ago. He could sense her nervous energy and noticed the way she patted her purse. She smokes, he surmised, and was disappointed.

"Neither have you, Levi. Right down to the clothes. Still wearing blue jeans and white T-shirts."

Only now his white shirts had pictures of cappuccino on the front. "It's sort of the uniform around here." He hated the way that sounded. As if he felt he had to apologize because he wasn't wearing a European suit and a shirt with French cuffs.

He cleared his throat and was about to ask why she was here, when he remembered his daughter. She was standing well behind Grace, doing a good job of blending into the background.

"Released on good behavior, were you?"

"Da-ad," Jess said in that new way of hers that sounded like a protracted groan.

"Well?" He looked back at Grace and had a scary suspicion. Impossible, surely. There couldn't be a connection. Or could there? "Don't tell me the two of you—"

Grace stepped forward and took his arm, bringing all his senses to immediate attention. Her scent, behind the faint smell of cigarettes, was sweet and expensive, and her hair felt smooth as it brushed up against the side of his face. He'd have known her by smell alone, or touch. For a second, he saw something in her eyes, in the softening of her lips, that reminded him of the way she looked the first time he'd kissed her.

But that was a long time ago. What would a woman like her want with a man like him now? Other than a mocha with whipped cream and chocolate shavings on top? On second thought, make that a double espresso with skim milk and cinnamon.

"We need to talk," Grace said in a low voice. "Privately."

Privately. His heart thumped, until he remembered his daughter standing behind them. "Right. We better go upstairs then." He led the way through the back room, up the stairs to their apartment.

Grace Hamilton. He couldn't believe it. Had Jess been up to something? Maybe this was some sort of coincidence.

"Nice place, Levi."

Over the years, he and Jess had fixed the upper story of the Victorian house into a comfortable home. An architect friend of his had helped. They'd opened up the front room so that only a long, curved counter divided the kitchen from the large sitting area. A narrow corridor, lined with favorite art pieces, separated the common rooms from the back of the house where he and Jess each had a spacious bedroom and bathroom.

The place was small, admittedly, but it worked for them.

Grace stood on the landing, not looking unsure of herself, but just a little cautious. The pool of sunshine from the skylight over her head picked out all the gold and bronze colors in her hair, giving her an almost angelic glow. He headed to the kitchen, then scanned the contents of the fridge and offered her iced tea or water.

"Iced tea, thanks," Grace said.

"Come and sit down."

He himself chose an armchair opposite his daughter, leaving Grace the long sofa. She sank into it gracefully, legs together, bending them slightly to one side.

"This had better be good, Jess. You know you have algebra this morning and your marks are nothing to be proud of."

"Yeah, well, it's kind of hard to explain."

Jess turned pleading eyes to Grace, he saw, which Grace seemed not to notice. Coolly, she crossed her legs—making him swallow hard—and swiveled her ice cubes with her straw.

Staring down at the carpet, Jess cleared her throat. "I had to skip my morning classes because I wanted to talk to her." She jerked her head in Grace's direction. "And I couldn't get an appointment any other time."

Grace choked as if she'd swallowed her iced tea the wrong way. Levi marked the point in Jess's story. Later, corroboration would be required; for now, he'd just let Jess continue.

"Why did you want to see Grace?"

Jess's face went pink. "I was afraid you were going to ask that."

Levi fought against his impatience and remained silent. Eventually, Jess spilled her story. It was so preposterous, however, that he had to ask her to repeat it. Jess, eyes still fixed to the floor, did as she was asked.

"I thought she was my mother. No." Her voice grew stronger at this point, admitting a touch of defiance. "I *knew* she was my mother."

It was like getting kicked in the stomach, only worse. Levi glanced from his daughter to Grace. She was still acting the part of a detached observer, sipping her drink as though attending a summer garden party or something. Well, why not? What was either Shanahan to her?

He turned back to his daughter. "Where would you get a crazy idea like that?"

Jess's complexion deepened from light pink to mottled rose. "I found those love letters she wrote."

"Love letters?" A mixture of mortification and rage spread through Levi. He brought a hand to his forehead, stood up and paced the room. Damn. Why hadn't he thrown those bloody things away years ago? What a sentimental fool. Grace had to think he was the world's biggest idiot. And Jess... "What the hell were you doing reading my private correspondence?"

Jess couldn't look him in the eye. "I found them when I was vacuuming and I couldn't resist—"

"Since when do you vacuum the top shelf in my closet?" He ran both hands along the sides of his head to the elastic that held his shoulder-length hair neatly at his nape. "What would you say if I went through *your* personal papers, Jess? I thought we had some mutual respect happening in this house, you know?"

Jess appeared contrite. "I know. I'm sorry, Dad. But I needed to find out about my mother. And you wouldn't tell me!"

He stopped his pacing. "What do you mean? I've told you everything I know about her."

"Except her name."

"Jessie." He perched on the side of her chair and gently drew a hand down her fine, straight hair. "You know I'm only trying to protect you."

"She ran out on me once, and you don't want me to give her the chance to do it again, is that it? But she isn't running away, this time. She came here with me to talk to you."

Jess looked over at Grace, and for the first time since she'd sat down, Levi detected a chink in Grace's composure. He noticed the rapid rise and fall of her silk-clad chest, the color rising again on her cheek-bones.

"I didn't come because I was your mother, Jess." Her voice, however, remained smooth. "I came so that your father could clarify the situation."

She gazed at him expectantly then, and he was only too glad to step in.

"Grace isn't your mother," he said, trying to be gentle.

Jess's eyes shone with defiance, suspicion. "We have the same color hair. The same color eyes."

He sighed. "And so do thousands of other people in the city."

Agitated, Jess stood. "But you didn't date any of them—you dated her! You're covering up for her, aren't you? Neither of you wants to admit the truth. Why?"

Levi hated to see Jess so hurt and confused. He wanted to pull her into his arms and tell her how much he loved her. Why was she so consumed about this mother thing anyway? Wasn't she happy, wasn't their life together good enough? Insecurity twisted his insides. "Jessie..." He didn't know what to say.

"One of these days, Dad, you're going to have to tell me the truth." She turned to Grace. "Both of you." Then, head held high, she went to her bedroom and slammed the door behind her.

Levi took off after her. At her closed door he paused. The barrier muffled, but did not block, the sound of her sobs, and his chest tightened with pain. Maybe he should go to her. He raised a hand to the doorknob but froze when music suddenly blasted out from within the room. Before he could decide what to do, he sensed Grace come up behind him.

With a gentle touch, she led him back to the living room, then went to stand by the French doors overlooking the small balcony where he and Jessie planted flowers and herbs in terra-cotta pots every spring.

"Give her some time alone, Levi. Let her cry it out."

He stared at her back, the slim, elegant line it made under her tailored jacket. Her calm assurance was bloody annoying. "Got a few teenagers of your own, do you?"

Her shoulders stiffened. "No. I'm not married."

He knew that. He'd read the articles. "Look, I'm sorry you got dragged into this. Jess has been asking about her mother a lot recently, but I didn't realize she'd become obsessed."

Grace turned. "So are you going to tell her?"

He picked up the empty glasses and took them to the kitchen sink. When he returned, Grace was still standing at the French doors.

"Are you going to tell Jess her real mother's name?"

He met the challenge in her eyes. "I wish it were that easy."

"Why isn't it?"

Levi shook his head. He could imagine how it looked to an outsider, but his hands were tied. This was about more than not wanting Jess to be rejected a second time by her birth mother, although that *was* one of his concerns. None of it, however, was Grace Hamilton's business.

Silence fell between them. He went to stand beside her but left a good two feet between them. Early spring was always beautiful in Vancouver with the abundance of greenery, the white and pink blossoms on the trees and, invariably, the hint of blue ocean beyond. He never tired of the view from his balcony. Today, however, the woman beside him held all his attention.

"Did Jess make an appointment to see you? Did you know what she was after?"

Grace gave a hollow laugh. "Hardly. She burst into my board meeting during the middle of my presentation and announced that she thought I was her mother. I was definitely the most shocked person in the room, let me tell you."

"Oh, God. That must have been embarrassing for you."

"Let's just say it was a little inconvenient."

"So then what happened?"

Grace leaned against the window. With her left hand resting against the ledge, he could see the perfection of her manicure, the absence of any rings.... She'd told him she wasn't married, but she might have a man in her life.

"I canceled the meeting and took her into my office to straighten things out. As you can tell—" she waved her right hand toward Jess's closed bedroom door "—I wasn't very successful."

He shook his head. "Ever since she turned twelve... Sometimes I feel I don't even know my own kid anymore." He looked away from the hand that he was longing to touch. "I'm sorry, Grace. She'll be punished for what she's done. You can count on that."

Grace's expression was troubled. "I'm not sure that's the answer."

"It's not the whole one," he admitted. "However, I can't let her go through my papers—" he caught the glance Grace flashed him and hurried on "—or cut school without some sort of retribution."

"I guess you're right," she said, but her eyes, as she gazed down the corridor toward Jess's room, were tinged with regret.

Hell, did she think it was easy? That he liked having to impose consequences when Jess acted up? He watched her take a deep breath, certain she was going to argue with him again, but all she did was check her watch.

"I ought to get back to the office."

"Right." He should have known where her priorities lay. "Where are you parked?"

"Across the street."

He walked her out to her car. It was a BMW. Light gray. Almost the color of her eyes. After opening the front door for her, he watched her slide into her seat gracefully, the way she did everything.

"It was nice seeing you again, Levi. Although the circumstances might have been more pleasant."

The sunglasses she slipped over her charming, perfectly formed nose made her appear even more remote than before. "It was good to see you, too." He heard the husky note in his voice and cleared his throat. "I'll make sure Jess doesn't bother you anymore."

"It was no bother, Levi. Just ask her to book an appointment next time."

She faced the steering wheel, leaned forward to start the engine. Levi felt an impulse to pull her from the car. He couldn't let her go, not now that she was close enough for him to reach out and touch her. What would she do if he hauled her into his arms, right now, right here, and kissed her the way he'd longed to do since he'd first seen her?

When she looked up at him, he saw his face reflected in her glasses. He smiled, noting with satisfaction that none of his inner turmoil showed in his expression.

"Goodbye, Grace," he said, then gently shut the

driver's-side door. With an elegant wave, she was off. He turned, not letting himself stare after her as she shot down the street, tires squealing in her hurry to leave.

"DO YOU WANT the long version or the short, Levi?" The attractive brunette paused as she stirred the light brown foam of her café mocha, her eyebrows rising.

"You mean I actually get a choice?"

"Long. Just as I thought. Well, you'd better grab a coffee. This is going to take a while."

Ten o'clock, Friday night, and they were doing a medium-to-heavy business. But since he had three experienced people on duty, Levi filled his dark green mug with freshly brewed java, straddled the stool beside Marian and prepared to listen.

"Well," she began, "there's this man at work I've been interested in for some time."

He held back a smile. Only one? "A banker, Marian? Your standards are slipping."

"Don't tease. He's impossibly good-looking, about my age— maybe a little closer to forty."

She said this without batting an eyelash, even though Levi knew, having once seen her driver's license, that she was forty-two this year.

"And he's single," she added, "which is the real zinger. I mean, how can that be? Of course, we all—"

She was referring to the other available women at the bank, who, from what Levi had heard, regularly discussed such things.

"—assumed there had to be a good reason for this. You know what I mean?"

"Not that there's anything wrong with that," Levi interjected wickedly.

"Exactly. But turns out he's not. Because he asked me to go to dinner with him tomorrow night."

"No kidding?"

Marian sighed. "I can't tell you how nervous I feel. Like a kid on her first date. It's been a while, as you well know."

He knew. Since Marian's divorce two years ago, she'd been going through a tough period trying to adjust to single life. Her ex-husband, Gordon, had been a friend of Levi's for years—they'd run several marathons together—but somehow, after the divorce, it was Marian he'd stayed friends with, while Gordon had moved to the States to start a new life.

"He got the car. I got the friends," Marian was fond of saying.

They'd had no children—something Marian blamed her ex for. "At least then I'd have somebody," she'd told him once. "And a decent excuse not to be having the time of my life. Why is it that every man I date turns out to be such a loser?"

He'd had no answer for her then, and now he could only hope that her luck had changed. "That's great news," he said, clasping her hand. "I hope this guy...?" He looked at her questioningly.

"Richard Craig," she supplied.

"Richard—thank you—appreciates his good fortune."

Marian made a face. "If this doesn't work out, I might start thinking something's wrong with me."

"Don't be crazy, Marian. Any guy would be lucky to have you." And he wasn't saying that just to make her feel good. She was petite, with thick wavy hair and large, expressive eyes; few men wouldn't find Marian attractive. And she had a gregarious personality that drew people to her. "One of these days, something will work out. Probably when you least expect it."

"Maybe."

"Let me get you another one of those," he said, standing up and reaching for her mug. "On the house."

"On the house" was a big expense item at the Jolt, but thanks to the booming business, they could afford it. Levi measured freshly ground espresso beans, his glance returning again and again to the front door.

Weekend nights Jess was supposed to be home by ten-thirty. It was quarter after now, and he was hoping she wouldn't pick tonight of all nights to exercise her newly discovered rebelliousness. The scene he'd had with her that afternoon after Grace left had worn him out. He didn't want to spend the next five years yelling at Jess, nagging, scolding, threatening. They'd always gotten along so well. Why did kids have to grow up, anyway?

He returned to Marian's table with her drink. "What about that legal matter you were talking about last week? Did you find out what the lawyers wanted?"

She laughed. "Did I ever. I can't believe I forgot to tell you. It seems I've come into a little inheritance."

"No! Really?"

"The last of my relatives on my father's side died and left me the family farm in Manitoba. My great-uncle Edward. I never met him—something I regret now—but somehow he'd heard of me, because I'm his sole beneficiary. I guess he didn't have a favorite charity."

Levi knew Marian well enough to recognize when

she was hiding deeper feelings behind self-deprecating humor. "Have you seen the place?"

Her expression grew pensive. "Just last week. I went to the funeral, of course. Flew down last Thursday and returned this Wednesday. Expenses will be covered by the estate, my lawyer tells me," she added sardonically.

Levi reached over and patted her hand. "So it was a family farm?"

"It's where my grandfather was raised. When my great-grandparents died, they divided the land between their two sons—my great-uncle Edward and my grandfather. My grandfather eventually pulled up stakes and moved to Edmonton, so Edward ended up with all the land."

Marian's expression softened, her eyes lost their focus, and Levi could almost see her thoughts lifting to her family's history.

He considered his own roots—his mother and all she had done for him. It was still unbelievable that she was gone. "What kind of farm was it?"

"Mixed. Grain and cattle. A neighbor is taking care of the livestock until we get an auction organized." She pulled in a deep breath and straightened her shoulders, almost as if physically shedding the past. "So," she said in a brighter tone, "I've had quite a week. An inheritance *and* a date. Things are definitely looking up."

"Couldn't happen to a nicer person."

"Thanks, Levi." She cast her eyes down to the table as though caught off guard by the compliment. When she raised her eyes, the smile was back. "Now it's your turn."

"What do you mean?"

"You seem worried. Want to tell me about it?" She followed his glance at the door and guessed its significance. "Is it Jess?"

"She has a new boyfriend," he confided. "Two years older than her. Even has his driver's license." He shuddered. "All of a sudden, we're fighting about issues I didn't think I'd have to deal with for at least a couple of years."

"Have you met the boyfriend?"

He shuddered again and nodded. "Want to know how many tattoos and pierced body parts he has? But that's not the worst of it. The kid is just plain lazy. I have yet to hear him utter one complete sentence. He doesn't play any sports, doesn't work out. Why, I'm twenty years older and I bet I'm in far better shape than him. Worst of all," he added, "the guy smokes. His clothes and breath reek. I don't know how Jess can stand him."

"He smokes? I didn't think kids were into that anymore."

"Yeah, unfortunately a lot of them are."

"It's almost like Jess handpicked someone just to annoy you," Marian said. "I mean, considering what a health freak you are and everything."

"Freak?"

"Oops. Excuse me. Poor choice of words."

"I'll say." He paused consideringly, then went on. "Want to know what else my sweetheart of a daughter has been up to today?"

"There's more?"

"There's more," he echoed grimly. "She went out hunting for her mother. Actually brought someone home. Not her real mother, of course, just someone she thought might be."

"Are you serious? Who was it?"

Levi tapped his blunt nails against the wooden table. "An old girlfriend of mine. Grace Hamilton." As the name rolled off his tongue, Levi wondered if he'd told this story to Marian just to have an excuse to say Grace's name.

"Grace Hamilton," Marian mused. "Isn't that the woman who was on the cover of *Vancouver* magazine the other month? President of Body and Soul, I think she is."

"The very one," he confirmed.

"God, she's gorgeous. But a bit of an ice-princess look about her, too, don't you think? Or am I just being catty? They did a cover article on her in *Chatelaine*. Did you really go out with her?"

"Last summer of university." He drummed his fingers on the table. It had been so many years; yet when he'd seen her today, the memories were so vivid. He could remember the way she had always smiled at him before she kissed him. The way her body had looked naked, curled up in his bed... She hadn't been an ice princess in bed....

"Is she Jess's mother?"

"Of course not." The image in his mind faded, then disappeared. Dreaming was for kids. He'd better keep that in mind. "Jess saw some old correspondence, drew the wrong conclusion." He sighed. "She's asked about her mother before, but I never realized how badly she wanted to know. I had no idea she was trying to find her behind my back."

"Why don't you just tell her the truth?"

"How can I do that?" Levi asked. "How do you think she'll feel if she learns her mother gave me custody on the condition that I never reveal her identity?"

"Well, she has to know sooner or later."

"I pick later," Levi said firmly.

"Well, you're her father."

"That's right. I am." Levi glanced at his watch. Ten-forty and she still wasn't home. Clearing the mugs from the table for the second time, he said goodbye to Marian, then began to prowl restlessly around the room, wiping tables, adjusting the merchandise displays. He'd told Jess she wasn't allowed to accept a ride from her boyfriend. They had to use public transportation, ride bikes or walk. At times like this, however, he wasn't sure he'd been wise to trust her.

Ten forty-five. He thought about the events of that afternoon. Grace Hamilton had walked into the café as if she owned it, head high, eyes bright. Of all his past girlfriends, why had Jess picked Grace as her mother? And why had Grace felt it necessary to drop Jess off, to stay and try to straighten matters out? It was none of her business.

Jess was looking for a mother figure in her life. In his calmer moments, Levi could understand that. There were things Jess would probably be more comfortable discussing with a woman. She used to confide in his mother, whom she adored, but his mother had died after a stroke. It probably wasn't coincidental that Jess's interest in her mother was following so soon after her grandma's death.

And so she'd gone searching for her mother. And come home with Grace Hamilton: sophisticated, elegant, cool and ambitious. Grace, president of Body and Soul, Entrepreneur of the Year. Grace, who had always kept her head and heart focused on one thing only—success.

He couldn't think of a less likely mother figure for his daughter.

GRACE DREW ON HER cigarette, exhaled, then took a sip of her martini. "My God, what a day this has been."

"You can say that again," her fellow board member Roberta Paxton concurred. "I tried to calm the waters, but I have to tell you the other board members were not impressed with the whole scene. Especially with your canceling the meeting. Someone even suggested it might be a ploy on your part to buy yourself time to find a way out of this mess."

Grace sputtered, then reached for a napkin. "That's ridiculous. Of course I have a plan. I'm the president of the company, after all. That's my job."

"I believe you, Grace, and I'll always stand by you. I can't say about the others, though. I'm sure you already know this, but Douglas Eberhart is sending out strong signals that he disagrees with your approach." The older woman stubbed out her cigarette, then lit another.

Thirteen years Grace's senior, Roberta Paxton was the epitome of what a woman could achieve in the modern business world. Executive vice president of a national communications company, single, wealthy and very influential in Vancouver business circles, Roberta sat on several boards, including Grace's. She'd offered Grace her first job out of university and been her mentor ever since. When Grace left Roberta's company to start her own, Roberta was generous with her support and encouragement. No one had been more pleased when Body and Soul made a successful initial public offering or when Grace was named Entrepreneur of the Year.

"Douglas has become a problem," Grace admitted. "He's supported the takeover from the start—and I don't think I'm being overly cynical in questioning his motives." After years in the business world, Grace thought she'd developed a tough skin, but Douglas's betrayal hurt.

Perhaps it had been inevitable, what with all those late nights working together, that eventually their business relationship had turned into something more. And resulted in the biggest professional blunder she'd ever made—dating a co-worker. It was against all the rules, and she had definitely known better.

"Maybe he sees this takeover as a way to get you out of the picture," Roberta said bluntly. "I've never known a man who didn't figure, deep down inside, that he could run a company better than any woman. The ironic part of it is, Douglas could no more be president of Body and Soul than lead the Canucks to the Stanley Cup."

Grace smiled. Roberta loved her sports analogies. "Well, maybe he'd be a little better at being president of Body and Soul."

"Don't say that even as a joke!" Roberta was suddenly serious. "Your relationship with Douglas may have been a mistake, but that doesn't mean you have to lose your company over it."

Roberta, of course, knew all about her affair with Douglas. In fact, on her advice, Grace had called it off when Douglas proposed that she move into his place.

"Why his place?" Roberta had asked. "Why not yours?"

When Grace had suggested as much to Douglas,

he'd been surprisingly reluctant to give up his down-town condo. It was almost funny to think that something so small as an inability to compromise on a place to live had destroyed their relationship, although maybe it was more pathetic than amusing.

The break had seemed amicable enough when it happened. But with hindsight, Grace realized that things were not the same at work and, over time, the situation had deteriorated. Culminating with this damned impending takeover attempt. Now Douglas's hostility was overt, and she could only wonder how long his resentment had smoldered beneath his calm exterior.

"Have you thought of letting him go? At this critical juncture, you can't afford to have employees who aren't team players."

"That's what I'll have to do eventually. But I have to pick the right time. If I did it now, imagine what the financial analysts would say. They'd be sure to interpret any changes in the upper echelon of the organization as panic in the face of the takeover. No, I need to present a united front to the shareholders."

"I guess you're right. Damage control. That's what you have to concentrate on. If I were you, though, I'd watch that man."

"I am." Grace twirled her martini, eyeing the clear liquid as if looking for answers in a crystal ball.

Roberta signaled the waiter for another drink. Grace shook her head, declining. They'd been there an hour and had three already—on empty stomachs. She didn't know how Roberta did it. She could feel her own thoughts becoming muddled, her voice starting to slur, but Roberta was as sharp as ever.

"Whatever happens, Grace, you can't lose control

of your company. You've accomplished something with Body and Soul that's an inspiration to ambitious young women everywhere. You've worked too hard, for too long—''

''I know, Roberta. I know.'' Grace felt a tightening in her gut, the beginning of an ache in her temples. That familiar enemy, stress, was reminding her there were some things in life she just could not control.

''And the girl?''

Grace's eyebrows drew together in her confusion at the shift in topic.

''The girl who interrupted our meeting. Who was she?''

Grace shook her head, feeling the effect of the three martinis on her equilibrium. ''Unbelievable, Roberta. She turned out to be the daughter of an old boyfriend of mine.''

An old boyfriend of mine. Somehow that designation didn't do Levi justice. Grace rubbed two fingers against her temple, remembering the stab of awareness, the sudden dizziness and the way her breath had stuck at the back of her throat when he'd first looked at her.

Although she'd been prepared for the meeting, *her* composure had cracked while he'd seemed unperturbed by her unexpected appearance. He'd brushed a hand against his jeans before offering it to her, and that had been the strangest moment of all—shaking his hand as if he were just an acquaintance or a business associate. On the drive over, she'd wondered if he would kiss her. Politely, on the cheek, the way old friends sometimes did. She'd been disappointed that he hadn't. Unless he'd been waiting for her to make the first move?

Grace kept massaging her aching temple. It wasn't like her to make such a fuss about something so trivial. Kiss, hug, handshake—what did it matter? And why was she thinking about him so much? She hadn't seen him in fifteen years. And it would probably be another fifteen before she saw him again.

"An old boyfriend? Sounds interesting."

"*Bizarre* might be a better word."

Roberta put her elbows on the table and propped her chin in her hands. "Don't be arch. Tell me all."

"Apparently, his daughter found some old love letters." Grace paused, then almost blushed as Roberta raised a brow. She didn't care if it *was* sentimental; she'd been touched to discover that Levi hadn't thrown them out. And unnerved at the thought of his fourteen-year-old daughter reading them.

"Love letters? Written by you?"

Grace measured the incredulity on Roberta's face. "Is it that hard to believe?"

"Having been the recipient of numerous memos, letters and business plans of yours, I would have to say yes. But carry on with your story."

"The letters were written about fifteen years ago. Which seems to correspond with Jess's age, so she determined from them that I had to be her mother."

"And of course you're not." Despite the actual words, the sentence came out sounding like a question.

"Of course I'm not. I may be focused on business, but I wouldn't go so far as to desert my own child. *If* I had a child, which I do not."

"Okay, okay." Roberta waved a hand, her perfectly manicured nails gleaming in the dim light of the bar like mother-of-pearl. "Go on."

"Unfortunately, nothing Levi or I said could convince Jess she was wrong."

"She didn't believe her own father?"

"No. But that's because he won't tell Jess her real mother's name. He said he couldn't, but I do think he's being unreasonable. The child has a right to know about her mother. And not telling her puts me in a terrible position, of course.

"Since Jess believes I'm her mother, she interprets my repudiation of her claim as just another rejection of her as a daughter. You see?" Grace knew she'd been called coldhearted by many an adversary, but she hoped the adjective applied to her strictly in the world of business.

"Not your problem, Grace."

Roberta was right, Grace acknowledged. But that look on Jess's face before she'd taken sanctuary in her bedroom…and those words… *One of these days, Dad, you're going to have to tell me the truth. Both of you.*

They *had* told her the truth—that Grace was not her mother. What would it take to make Jess believe them? Grace thought she had the answer. Jess needed to learn the whole truth about her real mother.

Why wouldn't Levi tell Jess? *Or her?*

How could Levi have conceived a child with another woman so soon after their relationship ended? And what had happened to this other woman?

Grace sighed and closed her eyes. There were too many questions, and maybe the answers weren't any of her business anymore. But then, why couldn't she put the affair out of her mind? It wasn't just Jess eating at her. No, that was the relatively simple part. It was Levi and how she had felt seeing him again that really had her confused.

Levi belonged to the past and he should have stayed there. So what if he was still as damn sexy as ever? There were other good-looking men around.

In her line of work, though, she never met men who wore jeans as if they were born in them; whose muscles bulged even under a thick cotton T-shirt. Men who dared to wear their hair long enough to be pulled back into a ponytail.

So what? She didn't like that look anyway.

Oh, really?

He had changed; she had changed. And even if he was interested, even if she was willing to take the chance, they could never make it work.

But in his eyes she could still see the soul of the man she had once loved.

She knew she was romanticizing. First love rarely lasted; the emotions were all illusion. That was part of what had made her relationship with Levi so special, why it had been so impossible for any man she'd met since to measure up.

Besides, in business, once you made a decision, there was no going back. Grace knew it was that way in everyday life, too. You made your choices, then you carried on. The magic she'd shared with Levi had been wonderful, but that time was gone now. And this weird, sentimental feeling she was experiencing would fade soon enough. Maybe even with the light of day.

CHAPTER THREE

GRACE FELT HAUNTED. She hadn't been able to sleep for the dreams; now she couldn't work for the memories. A ghost from the past had broken through to the present, and he was all she could think about. Levi Shanahan. It felt like they'd broken up fifteen hours ago instead of fifteen years.

Dressed in a business suit because she'd forgotten it was Saturday, Grace paced in front of the full-length window. Pressing work nagged from her desk, but all she could focus on was that face from the past, the man she thought she'd forgotten. In her hands she held the one picture she'd kept: Levi standing beside his red Mustang convertible. How he'd loved that car. How they'd loved in that car.

Why did she feel such a longing for that time?

Maybe it wasn't that strange. A woman was entitled to have fond memories of the first man she'd fallen in love with. And it had been a shock seeing him again. Grace sighed and tried to get a grip on her emotions. In a few days, life would return to normal. The memories would fade; real life would assert itself.

In a few days.

Grace jumped at the sound of her phone, shrill in the weekend silence. She wasn't expecting any calls, but most people knew she worked on Saturday.

"Hello?"

It was security. A young teenager said she needed to see her. Jess Shanahan.

Oh, Lord. Of course it wasn't over. Why had she thought it would be that easy? She remembered Levi's promise—*I'll make sure Jess doesn't bother you anymore.* Then she recalled the stubborn set of Jess's jaw as she'd barged fearlessly into the occupied conference room. No, Grace couldn't claim she was surprised that the girl hadn't given up.

Or even annoyed. Part of her wanted to see the teenager again. She didn't like how things were left between them. Jess's last words had stayed with her, an undeserved accusation but a poignant one nonetheless.

"Let her up, please."

Grace went to the elevator bank. After a few moments, a warning tone sounded, then the doors opened wide. Out stepped Jess, wearing a black ribbed top, flared jeans, black belt and platform shoes. Something sad and a little lost showed in her expression, a look not there yesterday.

"No watering can this time," she said, holding out empty hands.

"That's okay." Grace placed an arm around her shoulders. "I believe we had an appointment, anyway."

Jess smiled weakly.

"You look like you had about as much sleep last night as I did," Grace said, leading the way to the coffee room. She found a pop in the fridge for Jess and poured herself a cup of the coffee she'd put on to brew earlier that morning.

Jess just sighed.

"So how did you get here this time? The bus?"

Jess hesitated briefly before nodding.

"Does your dad know you're here?"

There was a cracking sound as she popped the tab on her drink. "Not really."

That figured. "Why did you come?"

Still looking at the can in her hands, Jess said quietly but with determination, "You know why I came."

Grace nodded. She believed she did. "You're not convinced that I'm not your mother, are you?"

"Yesterday after you left, Dad and I had a long talk, but I can't trust him to be open with me. Not about this. He's too scared of saying something that will scar me for life. As for you, well, if you decided to step aside after I was born, you'd hardly be changing your mind now, would you?"

Grace began to wonder if anything she or Levi said would ever convince Jess she was wrong.

"If I were your mother, and I'm not, but if I were—" Grace leaned against the counter, cupping her mug in her hands "—what would you want from me?"

"Just a little time." Jess, who had flopped down on one of the leather sofas, leaned forward over her knees. "My dad is great. I know I said that before— I just want you to know that I really mean it. But still, he's a man, you know what I mean?"

Oh yes. Levi was a man, all right.

"And I know you're busy and that you work almost all the time. I just thought we could do some girl things together. Like shopping and going for lunch. I used to do a lot of baking with my grandma Shanahan."

From the past came the sharp, sweet smell of cinnamon, so vivid it was hard to believe it wasn't real. Grace flexed her right hand, remembering how it had turned almost numb from beating together butter and sugar by hand because her mother had considered electric beaters an unnecessary extravagance. "But you don't bake with your grandma anymore?" she asked.

"She died. Last year."

Grace swallowed back regret. Levi had taken her to meet his mother a couple of times when he'd dated Grace. The woman's gruff exterior had hidden a warm and giving nature. Raising Levi on her own after her fisherman husband was killed in a boating accident must have been tough. But she'd seemed happy with her lot, and Levi had adored her. Judging from the emotion so apparent on Jess's face, so had his daughter.

"I'm sorry about your grandma, Jess. I bet you were really close."

Jess stared at the floor and nodded, her lips compressed as if she were fighting back tears.

Grace took a gulp of coffee. Lord, if she didn't feel like crying herself, and she'd barely known the woman. What was she doing? Sentimentality definitely wasn't her style.

Jess just needed a female role model. That was all this was about. Did it really matter if that female wasn't her mother?

No. Grace didn't think it did.

"Look, Jess, I'd be happy to do the sorts of things you were talking about. Except the baking. I'm not much of a cook—"

"That's okay. I don't really care what we do."

Seeing the happiness in the girl's face was a little frightening. "But it would have to be clear that I was spending time with you as a friend, not a mother. And your father would have to agree.''

''If it's okay with you, I know it'll be okay with him.''

Grace wasn't so sure about that. ''There's one more thing. You know how busy I am. I don't have that much free time.'' And now she was as good as committing what little spare time she had to a fourteen-year-old girl. Why didn't that seem more unappealing than it did? Well, Jess was a likable kid, and a pretty gutsy one at that.

Jess hesitated. Her large gray eyes were thoughtful. ''I can agree to all of that,'' she finally said.

''Just don't expect too much, okay? I'm afraid I don't have much in the way of experience with kids of any age.''

''Well, that's okay. Experience probably wouldn't help, because my dad always says I'm one of a kind, anyway.''

Grace smiled. ''I can believe that.'' She rinsed out her coffee cup. ''So how about I give you a ride home? It'll give me a chance to talk to your father.''

Grace tried not to feel nervous about the prospect. Spending time with Jess would automatically result in seeing Levi, too. At least occasionally. She had to admit the idea was not unappealing. Was that why she'd said yes to Jess? She didn't think so. She hoped not.

Levi. It was still difficult for Grace to think of him as a father. It was a role she'd never pictured him in. He'd been too much of a wanderer, a dreamer. The most impractical, impulsive, romantic person she'd ever known.

''He's going to be ticked off,'' Jess said when they were in Grace's car.

"How come?"

"He didn't want me to bother you again. And he's already in a bad mood because of last night."

"Last night?"

"I missed my curfew. But it was totally not my fault. He won't allow me to ride in my boyfriend Neil's car and the bus was behind schedule. We were only twenty minutes late, but he completely flipped out and said I couldn't see Neil for a whole week. But what could we have done?"

"Phoned to let him know where you were?"

Jess shot her an aggrieved look. "That's what he said. But if we left the bus stop to find a phone, we'd have been even later."

"Tough call," Grace admitted.

"He doesn't like Neil. Says he's too old for me. But there's only a two-year difference."

"At your age, two years is quite a bit. Sounds to me like your dad may have a point there."

"You wouldn't say that if you knew what most fourteen-year-old boys are like. They're so immature." Jess lifted her chin haughtily. "I think Dad is just obsessing because I finally grew breasts this year." Jess regarded her chest critically. "I was beginning to think it would never happen. All my girl-friends developed ages before me."

Grace kept her eyes on the road, her mouth closed. She had no idea what to say on the topic of Jess's new breasts. Were kids these days all so open? She was quite certain that when she was a teenager, she would never have voluntarily discussed her changing body.

"I'm sure your dad is just looking out for your best interests—"

"Then he shouldn't be so strict. Neil is the only

person who interests me and I'll go crazy if I can't see him for seven whole days." Jess raised her voice as a disastrous idea occurred to her. "What if Neil gets bored waiting for me and finds a new girlfriend?"

Then he probably wasn't worth your time in the first place. Grace bit back the words, deciding they would have no impact on the emotional fourteen-year-old.

"Do you think you could talk to Dad? Convince him he's being unreasonable?" Jess asked.

"Wait a minute here." Grace stopped at a red light and turned to face her passenger. "Let's get this straight right from the beginning. I've agreed to spend some time with you, but as a friend, remember? I'm not going to get involved with what goes on between you and your dad."

"But why not? I'm sure he'd listen to you—"

"Because it's none of my business how your father chooses to discipline you."

"But as my mo—"

"Stop." Grace held out her hand. "Don't you dare say the 'M' word. Okay? The only way I can see you is if you're willing to accept that I'm not your, well, you know. It just wouldn't be honest. Do you understand?"

Jess hesitated, then finally agreed. "Okay. I won't bring it up again. And I won't expect you to talk to my dad about my being grounded. Even though it means I'm going to miss the best party of the entire year tonight."

"Of the entire year?"

"Actually, of my entire life. All my friends are so jealous that I'm going with Neil. We've only been seeing each other for about three weeks, and he's absolutely the coolest guy around."

As a teenager, Grace wasn't allowed to date and so she didn't have any boyfriends until she left home. But she remembered the feeling Jess was talking about. Oh, yes, she remembered.

In fact, it was awfully like the feeling she had right now, pulling up beside Levi's Jolt O' Java.

LEVI DIDN'T LOOK HAPPY to see her. Or maybe it was his daughter he was scowling at. Either way, Grace felt her courage wane as she and Jess pushed past the door and went inside, only to find him glaring at them.

Levi's eyes barely touched on Grace before settling on his daughter.

"Hi, Dad."

The slight waver in Jess's voice revealed something. Nervousness? Fear? Grace's back stiffened. "Hi, Levi," she said, moving forward with a confidence she hadn't possessed fifteen minutes ago. "I wonder if we could talk privately for a few minutes."

Levi's attention focused on her then. His silent contemplation was almost more than she could bear. How could he give the impression he knew every thought in her head without revealing any indication of his feelings at the moment? He turned back to his daughter.

"Didn't I tell you not to contact Grace again?"

Jess said nothing, just glared at him defiantly.

A few seconds passed. Levi was obviously waiting for some explanation from his daughter. When it was clear that none was forthcoming, he said, "Go to your room, please, Jess, and wait for me. I see we need to have another talk."

Jess didn't argue. With one final pleading look at Grace, she complied with her father's request and went upstairs, leaving Grace alone with Levi and even more uncomfortable with the role she'd agreed to assume.

"And so we meet again." Levi's expression was not angry, but it was definitely grim. Today, Grace noticed the lines that fifteen years had added to his face, lines that marked the character of the man and attested to strength, humor and maybe worrying a bit. She had no doubt about the cause of the latter.

"Your daughter is one determined young lady."

Levi nodded slowly, still not smiling.

Silence could be a strong negotiating tactic. Grace had often used it to her advantage in making business deals. Now, with Levi regarding her quietly, expectantly, she felt an unaccustomed uncertainty.

"I hope you don't mind that Jess came to see me. I really wasn't that busy today."

Levi sighed. "That's not the point, is it? Of course I don't want her to be a nuisance, but it's Jess's well-being I have to be most concerned about."

What did he mean by that? Was he implying he didn't think she was worthy to associate with his daughter? Grace frowned. "Can we sit outside for a moment and talk?"

He didn't look happy with the idea, but in the end he nodded his agreement and led her out to the front patio, where little wooden tables with folding wooden chairs lined the front window of the café. On each table, a single, freshly cut daffodil bloomed brightly in a slim blue vase.

"I'm not sure if I was able to convince her last night that you're not her mother." With the air of someone whose mind was miles away from his body, he watched the people passing by on the sidewalk next to them. "I told her not to bother you again. Obviously to little effect. I must say I'm getting to the end of my rope.''

He set an elbow on the table and propped up his head with a hand. She could see signs of a restless night and worry around his eyes. The stubble on his face had grown about a quarter of an inch. Feelings stirred inside Grace at being so close, his face within touching distance. She reminded herself of the purpose to her visit.

''I think the reason Jess is so desperate to find her mother is that she misses her grandma. I'm sorry about your mother, by the way.''

Levi stared down at the tabletop. ''Yeah. We both miss her.'' He looked up then, his eyes the same startling blue as the vase that held the daffodil. ''Not much I can do about that.''

''Maybe, maybe not.''

''What do you mean?''

''Maybe Jess needs a female role model in her life. Especially considering her age.''

''And I should do what? Look under Female Role Model in the Yellow Pages?''

''No, of course not,'' she replied, shaking her head. ''But Jess can be quite persuasive.''

Levi stared at her blankly.

''Do you have to make this so bloody difficult? Isn't it obvious I'm applying for the position?'' Now she couldn't look at him. She could sense the heat in her cheeks. Lord, how ridiculous she felt.

And she wondered what good she could possibly be to Jess. As she'd told the girl, she had no experience with kids. And when she'd lived at home, not only had her father forbidden her to see boys, but he'd also required her to dress plainly. No makeup or special hairdos, no frills of any kind.

It might not have seemed so unfair had he been equally strict with her older brother but her father had been of the old school and felt daughters had to be protected, whereas sons should be free to "sow their wild oats."

And his old-fashioned views had extended to education, too. Her brother went to agricultural college so he could become a better farmer and provider. Grace, her father claimed, didn't need an education to get married and raise kids; being female, she probably couldn't have handled the pressure of university. Grace had never resented having to pay for her own schooling as much as she'd resented the limits her parents had always set on her.

"I knew it would be a waste of time coming down here. Why did I let Jess talk me into it?"

"Exactly."

Damn him, he looked so smug, so sure of himself. "All right, just what is it you have against me?"

He crossed tanned, muscular arms over his chest. "Why, I have nothing against you, Grace. I just find it funny how people without children are always ready with pearls of wisdom when it comes to raising them. Too bad you'll never get the chance to put all your knowledge to practical use. Unless you've changed your mind about having a family."

"No. I haven't." He knew damned well kids had never been on her agenda. And she was not going to let him make her feel guilty for her choice.

"It's easier managing subsidiaries, isn't it, Grace? Plus you get to give others less wise than you the benefit of your sanctimonious advice."

Pushing against the table, Grace slid her chair back and stood. They were getting nowhere. In fact, the situation was deteriorating at an alarming rate. "What do you want me to do, Levi? Apologize because I never had children, because I always put my career first? Well, why should I? At least I was honest enough to say what I wanted from life, then go ahead and get it.

"What I don't understand is you. You were the one who was going to sail the Seven Seas, cycle across India, explore South America. What became of the great adventurer, Levi? What happened to that man?" She picked up her briefcase and started down the sidewalk before remembering she'd parked in the opposite direction. Chagrined, she stopped and turned around...

And marched right into Levi, crashing against the solid wall of his chest. Automatically, he put out both hands to her shoulders not having any idea, or so Grace hoped, how his touch sent her panicked central nervous system into overload. Their eyes met, and the memory of a hundred different kisses and embraces flooded Grace's consciousness.

She knew her face was suffused with color; she could feel her cheeks burning. And in that instant, she wanted to deny the years that had passed between them, to close her arms around Levi and pull him to her, claiming him as her own. He knew it, too; she saw the comprehension in his eyes as he tugged her nearer, secure in the knowledge that this was what they both wanted.

Or was it?

Weariness slid over the heated passion she thought she'd glimpsed in his eyes.

"Don't come back here, okay, Grace? It's better for Jess if you just stay out of her life."

Grace lifted her chin as if she could ward off the hurt his words inflicted. Say what he would, she could tell he'd reacted to her physically. Even if only for a few moments. Maybe the feelings had frightened him as much as they had her. "Better for Jess or better for you?"

He dropped his hands. "Jess needs limits right now."

"Agreed. But do you really think grounding her for a week is going to solve all her problems?"

He narrowed his eyes. "This is none of your business, Grace."

She realized it. But perversity drove her on. "You just don't want to admit that you need help raising her. That a father sometimes isn't enough."

He leaned forward. There was no hint of passion in his face as he looked down on her, inches separating her mouth from the thin, angry line of his lips.

"That's dangerous ground you're stepping on. Do you know how Jess really got to your office today?"

"She said she took the bus."

"Well, she lied. Her boyfriend drove her. I saw him pick her up at the end of the block about five minutes after she left the house." Levi's dark brows rose, mocking her naiveté. "Why don't you leave raising her to me, Grace? You go home and do something easy, like run a multimillion-dollar corporation."

LEVI TOOK THE TWO ORDERS of vegetarian stew, with whole wheat bun on the side, to a table at the back of the Jolt and sat down opposite his friend.

"Here, Phil." He slid one of the large, shallow

bowls to the other end of the table, then dipped his spoon into the rich, aromatic stew. They'd just returned home from sailing. Jess had taken her dinner upstairs so she could work on school assignments due tomorrow morning.

Spending the day on the ocean had been invigorating as usual, and Levi had appreciated the chance to have some time with his daughter away from the stresses of everyday life. Out on the ocean, her boyfriend couldn't call, her girlfriends couldn't drop by for a visit. With the sea wind in her hair, she didn't care about makeup or hair gel or any of those godawful rings she liked to clip on her nose and ears.

They were pals again, like in the good old days, before hormones and peer pressure had taken hold of his little girl.

"Thanks for letting Jess and me crew for you today, Phil. We really needed the break."

"I could tell." Phil ran a tanned hand through his thinning blond hair. "We brought home a different girl than we took out."

Jess had initially put up a fuss about being out on the boat all day Sunday. She was still in a huff over missing some party on Saturday night, and she'd wanted to hang out with her girlfriends. But he'd insisted she come. They didn't often get opportunities like this, and he knew she was objecting more out of principle than anything else. Jess had always loved the water. And like her old man, she had a hankering for adventure.

Phil stopped eating for a moment. "I still say you should pull up stakes and come with me when I finally have enough money saved to ditch my job. Think of it—sail anywhere we feel like, whenever we want.

Nothing but the boat, the sky and the clear blue ocean.''

"You make it sound so simple. But I've got responsibilities. The business. Jess.'' The objections were rote by now; the two of them had carried out the same conversation so many times. And yet, even though he knew there was no feasible way he could leave, Levi got an adrenaline rush just thinking about it.

A lifelong dream come true. That was what it would be for him. And now, with Grace's taunting words still ringing in his ears, the bitter knowledge that traveling the world in search of adventure would only ever be a dream, haunted him even more than before.

"Sell the business,'' Phil said, as he'd told him so many times. "That's how you finance the expedition.''

Levi tried to shut his ears. He'd gone shopping with Phil for Phil's first boat, and it had been murder. He'd wanted desperately to go halves with his buddy. Possessed of a healthy savings account, he could have swung it, but the money was earmarked for Jess's education.

"We'll come for a month in the summer,'' he said, dragging a chunk of the bun around the perimeter of his bowl to soak up the gravy. A consolation prize, he told himself.

Phil shook his head. "Well, you'll have to make up your mind for good before long. My pension fund did quite well last year. I'm not that far from my target. If the company pulls through with the profit-sharing plan, I could be sitting pretty a month from now. In fact, I'm meeting with a real-estate agent tomorrow night to put my house up for sale.''

"That's great, Phil.'' Levi tried to feel pleased for

his friend. Just because he couldn't go didn't mean he should begrudge his pal the opportunity to live out his dream. Phil, like Levi, had never hankered for the traditional trappings of success. He hated routine and schedules above all else. Levi was certain the life of a nomad would suit him just fine.

Whereas Levi, despite his occasional yearnings, was actually happy with his lot. The realization that his life suited him had come on him suddenly several years ago. He liked being a father, and he liked running the coffee shop. Admittedly, he didn't have much time or money for travel, but people more than places had always intrigued him foremost.

"Want seconds?" he asked Phil, but his friend's attention was elsewhere, on someone or something at the front of the room.

Levi turned, and for a second he froze. It was Grace. She was wearing tan shorts, a long-sleeved white top and white sling-back sandals. As usual, her legs drew his eyes first, then her hair, swinging down past her shoulders as she bent to survey the baked goods on display beside the till. Levi's stomach clenched around his dinner, making him wish he hadn't eaten a thing. He'd thought the final chapter had ended. He was wrong.

"That isn't Grace Hamilton, is it?"

Phil had been his friend since high school. He'd witnessed Levi and Grace's short but intense affair, and was the one to help Levi get his life back together after it was over.

"None other."

"What's she doing here?" Phil shot a concerned look at his friend. "I hope you're not getting involved

with her again. I warned you the first time that she
would only bring you trouble and—''

"And you were right. But her being here now has
nothing to do with me. Jess found some old letters and
jumped to the wrong conclusion. She's convinced
Grace is her mother.''

"Grace? Fat chance. If that woman got pregnant,
I'm sure she'd give birth to a batch of black widow
spiders.''

"Cut the flowery compliments, Phil. Why don't you
just admit you don't like her very much?''

Levi cleared their plates, then headed for the
counter. What *was* she doing here? He thought he'd
made it very clear to her that he didn't expect their
paths to cross for a mighty long while. But Grace
never gave up easily. And, he had to admit, part of
him wasn't at all sorry to see her again. Probably the
same part of him that wanted to go off sailing with
Phil. If that area of his brain had a name, he knew
what it would be called— Warehouse for Impulses
Not to Be Acted Upon.

"Don't lose your head, buddy,'' his friend said quietly from behind.

But Levi ignored the warning as he closed in on his
target. Obviously, Grace wasn't used to hearing the
word *no*.

It was about time she learned.

CHAPTER FOUR

"I'LL TAKE THE LEMON POPPY—" Grace stopped speaking abruptly when she saw him. "Levi."

Using a pair of metal tongs, he set a lemon poppy-seed muffin on a plate and handed it to her. To his right, one of his staff had just finished frothing her cappuccino.

"On the house," he said as she reached for her purse.

She paused with her fingers on the clasp. He noticed the plum-colored polish on her perfectly manicured nails.

"I didn't really come for the food," she said. "I thought we might talk."

He felt his heart speed up at her words, and that alone was enough to convince him this was wrong. Generally, he kept his cool around women. But that had never applied to Grace. Phil was right. He didn't need this woman messing up his life. Not to mention Jess's.

"We did that last time, and you know how it ended." With him longing to kiss her but knowing he didn't dare. Not because he was afraid of her reaction but because he was afraid of his.

"Look, Levi, I don't have time for more of this cat-and-mouse. I'm here because Jess called me. And this time I thought I'd better check with you before I agreed to see her.''

He went still. "Jess called you? When?"

"About twenty minutes ago."

As soon as they'd returned from the sailing trip. Levi frowned, thinking of his daughter, who supposedly was upstairs studying. Did she ever tell him the truth anymore? He thought she'd enjoyed sailing with him and Phil today. But if that was true, why had she felt the need to talk to Grace the minute they got back? Feeling defeated, Levi followed Grace to a table.

"What did she want this time? To complain some more about what a lousy father I am?"

"Not at all. She said you had a great day sailing."

"So why'd she call?"

"To invite me to go shopping with her tomorrow. She said she wanted my advice on a dress she was thinking of buying."

"A dress…?" Levi stared at Grace, feeling stunned. "Jess has refused to wear a dress for years. What's going on here?"

"I suspect she just wants an excuse to get together. She's trying to establish a relationship between us."

"You know how I feel about that."

"Yes. You made things quite clear the last time we talked. But think about this from my point of view. Even Jess's. This kid comes to me asking nothing but to spend a little time together. How can I say no? She knows her real mother backed out of her life almost from day one. And she's missing her grandma. Does she really need more rejection from another female in her life?"

Oh, God. How was he supposed to react to this? Of course he didn't want Jess to suffer. But an alliance with Grace of all people? "Fine, if it's as simple as that. But what if deep down she still believes you're her mother? I don't want her to build up false hopes."

"She wouldn't build up false hopes if you'd tell her the truth about her mother."

"I already said I can't do that." So she'd think him a bastard. What choice did he have?

"Then let me spend some time with her. The occasional shopping trip or lunch. What can it hurt?"

He stared at her for a long moment. Something wasn't adding up here. "I don't get it, Grace. Why would you go to all this effort for Jess? She's nothing to you."

Unbelievably, Grace looked hurt at his words. "That's not fair, Levi. This girl came to me for reasons beyond my control. Nevertheless, I can't wash my hands of her."

Did any of this come from her feelings for him? Because Jess was his daughter? Levi dismissed the idea the second it occurred to him. Grace's feelings for him had never fallen in the same category as his feelings for her.

"So what are you proposing?"

As if making a presentation to a potential financial backer, she cleared her throat and straightened her back. "Nothing too drastic. Just spending time together, maybe once or twice a week. I've told you before—I feel Jess is looking for a female role model more than her actual mother. And whatever you think of my nurturing abilities, you must at least be prepared to admit I am that—a female."

Oh, he'd admit that much, all right.

"And you're also a very busy president and chair of the board. Are you sure you'll have the time?"

He saw a flicker of doubt cross her face and stopped her before she could sputter out some false reassurances.

"It's a bad idea, Grace."

"How can you say that? You're not even giving me a chance to answer. Yes, I am busy, I'll grant you that much. But one or two visits a week should be manageable."

She sounded so cool, so sure of herself, Levi mused. He could imagine her blocking off a couple of squares on her agenda, penciling in his daughter's name. "And what about when it isn't manageable? What if there's a big crisis at work and you can't get away? The needs of a kid can't be flicked on and off like an electrical switch, you know. You make a commitment to Jess, then you've got to be there for her."

She seemed taken aback by his intensity. Just as he'd figured. She hadn't really thought this through, didn't understand the importance of what Jess was asking of her.

"Why are you so certain I'm going to let Jess down?"

"Because I know you." He knew her, all right. Hadn't she done the very same thing with him? He'd never forget the day she calmly told him about her new job. He'd just finished writing one of his final exams and had planned on celebrating with her that evening.

She had the worst sense of timing. *Time to go our separate ways,* she'd told him. *But I'll never forget you.*

He'd felt as if his insides were being wrenched from his body, but he'd struggled to keep his reaction from her. *Sure. Cool,* he'd told her. He had his own road to follow.

"So are you saying you don't want me to see her?"

She had him in a corner and she knew it. He was already the bad guy. He'd given Jess a week of kitchen duty as added punishment for having allowed Neil to drive her to Grace's on Saturday. If he told Jess now that she couldn't see Grace, she'd really be steaming. Not that he couldn't take the heat, but maybe this was one lesson his daughter would have to learn the hard way.

And she would. Depending on Grace Hamilton was a little like banking on Vancouver weather. Eventually, the rain would fall. It was just a question of when.

"It was, like, totally the best."

Jess groaned into the phone. "I can't believe I had to miss it." She was sprawled backward on her bed, both feet propped above her on the wall. She could see that the blue polish on her toenails was beginning to chip.

"I know. And your dad is usually so cool."

It always made Jess feel good when her friends said things like that. A lot of her girlfriends, like Amanda, thought her dad was a real hunk. That was a little weird, but kind of neat, too. "He said it was because I missed my curfew, but I know it's really about Neil. Dad doesn't like him at all."

"I don't get it," Amanda said. "Neil's so great. He was wearing this awesome leather jacket at the party."

So he'd been there. Jess had been afraid to ask. "Did you talk to him?"

"A little."

Amanda sounded hesitant. Jess sat up in bed, alert.

"Did something happen at the party that I ought to know about? Come on, Mandy. If it did, you've got to tell me. You're my best friend in the whole world."

"Nothing happened. Not really." Amanda's reassurances were not convincing.

Jess clutched a hand to her breast, preparing herself. "Did he meet someone new?"

"No. Nobody new."

Jess's control snapped. "Then what was it? You've got to tell me. The suspense is killing me."

"Okay, okay, I'll tell you. But it's probably nothing, all right? In fact, everyone else is going to be mad at me because we all decided not to say anything, since it would only get you worried."

Worried? Jess was almost beside herself now. "Everybody knows but me? Knows what?"

"Well, it was Karen. She was looking really good. She got her nose pierced on Friday. It's way cool."

"Amanda—" Jess could feel her jaw muscles tightening "— forget the nose and tell me what happened with Neil."

"Well, nothing happened, Jess. Like I said."

"Then what was it *everyone* decided not to bother telling me? That Karen got her nose pierced?"

"No, of course not. It's just that Neil did talk to her for quite a long time. Almost the entire party, actually."

Jess covered her face with her free hand. It was worse than she'd thought. She and Karen had never gotten along all that well. They were both too competitive. Nothing would give Karen greater pleasure, Jess was sure, than to steal Neil away from her. "Did they leave the party together?"

''No, and I'm sure about that since Karen took the same bus as me.''

Thank God for small mercies. Jess listened to a couple of other details about the party, but she wasn't very interested and soon said goodbye.

After hanging up, she paced her bedroom, not sure whom to be more furious at—Neil for talking up Karen, or her dad for not letting her go to the party. She'd known something like this would happen if she wasn't there. And the worst thing was, she couldn't even call Neil and confront him. No contact for a week included phone calls. It was so unfair. She *needed* to talk to Neil right now.

Her dad would never know if she made just one teeny little phone call.... It was so tempting. Jess picked up the phone, then rapidly punched in the first six digits of the number she knew so well. She hesitated over the seventh, remembering the week of kitchen duty she'd ended up with when she'd asked Neil to give her a ride to Grace's.

Of course, this was different. Her dad wouldn't find out this time. How could he? The phone bill didn't note local calls. So why not go for it?

Still she hesitated, flashes of things her father had said recently coming back to her: *I thought we had some mutual respect happening here. I thought I could trust you, and I hope I still can.*

The phone in her hand began beeping. She was told her call could not be completed as dialed. Jess hung up.

And tried to prepare herself for a week of mental torture.

JUST A FEW EMBERS, Grace told herself. *Nothing hot enough to restart the fire.* She was still trying to justify the way she'd melted when Levi placed his hands on her shoulders the other night. The impulse to kiss had been irrational, and fortunately neither one of them had carried through with it. He had sensed it, too, hadn't he? Lord, she would feel such a fool if her desire had been obvious and he had experienced no matching attraction. But that flash of heat in his eyes— she couldn't have imagined it. Or was she merely projecting her emotions on him?

"Everybody's waiting, Grace. Finished polishing your nails yet?"

Douglas Eberhart regarded her condescendingly from the doorway. Grace closed the file in front of her and stood up, then slowly and deliberately gathered the materials she needed for the board presentation. As she eased past him, she stopped briefly to glance at his left hand, which still gripped the handle of her door.

"Looks like yours could use a little buffing, Doug."

He fell in beside her as she headed down the corridor to the conference room. "Really, Grace? You used to think I was just fine the way I was."

Grace refrained from responding in kind. His sly references to their past relationship had increased lately. Together with her other problems, his insubordination was becoming more than she could deal with. He would have to go, she decided. But not until she'd immobilized this takeover attempt.

The double doors that led to the conference room were open. Grace nodded at Jackie.

"Everybody's here, Grace," Jackie said. "And don't worry. There won't be any interruptions today."

"Good." Grace paused a moment before entering

the room, letting Douglas precede her before she shut the maple doors firmly behind her.

Roberta's words came back to her as she settled herself at the head of the oval table. *Whatever happens, Grace, you can't lose control of your company. You've worked too hard, for too long,* she reminded herself.

She looked around the table, making eye contact with each board member before commencing. "Thanks, everyone, for taking the time to fit in another meeting. Today I'd like to outline my plan for evading the recent takeover attempt by Jarvis Enterprises. It will require bold action, but I believe those of us here are best positioned to make Body and Soul the foremost beauty store in the country."

Excitement and confidence, mixed in equal measure, poured through Grace's veins as she warmed to her subject. This was where she belonged, doing what she did best. She could triumph; she knew she could. All she had to do was convince the board....

"How old were you when you first slept with a guy?"

Grace stared blankly at the row of mauve polyester-silk dresses Jess had wanted to try on. They were searching for a size four. "I thought we were shopping for a dress." Although, in Grace's opinion, these were more like slips than dresses.

"What's the matter, Grace? Don't you want to tell me?"

Oh, sure. Nothing she'd like more than to discuss her first sexual experience with a fourteen-year-old girl she'd met only one week ago. Especially since the person she'd had her first sexual experience with had been Jess's father. "Is there a point to the question?" she asked evasively.

Jess shrugged. "Sort of."

Sort of. Grace didn't like the sound of that. Luckily, she found the dress she was looking for just then and could drop the subject. "Here's one. Size four. Want to give it a try?"

"Sure." Jess took the hanger and went into a change room.

Grace sat on a chair outside by the three-way mirror and waited, mulling over the possible reasons why Jess was so interested in the topic of sexual intercourse.

Was it curiosity? Or was there a more practical point to her question? Was it possible she was actually contemplating sleeping with her boyfriend, Neil? The very idea made Grace cringe. Surely not. At fourteen, Jess was still so very young.

Five minutes later, the door to the change room opened, and Grace's mouth dropped open in astonishment. The deceptively simple dress had completely transformed the slightly awkward adolescent into someone Grace wasn't sure she was ready to meet. The silky fabric clung to Jess's youthful curves, revealing faithfully the shape of her new, firm breasts, the flat plane of her belly, her slim but rounded hips. Unselfconsciously, Jess stood before the triple mirror, turning from side to side, allowing the fabric to swish gently against her legs.

"Nice, isn't it?"

Grace swallowed. She could not allow Jess to buy that dress. Levi would kill her. If she didn't kill herself first. "Maybe it's a little old for you, Jess. That's quite a sophisticated style for a girl your age."

Which was, of course, exactly the wrong thing to say.

"Really?" Jess's eyes gleamed. "I wonder what Neil would think of me in this."

Grace didn't wonder. She knew.

"It doesn't come with a jacket or anything, does it?" she asked a salesperson strolling toward them.

The young woman shook her head. "No. But that looks fantastic on you," she told Jess.

Thanks a lot, Grace thought. Now, how was she going to talk Jess out of this dress? In the end, fortunately, it was the price that did it.

"Wow!" Jess had dipped her head under her shoulder to look at the paper tag hanging out at her armpit. "Dad didn't give me this much money."

"Oh, well. I'm sure we'll find something else."

"Maybe." Jess changed back into her own clothes and left the dress behind in the change room with a longing glance. "Maybe Dad will give me an extra forty dollars."

Not once I tell him about the dress, Grace vowed silently. Aloud, she said simply, "I'm feeling a little hungry. How about you? Have you had dinner?"

"Yeah. Dad made me have something before I left. I could use a little dessert, though."

They took the escalator up to the food court, where they each got their own food then met at a little table. Grace dug into her chicken Caesar salad, privately salivating over the large hunk of cheesecake Jess had picked. Those were the days, she mused, remembering her teens and how she'd been able to eat anything without gaining weight. Although the truth was that she still didn't have to worry about her waistline. Stress and work did the trick. It certainly wasn't healthy eating and exercise that kept her in a size eight.

Once her salad was gone, Grace fought an unexpected urge to light a cigarette—which concerned her because she didn't consider herself addicted to smoking. Generally, she smoked only during business gatherings. Logical or not, she felt it gave her an added edge in dealing with men, and it was something Roberta had suggested in the early years when they'd worked together. Grace played with her fork, ignoring the irrational impulse. Smoking in the company of the impressionable teen was the last thing she'd do.

"So how was the board meeting?" Jess asked when all but a few crumbs remained of her dessert. "You said you were going to talk about how to stop that other company from buying a bunch of your shares and taking control of Body and Soul."

Grace was impressed that Jess seemed interested. "Not as well as I'd hoped, unfortunately, although I gave a dynamite presentation." She smiled, mocking her lack of modesty.

"What happened?"

"It's not so much what happened but who. Douglas Eberhart." Just saying his name gave Grace a sense of helpless rage. She should have guessed he'd try to sabotage her plans in a move to discredit her. Who would have thought he'd be so bold, though, as to openly oppose her at one of their board meetings?

"Is he that guy who came to your office when we were talking?"

"Exactly. Douglas is the vice president of finance. He's been with Body and Soul from the beginning. I used to think of him as my right-hand man."

"What did he do?"

"He tabled a statement that showed our company going bankrupt in about eight months if we followed my recommended course of action." Grace took a sip of water to rid herself of the acrid taste that had come to her mouth.

"Was he right?"

"Of course not. I could never put forward a plan of action so obviously harmful to the company's future." Grace shook her head. "The problem is you can use numbers to draw any conclusion."

"Why would he do something like that?"

"I don't know, Jess." She had her suspicions, of course. Jealousy, ambition, greed...not to mention leftover resentment from a love affair that never should have happened. None of which seemed appropriate to share with a young teenager like Jess.

Grace recalled the day—over a month ago now—that Stephen P. Vanderburg, chief executive officer at Jarvis Enterprises, had asked her to lunch. He'd laid his plans on the table next to the fettuccine and red wine. Body and Soul's unique product mix perfectly complemented his other retail operations. He wanted to buy out a percentage of her shares and give her divisional control over the company. They would integrate the Body and Soul package with his department stores and eventually phase out the independent franchise operations.

What did she think? He named a share price that he obviously thought would make her swoon. It certainly would make her a multimillionaire.

But she hadn't swooned. She'd stormed. The concept behind Body and Soul was completely incompatible with large-retail mentality. And what about her franchise owners, the people who had risked their capital and time because they believed in her idea as much as she did? She wasn't about to sell them out.

"I already own just under ten percent of your shares," Vanderburg had told her.

She'd been dismayed he'd built up so much equity in her company while strategically remaining below the ten percent threshold at which he would have to declare his ownership publicly.

He'd stayed calm in the face of her outrage, even going so far as to polish off the bottle of wine; where as she barely touched her glass.

"And soon I'll own even more," he'd continued. "I'll give you a couple of weeks to mull this over. If you don't come to see things my way, then I'll have no choice. I'll have to launch a formal takeover bid."

A takeover bid would give Jarvis Enterprises a minimum of twenty-one days to collect the shares they needed to gain control of her company.

Grace knew that with a high enough offer, Jarvis could convince most of the smaller shareholders to sell out to him. But even if he did that, and if Douglas sold his shares, as well, they would be short of their target of an additional forty-one percent of the total number of shares.

Grace was confident that neither she nor her loyal franchise owners would ever sell their shares. That left the balance of control with her remaining board members, each of whom owned small blocks of shares. In order to obstruct Jarvis's takeover, she had to convince those board members that she had the vision and the ability to maximize Body and Soul's potential.

"I hope they don't take your company away from you," Jess said.

"Thanks, Jess. But it's not a question of hope. It's

up to me to make sure it doesn't happen. I've got to convince my board of directors they'll do better to leave the company in my hands than to sell out to Jarvis. The way I'll do that is to develop an expansion plan that will more than double our size in the next five years.''

''Sounds risky to me.''

''Of course. But that's what business is all about, Jess— taking risks. If you never stick out your neck, you never get anywhere. Of course, you can't take stupid risks.''

''I think I know what you mean,'' Jess said, nodding. ''I sort of feel that way about Neil.''

Grace blinked. Jess had the most confounding ability to turn conversations around in a second. ''How so, Jess?''

''Well, he's a really cool sixteen-year-old, and I'm only fourteen. To keep him interested in me, I have to be willing to take some risks, you know. Or he'll get bored.''

''I don't think I follow. The rules that govern business don't necessarily apply to relationships.''

''Don't they?''

Grace stared at the girl across the table from her. They were heading into uncharted waters here, yet how could she, in all good conscience, back down at this point? ''What sort of risks are you talking about, Jess?''

Suddenly, Jess turned evasive. ''Oh, I don't know. I guess you'd think it was dumb, kid stuff.''

''No, I wouldn't.''

Jess shrugged. ''Just learning to like different music, trying to be interesting and more grown-up. You know what I mean.''

Grace suspected more was at stake here than just music. Yet part of her couldn't help but feel relieved that Jess hadn't confided in her any further. "I think you're great the way you are. You don't need to change to please anyone else."

"Really?" Jess smiled, and her cheeks flushed. "I hope I grow up to be as beautiful as you."

"You *are* beautiful," Grace replied, discomfited by the keen and hungry way Jess was looking at her, as if memorizing each feature of her face. Did Jess secretly harbor the belief she had some genetic expectation of resembling Grace when she grew up? Grace had hoped they were past that, that Jess was ready to accept their relationship for what it was. "Your real mother, whoever she is, must have been very pretty."

Some of the spark went out of Jess's eyes. She glanced down at the table, then raised her head. "I know my dad thinks you're beautiful, too," she said quietly. "I can tell by the way he looks at you."

Now it was Grace's turn to flush. Levi still found her attractive? "I don't think your father—"

"You don't have a boyfriend, do you?"

"Not really, although there are a few men I see occasionally." She thought of Ben Ryan, a lawyer who'd made it clear he'd be happy to see her more than the once or twice a month when she could fit him into her schedule.

Jess appeared worried by this answer. "You're not in love with any of them, are you?"

Grace stared down at her plate, fighting the smile of amusement that she knew would hurt Jess's feelings. She was not deceived by Jess's interest in her love life. She'd seen the movie *The Parent Trap*. So Jess thought she could get her parents back together, did she? Never mind that she had the wrong mother. And that Grace and Levi were ancient history.

"I'm not in love with anyone. And that includes your father. Don't think I can't see where you're headed with this. You have to understand your dad and I dated a long, long time ago. We've both changed a lot since then."

"But you had the kind of love that lasts forever!" Jess burst out, then suddenly looked sheepish. "Remember, I read your letters."

As usual, Grace felt a pang when she thought about those letters. She had poured everything into those pages. Now she could see that the writing had been cathartic, opening the dam on a lifetime of tenderness and love she had never shared with anyone before. Or anyone since. "You say all sorts of things when you're in love. They seem true at the time." Grace smiled gently. "Now I think I should take you home. Your dad did say to be back by nine."

"WHAT THE HELL IS THIS all about, Grace?" Levi asked angrily. He kicked at the ground, sending a cloud of sand scattering. "You had your little shopping trip. What do you need to talk to me for?"

Grace wondered if she would have been better off having this discussion at the coffee shop. She'd thought the peace and quiet of Kitsilano Beach would be conducive to a calm, rational conversation about Jess. Perhaps that had been too much to hope for. Levi had made it clear he wasn't pleased she was spending time with his daughter.

Jess was in her room right now, returning a couple of phone calls from her girlfriends and getting ready for bed. Grace thought about the issues that had come up earlier that evening and sighed.

"I didn't suggest this walk for the fun of it." Could she help it if she sounded bitter? They were walking northeast along the pathway, heading toward Granville Island. The ocean lay to their left, the reflected lights from the city sparkling on the dark water like diamonds tossed onto black velvet. Nearby, waves broke, pulsing with a rhythm that reminded Grace of other nights, on other shores, spent with this man by her side.

"That goes without saying." Levi sank his hands deep into the pockets of his khaki-colored shorts. His lean, muscled legs moved with deceptive languor as he set a pace just a little too fast for Grace.

She followed, though, strangely feeling that the narrow trail they were walking symbolized an emotional tightrope. She had to keep fighting the urge to reach out a hand to him in the hope that he could keep her steady. Instead, she tried to concentrate on the cool evening breeze as it danced through the weave of her knit top.

"Jess and I talked about things I thought you should be aware of."

She could sense the pricking of his interest, although he didn't say a word.

"Starting with the dress she wanted to buy. It was over her budget, thank goodness, but she might ask you for the extra forty bucks. If I were you, I wouldn't give it to her."

"Oh?"

"At least that's my opinion. Of course, if you want, you could go take a look at it with her and see what you think."

Overhead illumination as they passed a streetlamp revealed trepidation in his expression. "Is it too old for her?"

"That's part of it." Grace hesitated, searching for the most tactful way to explain that it simply made Jess look too sexy. "Although I think a woman would have to be young to wear the dress. It doesn't exactly hide the effects of gravity on a woman's body or the passage of time. My first thought when I saw it was that it was a slip, not an actual dress."

"A slip. I think I know the style you're talking about." He gave her a sideways glance. "And did the dress, um, fit her?"

Grace knew what he meant. "Yes. It definitely fit her. She looked beautiful in it."

"Beautiful in a fourteen-year-old-girl way?"

Grace paused. "More like an eighteen-year-old-girl way."

Levi cleared his throat. "So no extra forty bucks."

"I think that's wise."

The path broadened as they rounded the curve past the park, and Grace felt her energy pick up. Suddenly, Levi's pace wasn't too fast anymore. She enjoyed the feeling of her arms swinging through the air. If only she and Levi could keep on like this. She felt no need to talk, or even to hold hands. Levi's presence beside her was a palpable thing.

Ten minutes likely passed before Levi spoke again. "Why is it young girls are always in such a big hurry to grow up?"

Grace couldn't answer. He knew, better than anyone, how little experience she'd had with growing up until she finally broke out of her protective family circle at age eighteen.

"Do you suppose Jess still thinks you're her mother?"

Grace thought about the moment in the food court when Jess had scrutinized her as if trying to guess which features she might have inherited; then, later, Jess's not-so-subtle attempt to figure out Grace's feelings for Levi. Did Levi need to know any of that? She had no idea how she could even begin to tell him. "I'm not sure. She didn't say anything specific. We just shopped."

"Right."

Maybe she'd sounded dismissive, as if she didn't want to tell him about her time with Jess. Well, the truth was that it would be awkward—particularly when it came to Jess's questions about Grace's first sexual encounter. How could she broach a topic like that with Levi? Not that it was even necessary. She'd probably overreacted. And Levi seemed to be doing a good job of keeping tabs on his daughter. He certainly didn't need her advice or help. She was sure, in fact, that he would be quick to tell her so if she brought up the topic.

"What about you, Grace?" Levi asked. "Did you buy anything? Maybe *you* should have tried on that dress. Gravity and the passage of time haven't made much of a mark on you."

Oh, really. Grace was surprised he'd noticed. He seemed so indifferent to her presence, while she felt almost foolish in her adolescent awareness of him. "Nor you," she said softly. "You're even fitter than when—than when you were in university." She'd almost said *than when we were going out,* but in the end the words wouldn't come. Maybe if she never mentioned it, she could pretend it never happened.

Maybe then she could regain her equilibrium and relegate Levi to the far recesses of her mind, where he belonged.

"That's running for you. Jess says I'm addicted and she's probably right. What do you do for fitness?"

"Not much, I hate to admit." As if there were any time in her life for the gym or sports.

"But you're still so slender. Maybe even thinner than before."

"I skip more meals than I should," Grace said. "Unless I have a luncheon or dinner meeting, it's hard to take the time to eat." She sensed his disapproval of this as well as the lack of exercise she'd admitted to earlier. What was it to him how she lived, anyway? She had her answer in his next remark.

"I hope your food habits don't rub off on Jess. It's hard enough to get her to eat proper meals. She's only fourteen, but already she worries about her weight."

"So what am I supposed to do? Pin a Canada Food Guide to my fridge when she comes over?" Grace felt an unaccountable desire for a cigarette. She reached for her purse where she kept the pack that usually lasted her all week, then pulled her hand away, suddenly reluctant to smoke in front of Levi.

But he'd already noticed and correctly interpreted her gesture. "When did you start?" he asked quietly. Disapprovingly.

"Years ago," she told him defiantly. What right did he have to pass judgment on her? It wasn't as if she smoked very much. Smoking was just a behavior she engaged in occasionally—like drinking martinis—that helped her to be taken seriously by the business crowd.

"I hope you don't plan to smoke in front of Jess."

That remark stopped her in her tracks. "You've really got your nerve."

"That may be how you see it. But as Jess's father, I have to watch out for her best interests. She thinks you're the greatest, you know that?"

He was looking at her as if it were totally inconceivable.

"At this point in her life," he continued, "I don't think anyone has more influence over her. She's even trying to walk and talk like you now."

Was that true? Grace hadn't noticed.

"If she saw you smoking, you can be sure it would make a big impression on her. And not the sort of impression I would be very happy about."

Grace appreciated his rationale, but she fumed at his condescension. Facing him on the path, she resisted the urge to shake him by the shoulders. "I don't suppose it's occurred to you I might actually have the good sense to figure that one out on my own. Next you're probably going to tell me not rob any banks, jaywalk or litter when I'm with her...."

She turned around and began walking rapidly back toward the Jolt O' Java and the parking spot where she'd left her car, her earlier excitement that the night might last forever reduced to cinders by the anger that now burned inside her. Why had she suggested this foolish moonlight stroll? While she was fantasizing about their past relationship, all he could think about was how unsuitable she was for his daughter. Why did he disapprove of her and her lifestyle so much?

Behind her, she heard his footsteps on the path, fast enough to overtake her but not a full-out run. As he drew near, the quick in and out of his breath became audible.

"I'm sorry, Grace. I guess I got carried away."

He was beside her again, had taken her arm. *It wasn't fair how good it felt.*

She pulled away. "I'm surprised you didn't ask me for references before you allowed me to go shopping with her."

"Enough, Grace. I've said I'm sorry."

Grace's chin rose higher. *He* was angry now?

"I know I have no right to grill you like that. But try to see things from my perspective. From the beginning, it's been Jess and me. Just the two of us. Up until the past couple of years, Jess seemed to think the world revolved around me. Whatever I said had to be right. I was always the final authority, the big hero. Nothing made her happier than when we spent time together.

"Now, suddenly, everything has turned around. She's wearing makeup and has a boyfriend. Spending time with me has become a big sacrifice—she'd really rather be with her friends."

Grace's anger evaporated as she recognized the pain behind Levi's words. "It's just a stage, Levi. The first time I met her, she told me what a fantastic father you are."

"I know, Grace. But—" Levi let out a deep breath "—well, I guess I feel a little jealous. You're all she talks about these days. The prospect of spending time with you is the only thing I can use to distract her from the misery of not seeing her boyfriend for a week."

"Oh, Levi. I'm just the flavor of the month. You're her *father.*" The comment, which she'd meant as reassurance, did not go over as planned. She saw the mistrust in his eyes when he repeated the phrase.

"Flavor of the month."

She knew what he was thinking—that she'd even-tually abandon Jess. "It's just an expression, Levi. I didn't mean it literally."

"Are you sure, Grace? Maybe you already resent the time Jess is taking from your work."

"Don't try to second-guess me. I told you at the beginning that I wouldn't let Jess down, and I meant it."

Levi stopped walking and turned to her. They were between streetlights now, and deep shadows hid his face. She was aware of him on a level that had nothing to do with his daughter and everything to do with their past. She heard the intensity behind his softly spoken words.

"I'm sure you meant it, Grace. But can you live up to it? That's what I'm wondering."

"I know." Grace didn't bother with more reassur-ances. Suddenly, despite Jess's having been the subject of their conversation, she was the last thing on Grace's mind. Maybe it was the darkness that allowed her to stand her ground, neither turning nor walking away from Levi, but she waited quietly for him to reach out and touch her. They were so near to each other it wouldn't take much movement from either of them.

Didn't he feel how inevitable it was?

Didn't his body feel the same gravitational pull as hers?

Didn't he wonder what it would be like to kiss her again?

"Grace..."

There. She heard what she wanted in just that one word. She leaned nearer. Yearning...

"You're going to drive me mad. You know that, don't you?"

Yes. That was her aim. She lowered her eyelids, parted her mouth… Nothing happened. She felt her body waver, then he reached out his hand to steady her. Not to pull her nearer. Just to steady her.

"You're a very beautiful woman, Grace."

What was that supposed to be?—her consolation prize? Her sight now adjusted to the murky light, Grace inspected his face, searching for the emotions he'd always allowed to stay close to the surface. Tonight she couldn't see them. It wasn't the darkness; it was Levi. He was purposely shutting her out.

"We could kiss right now, Grace," he said. "I could even take you home and we could make love."

Yes. Grace's rational mind had shut off and she knew it. What was more, she didn't care. Desire danced on her nerve endings, luring her forward and into his arms.

But he was still standing back from her.

His eyes never veered from hers. Dark stubble outlined his jaw and chin, highlighting lips she longed to touch.

"We could do that for old times' sake and it might be kind of nice—it might even be fantastic."

It would be fantastic. She knew it would.

A gust of wind came up from the ocean then, lifting the corner of his T-shirt, flattening the silky fabric of her top against her breasts. And with the wind came a moan and the whisper of a name. Jess. The name hovered between them long enough for Grace to be quite sure.

It wasn't going to happen.

Not now. Maybe not ever.

"Levi." She tried not to sound as though she was pleading.

This time, he placed an arm around her shoulders—a gesture almost brotherly in nature. She leaned against him, as close to collapse as she'd ever felt in her life.

Levi Shanahan was her ex-lover. And it appeared he was determined to stay that way.

CHAPTER FIVE

JESS HEARD THE KEY scraping in the lock, the footsteps to the kitchen, the fridge door sighing open. She knew it was Levi, back from his walk with Grace. A few moments later, he made his way down the hall and stopped in front of her door.

"Come in, Dad," she said before he had a chance to knock.

"Hey, Jess." He stood in the doorway, a beer bottle in one hand, the other hand resting against the door frame. "Still awake?"

"Can't sleep." She rolled onto her back and put her book facedown on the pillow beside her.

"Yeah?"

Her father settled on the edge of the bed and ran a hand over her head as though checking for a fever or something. Of course, the thing that was wrong with her wouldn't show up that way.

"Feeling okay?"

"Not bad." She shrugged. There was no sense telling him how worried she was about Neil and Karen. He'd just figure she was blaming him for not letting her go to the party in the first place. And anyway, he'd probably think it was good news. He'd made no secret of his dislike for Neil. Which was just so unfair.

"I've been giving some thought to the dress, kid,

and I'm sorry, but I'm not going to give you the extra forty. I'd like you to keep to the original budget."

He looked as if he expected her to protest, but the truth was, she wasn't sure she even wanted the dress. Observing herself in the mirror, she'd felt that she was meeting a stranger. She'd liked what she'd seen, but she wasn't sure she was ready to be that person yet.

"That's okay. I'm sure I can find something else. I saw a nice long velvet dress that I might go back and try with Amanda."

"Good. Great." He bent over to kiss her forehead. "Good night, Jess."

"Night, Dad." She watched him walk back to the door. "Oh, Dad?"

"Yes?"

"How was your walk with Grace?"

The tender expression on her father's face vanished. Something cold, almost empty, took its place.

"It was okay."

They hadn't been gone long. He'd returned home alone. It wasn't what Jess had hoped for when she heard Grace issue the invitation.

Grace and her dad, together again. The idea had appealed to her from the moment she'd met Grace. Grace was everything Jess wanted to be when she grew up. Beautiful, sophisticated, independent and smart. Jess just knew that she was her mother; it felt right. And she knew that her father and Grace were attracted to each other. The vibrations were heavy whenever they were together. So what could make more sense than their becoming a family, the family they were always meant to be?

"I had a lot of fun shopping with her. It was even

interesting talking about her business. She's real smart, isn't she, Dad?''

He nodded, still not smiling. ''Yeah.''

''Beautiful, too.'' She was pushing it, she knew. It wouldn't pay to be too obvious.

''G'night, Jess.''

She watched as the door swung behind her father, then listened to it click tightly shut. With a sigh, she turned off the lamp and settled back into her pillow. Grace and her dad belonged together; she was sure she was right.

But so far, she seemed to be the only one who thought that way.

MARIAN WAS WEARING a new dress, Levi noticed later that week. And she'd done something to her hair.

''The date was a success?'' He placed her cappuccino on the table.

''I'll say.'' Her eyes were sparkling with sass; her smile was broad. ''We went to Umberto's and had the best risotto ever. And a bottle of wine with dinner, then champagne later. At Richard's house.'' Marian winked. ''We went to a movie on Tuesday and we have another dinner date tomorrow.''

''Sounds great, but are you sure you're not moving just a little too quickly?'' He was glad things had gone so well, but that bottle of champagne at Richard's sounded a bit too cozy for a first date.

''You're forgetting we've known each other for years, Levi.''

''Yeah, I guess.'' He just didn't want to see Marian hurt again. Her impulsiveness had done it to her before.

''You worry too much, you know that?'' She took

his hand. "But I appreciate your looking out for my interests—I really do."

Phil came in then and pulled up a chair. He knew Marian; Levi had introduced them after her divorce, thinking something might come of it, but it never had. They liked each other well enough, but, as they'd both confided to him privately, there just weren't any sparks.

"You're looking good, Marian," Phil said. "Do something to your hair?"

Another woman might have accepted the compliment and let it pass. Not Marian. "Yeah. I had it highlighted on Monday. It took two frigging hours and cost me over a hundred bucks, so it oughta look good, don't you think?"

"Of course you're rolling in dough these days, aren't you? Levi told me something about an inheritance."

"That's right. The family farm in Manitoba. It goes on the auction block next month."

"How much do you think it'll bring?"

"I don't really know. I'm supposed to get some estimates in a week or two."

"Excuse me a minute." After leaving his coffee cup on the table, Levi went up to the front of the café to serve a couple who had just walked in the door.

It was a pleasant spring evening, not quite dark, and the place was hopping. Going for a stroll after dinner, then stopping for a cappuccino, was becoming a way of life for a growing number of urbanites. Levi thought it was a mentally healthy trend— anything to get people away from their televisions and out mixing with the real people they lived among.

"Can we sit outside?" the man asked after Levi had given him his change.

"Sure." Levi grabbed a dishrag and led the pair out the door to the only available table. He cleared the dishes, then wiped down the table for them. "Here you go. Enjoy the evening."

As he carried the dirty cups and plates to the dishwasher, he passed Marian and Phil on the way. They were so engaged in their conversation they didn't notice him go by. He hoped the negative feelings he had about this Richard Craig would prove wrong with time. He didn't know why he felt so distrustful of a man he'd never met, but his instincts warned him that Marian was headed for trouble again.

Maybe it was because he was a father. Having a teenage daughter had forevermore changed his views on romantic entanglements. For sure, he didn't want to be a hypocrite—advise Jess one way, then condone a different behavior for himself and others. Not that he'd been one to sleep around, but now he was almost paranoid in his choices.

With the result that it was now eight months since Cynthia had walked out on him in frustration at his unwillingness to commit beyond a day, a week or a month. She'd made the right decision because he'd missed her only for a month or so, and even then not too badly.

When love was the real thing, breaking up hurt a hell of a lot more, he knew.

Did Grace have any idea that his feelings for her had become the standard by which he measured all his liasons? It wasn't that he remained single because he harbored secret fantasies that somehow he and Grace would end up together again. When she walked out on him, he'd accepted that it truly marked the end for them. Nor did he believe there was only one person in the world he could ever be happy with. He wasn't that idealistic.

But he was enough of a romantic to be unwilling to settle for anything less than that feeling of total involvement with another human being. He'd had it with Grace, but no one since.

Odd, because as his friends, and Phil in particular, had been so quick to point out, he and Grace were so unlike each other. They had different interests, priorities and goals in life. So what was it between them? After all these years, he still didn't know. He knew, however, that whatever it was, it hadn't gone away.

The silken thread connecting them when they were younger may have stretched, but it hadn't broken. Did she feel that, too?

He'd never been quite sure of Grace, not even during the height of their romance. Purposefully or not, she'd always kept something back, her eyes and words never admitting the depth of what *he* felt between them.

Which had to explain what had happened the other night on the beach. Or almost happened. The word *temptation* didn't begin to describe the way he'd reacted with her body only inches from his and that open invitation in her eyes. Why hadn't he just taken her in his arms and kissed her? It was what they'd both wanted at that moment.

But he was the father of a teenage daughter. And he could no longer think only of the moment.

Obviously, Grace could contemplate life apart after spending a night with him, whereas he realized it would tear him to pieces to hold her once more, only to have to let her go again.

Even knowing that, however, hadn't made the decision an easy one. She'd looked bewitching in the glow of streetlamp and moon, and he was only human after all. Which made him wonder where he'd found the strength. And where he would get it the next time he needed it.

"Hey," Phil called.

Levi emptied a bag of muffins into a wicker basket and placed them in the display case. He knew he was preoccupied with Grace; she was quickly becoming an obsession. He had to get a grip, keep his life under control. Once he'd filled his mug with fresh, Java-blend coffee, he rejoined his friends.

"What's up?" he asked.

"I was just wondering about Grace. She been around since the last time I saw her?"

Mind reader—that was what Phil was. Of course, Levi knew reading *his* mind these days was pretty easy. All he ever thought about was Grace. If you didn't count the worrying about Jess. Still, it wasn't a subject he wanted to discuss. "If you're thinking of asking her for a date, forget it. Her corporate calendar is pretty full."

"As if I'd do that to my oldest buddy. As if she'd be interested if I did."

"What's this?" Marian looked from one man to the other. "Are you talking about Grace Hamilton?"

Phil smiled knowingly. "None other."

"She's the one we were talking about the other day, isn't she, Levi? The one Jess thinks is her mother?"

Phil raised an eyebrow at his friend. "Poor Jess will soon figure out Grace's maternal instincts are limited to buying a padded carrying case for her laptop computer.''

Levi had to smile. ''God, Phil. I hope I never end up on your bad side. She's not quite that awful, Marian.''

Phil shook his head. ''Don't let his casual attitude deceive you. There never was a woman could tie our Levi in knots the way good old Grace could. Which brings me back to my original question. Have you seen her lately?''

''Define 'lately.'''

''Jeez, you can be a stubborn—''

''Oh, let it drop,'' Marian said. ''He isn't going to tell you anything anyway.''

''Smart woman.'' Levi patted her hand, then looked at Phil. ''You could learn a thing or two from her.'' The trouble with a friend dating back to high school was he thought he could talk to you about anything. Phil had always been generous with his advice, even though Levi rarely chose to take it. If he'd listened to Phil, Jess wouldn't even be here right now. She'd have been put up for adoption or shipped out to some foster home.

''I just don't want to see you make the same mistake twice,'' Phil said.

Marian looked at Levi thoughtfully. Clearly, she was intrigued by the subject. ''Does Jess still think Grace is her mother?''

Levi frowned at Phil. ''Look what you've started.'' He turned to Marian. ''I don't know. I hope she doesn't. She *says* she doesn't. But deep down...well, I just don't know. She and Grace went shopping the other day.''

''Shopping?''

"Yeah. Grace says Jess isn't necessarily looking for her mother. What she really wants is a female role model." Levi could feel his lips twist as he pronounced the last three words with a decidedly sarcastic edge.

"Let me guess. Grace is the role model?" Phil asked.

"For the time being." Levi stared at the dregs in his cup. "I think she feels sorry for Jess, but I'm sure it won't be long before she gets either too bored or too busy to find the time for her. I'm just standing on the sideline, waiting to pick up the pieces when that happens."

Marian appeared puzzled. "What makes you so sure Grace is going to let her down?"

Phil exchanged a knowing look with Levi before replying on his friend's behalf. "Experience."

GRACE SHUT HER office door with her elbow, dropped her briefcase onto a chair and set her coffee and Danish on top of the desk. It was one of those rare mornings when she had a couple of hours before her first appointment, and she intended to start working on the budget for her expansion plans. If she couldn't count on Douglas to do his job, she'd darn well have to do it for him.

After shrugging out of her navy silk blazer, she hung it carefully on the back of her chair. Would she ever forget the humiliation of that moment when Douglas had stood up in front of the board and pronounced her plans not only unfeasible but downright financially irresponsible? Lord help her, she was going to get him for that.

With the edge of her polished thumbnail, Grace

pried the plastic lid off her foam cup, then took a sip from her jumbo-size java. Why had she selected the brew Levi favored? Why did he seem to influence almost every decision she made these days?

She pushed those questions away with a bite of the gooey strawberry Danish. Until this moment, she hadn't realized just how hungry she was. Had she had dinner last night? She couldn't recall.

Not sleeping much, however, she did remember. It had been that way since Levi had rejected her so unequivocally that night at the beach after she'd been shopping with Jess. She didn't know whom to be more angry with—herself for making it so obvious she still wanted him, or him for being so maddeningly immune to her. She took another sip of coffee, another bite of Danish.

Levi. The name—the man—was on her mind far too often. The fact was, she just didn't have time to fixate on the situation between them. Okay, she'd practically thrown herself at him. And he had turned her down. *Get over it,* she warned herself. Work was her priority now, and she had a lot to accomplish today. So what if she felt as if she hadn't had a decent sleep in days? That could always be compensated for with a heavy dose of sugar and caffeine. Besides, she was used to running on adrenaline.

Grace opened her folio and glanced through the budget numbers Douglas had cooked up for last week's meeting. He'd developed estimates of the revenues and expenses they could expect at each of Grace's proposed expansion sites. Even a quick review assured Grace his results were absurd.

Their worst location had never done sales at the low levels he'd chosen to project his revenues. As for the expenses, everyone knew interest rates were not going to rise that high in the near future. Grace reached for her calculator with one hand, the Danish with the other. Punching through the numbers, she found a simple adding mistake, one that didn't work in the project's favor. Was it an honest error, or was Douglas using every trick in the book?

After a final gulp of her coffee, Grace gathered up her papers and went across the hall to confront him with the obvious errors she'd uncovered. That there were more, she had no doubt, but at least this was a start.

His office, however, was empty. His secretary said he wouldn't be back until after lunch. Frustrated, Grace scanned his desk to see if she could locate the support for his numbers. Tucked in a corner, under the morning paper, sat a file labeled "Expansion Projections" that appeared promising.

Her first conclusion was that she'd found what she was looking for. But after skimming over the budget numbers, she realized this was a completely different version. While the figures he'd presented to the board had shown losses for the complete five-year time span, these indicated not only profits but an investment payback of only four years.

Grace sank into Douglas's chair to examine the figures more carefully. She saw they were based on the assumptions and hypotheses she had outlined to him several weeks ago. As she flipped through the pages, she fought her growing disbelief. When had Douglas done all this work? There hadn't been time since that muddled board meeting, had there? And even if he'd had time, what could possibly have motivated him?

Had something happened to change his mind about the takeover?

Instinctively, Grace picked up the phone to call Roberta.

"Good news. It looks like Douglas has developed the projections the way I asked him to. We're showing a positive cash flow right from the first year. I'm sure the board will approve my ideas now that we've got realistic numbers."

"That sounds great, Grace. I'm glad to hear it." There was a muffled sound of Roberta coughing, then she continued, "The sooner you put out a press release, the better."

"It won't be for a while. I can't get everyone together for another meeting for at least a week or two."

"So you'll hang tight until then?"

"Right. Thanks, Roberta." Grace hung up with a sense of calamity averted. Douglas's animosity was not as far gone as she had assumed. Perhaps he'd realized that by hurting the company, he would only be harming himself and his own prospects in the long run.

In which case, she would have to rethink some of her more recent decisions. Maybe she wouldn't have to get rid of Douglas after all.

Caution, nonetheless, made her review the numbers once more, this time using a calculator to check all the math. Douglas walked in the room when she was on the last page.

"Excuse me?" He looked profoundly offended to find her at his desk.

"I'm sorry, Doug. I was just so excited to see these figures you developed." She tapped the file folder in front of her. "This was exactly what I wanted. You've done a very good job." She stood up, waving him to his seat. "I just called Roberta. We'll schedule another board meeting and you can present this information then. Perhaps you could get transparencies made up…?"

"Sure. No problem." Douglas seemed more comfortable now that he was back in his chair. He glanced down at the file folder, then back at her. "Did you get a chance to examine the whole package?"

"Enough. I saw the budgets and the list of assumptions I asked you to work with. I might have used a slightly lower growth factor, but I think it's fine the way it is."

"Good. I'm glad you're satisfied."

There was nothing insubordinate in what he said, but the gleam in his eye made her feel slightly uncomfortable. Not willing to jeopardize the positive shift in their relationship, however, Grace told herself not to be overly sensitive.

"I'm glad you decided to be cooperative, Douglas. If we work as a team on this expansion, nothing and no one will be able to stop us."

"Yeah. We make a good team, don't we, Grace?"

There it was again. That glimmer of something she couldn't quite identify. Was it more of his sexual innuendo? Maybe she was just imagining it.…

"I'd like to see those transparencies before the meeting," she said, her hand on the doorknob.

"Sure thing." He got up and walked to where she stood by the door. After placing one hand over hers, the one about to pull open the door, he turned it into his palm.

"I'd forgotten how nice working with you can be, Grace. Do you ever think we made a mistake? You know, in deciding to end our after-hours partnership?"

Grace eased her hand from his. "I do miss the comradeship we shared in the early days." She backed away from him slightly, repositioning her hand on the doorknob, pulling it toward her so she could glimpse the corridor beyond. "But as far as our relationship went, the mistake was in starting anything in the first place."

"Oh, really?"

"Not a good idea to mix business and pleasure. Surely you agree."

"I don't know. I always thought business was pleasure. And I thought you thought the same way."

"I guess I did."

"But not any longer?"

Grace opened the door wider, feeling a desperate need to escape. "I just believe that a purely business relationship is more professional. I'll look forward to seeing those transparencies." Then she closed the door, instinctively checking the corridor to see who might have overheard her parting words.

Her executive assistant, Jackie O'Connor, was the only one nearby.

"Watch that one," she said warningly as Grace passed by.

"I always do," Grace replied.

CHAPTER SIX

GRACE SPREAD HER SWEATSHIRT on the damp grass and settled herself on top of it, facing the beach. The rising sun was at her back, but she kept her sunglasses on and her baseball cap low over her forehead. Dawn had broken only an hour earlier and the city looked dewy fresh in the glow of the morning light. To be out this early was unusual for her unless she was at work. She felt guilty, then wondered if it was because of the unattended paperwork in her briefcase or because of what she'd come here to do.

She closed her eyes, focusing on the sound of the waves splashing on the rocks in front of her and the squawks of the seagulls as they coasted on airstreams above her head. With deep breaths, she filled her lungs, slowly pushing away her concern about work— that ever-present anxiety that something was about to go seriously wrong.

When she tried hard enough, she began to pick out the smells of the world around her. The tang of the ocean and the musty scent of trees, grass and dirt. Gradually, she felt a change wash over her body. Her limbs became heavier; her head relaxed with somnolence. Close to sleep but not quite there, she experienced a peaceful relief from the tension headache that had hit her last night and had not quite been gone when she awoke that morning.

Serenity. It was such an unfamiliar sensation.

Grace had occasionally felt a sense of happiness that bordered on elation—the first time she'd sat at the desk in the office of her own company; cutting the ribbon on her first retail outlet; seeing her company's name listed on the Toronto Stock Exchange.

Those had been momentary high points, though. Gone almost as soon as they arrived. Sometimes Grace thought they might have been less elusive if she'd had someone to share them with. *See, Mom, Dad? I told you I could do it!*

But her parents were dead—killed in a car crash just three months before her graduation. They'd died thinking she'd ruined her life; now they would never know how wrong they'd been. She had more money than they could have dreamed of. She had power and influence, was a woman who had made her mark, not through her husband and a good marriage but because of her own accomplishments.

Waste of good money to send a girl to university.

Her father would never eat those words now.

But it seemed that no matter how great an achievement, the feeling of satisfaction was all too transitory, leaving her with longings she could quell only by hurling herself toward the next goal, searching for the peak that would finally be high enough to fill her entire being with a sense of worthiness.

The truth was, despite all the accolades she'd received, Grace still felt she was somehow not good enough. That she was a fraud. That good luck, not intelligence and hard work, was responsible for her achievements.

And it wasn't fair, because she'd paid the price for her success. Living alone, sacrificing her social life, working horrendous hours—these had been her conscious sacrifices. Of course, she had her colleagues and her business associates, but they occupied a realm that could never be confused with family or friends.

Even her relationship with Roberta could not truly be considered a friendship. She couldn't imagine, for instance, the two of them sharing a Thanksgiving dinner. Partly that was an extension of the kind of person Roberta was. She'd always said there was time for success or time to have fun, never time for both. Roberta had sworn off holidays years ago. And Grace had never forgotten the first thing she'd told her on her first day of work.

"You probably think you have to be as tough as nails to survive in the business world, Grace, but that's not true. If you hit a nail with a hammer the wrong way, it bends. You can't let that happen to you. No matter what, you can't allow yourself to bend. Because then someone's going to yank you out of the wall, and what'll you be good for then?"

Tougher than nails.

Grace had tried. She'd thought she was.

Then Jess had showed up. And she'd seen Levi again. The stronghold was crumbling at the foundations and she had no idea what to do about it.

A month ago, she never would have guessed how a fourteen-year-old girl could get under her skin. She'd never been one for maternal cravings, never felt the relentless ticking of her biological clock. In fact, babies frightened her.

But Jess... Something deep inside Grace responded to the girl—to her trust, her openness, her vulnerability. It wasn't just that Jess wanted to spend time with her; it was the way she seemed to *need* to spend time with her. Grace wanted to take her by the hand and introduce her to the possibilities before her. She could be anything, go anywhere, do what she pleased. There were no limits, beyond her imagination. These were the gifts she longed to give Jess, to show her what a young woman could accomplish if she was encouraged to succeed, rather than discouraged at every turn.

Not that she suspected Levi of being the sort of parent to Jess that her father had been to her. But the world was still largely dominated by men. Jess was going to have to face some hurdles that only another woman could understand. And Grace wanted to be the woman who helped her; she felt a protective concern for Jess that she had never experienced before.

She didn't know why. Was it that Jess was Levi's daughter? Was it that she'd never felt for any other man anything like what she felt for Levi? Grace hoped not. She knew better than to assume her motives regarding Jess were entirely altruistic. But she didn't think she was merely trying to leech onto a part of Levi's life.

And even if she was, she was smart enough to know any such attempt would not meet with success. Anyone could tell Levi wasn't looking for a woman to make him complete; his life was already in balance. Sure he'd been thrown a few curve balls, but he still gave the impression of being in control, just as he'd been when she first knew him so many years ago. Grace envied him that inner strength, the confidence that no matter what happened, he could make everything turn out right.

She'd thought she had that same confidence, but now she wasn't sure. Levi, not she, had been the one wise enough to step back when she'd thrown herself at him the other night. It was he who had understood there was no sense in the two of them searching for a connection that no longer existed. He who had moved on, unencumbered by the past the way she was.

Tucked up against a tree, Grace straightened her spine as the man in her thoughts suddenly came into view. Her body went on alert—her breathing quickened; her pulse picked up. To see him was why she had come to the beach so early on a Saturday morning, dressed in clothes meant to conceal.

Feeling guilty, like a spy, she'd questioned Jess about her father and found out that a morning run was part of his routine. She'd come here specifically to watch him without his knowing. To have the luxury of a few minutes where she didn't have to guard her expressions and reactions. She could stare if she wanted, absorb all the details that fascinated her, and no one would know.

Grace realized she was acting like a person obsessed, but she was unable to shake this new compulsion. It had been over a week now and he was still almost all she thought about. If anything, it was getting worse. She longed to reestablish the connection between them. Not that she was foolish enough to think it was something that might last. No, she'd be happy with just a night, one night to remember and experience everything that being in love could mean.

Which was foolish, of course. You couldn't turn back the clock, and she and Levi would never be the people they once were. She ought to be grateful he had appreciated that fact and had the good sense to maintain the distance between them.

But she wasn't. Ever since their moonlight stroll on the beach, she'd dreamed of how things might have turned out. She could sense he was still attracted, at least physically, and in her mind she'd replayed scenes from their past, invented scenes for the future. It was like a progressive disease, to the extent that Grace wondered if something was fundamentally wrong with her. She knew she needed a reality check, but she didn't know how to get it.

Levi was running along the path that separated Kitsilano Beach from the park, his chest bare, his hair pulled back as usual. His body was lean, the muscles well defined, the skin tanned dark, almost like espresso. As he ran closer, she could hear the *huff, huff* of each breath he let out. Sweat glistened, particularly on his face and chest, reminding her of the baby oil they'd slathered over themselves in younger, more foolish days.

Closing her eyes and hugging her knees to her chest, Grace could almost feel his hands on her sunbaked body, gliding with the oil down her back to meet with her bikini bottom, one finger sliding suggestively under the thin fabric and rubbing seductively. He had nibbled her ear while doing this, suggesting in short, blunt phrases what he would do if they weren't on a public beach.

Suddenly, a woman running from the opposite direction with a large golden retriever lost control of her leash. Her hot, tired dog dashed for the ocean despite her cries of dismay.

"Max! Max! Come back here, Max!"

With long, even strides, Levi swerved from his route and came up from behind just as Max stuck his nose in the surf. Lunging gracefully, Levi grabbed the leash. "Sorry, Max. No fishing today," he said good-humoredly. Then he handed the leash to the grateful woman, who tried to detain him with a hand on his arm and words Grace could not hear.

The woman was attractive and young, her fit body encased in Lycra shorts and a sports bra, and Grace hated the instant jealousy that curdled in her stomach with the cup of coffee she'd gulped down on the drive over.

Levi was doing a slow backward jog so he could keep up his heart rate while talking to the woman. She was waving her one free hand, taking occasional steps forward to keep the distance between them from increasing too quickly. But Levi shook his head to whatever offer she was making him or maybe he was just brushing aside her thanks, before he turned and dashed back to the path.

Grace watched the whole thing feeling as if someone had taken a bicycle tire pump to her heart and expanded it way beyond its normal capabilities. She knew he'd done nothing extraordinary, nothing even remotely heroic or courageous.

He was just being decent and kind.

In other words, himself.

Gradually, he disappeared around the curve of the small peninsula, and Grace allowed herself to fall back against the tree trunk. What had she just done? Sure, this was a public beach and she had every right to be here if she wanted. But she knew she'd only come to see Levi. And now that she had, an unfamiliar emotion made her want to run for her car and hide. After a few uncomfortable seconds, she identified the feeling. It was shame.

She balled up her sweatshirt and made her way to the street. She had hours to pass before her lunch date with Jess. Just the opportunity she needed to go over

the sales reports for last month. The image of Levi
running on the beach burned in her mind as she unlocked her car and pulled down the visor against the
low morning sun.

She'd planned to pick Jess up, but maybe it would
be better to ask Jess to meet her at the restaurant, so
she wouldn't have to face Levi. She had a hunch it
would be simpler that way.

"GRACE, HOW DO YOU KNOW when you're in love?"

Grace sputtered on her mouthful of vegetable soup
and vowed vengeance on the teenager across the table
from her. "Why do you save all the easy questions
for me? What about your father?"

Jess leaned forward, rested her elbows on the small
table and asked another one. "Do you have to be *in*
love to *make* love?"

"Yes!" This one, at least, was easier. Or was it?
Had she really loved Douglas before making love with
him? Or even during or after, for that matter?

Of course, it was different when you were an adult.
But why?

"The whole experience is meaningful only if you
care intensely about the other person," she said finally, feeling acutely uncomfortable and unable to
look Jess in the face as she said the words.

"The way you felt about my dad," Jess elaborated,
just a hint of slyness in her smile.

Grace nodded, breaking the whole wheat bun on her
side plate into small pieces. She'd selected a healthy
lunch as an example for Jess, but it couldn't have
made much of an impact because Jess had ordered a
pop and French fries.

"That's how I feel about Neil," Jess confided.

"Are you allowed to see him again?"

"Yes. Last night was the first time. We went to a movie, then back to his place for a while."

His place. Grace wondered if Levi had known about that. "Were his parents home?"

Jess shook her head. "He lives with an older brother."

"I see." Oh boy, did she ever. Grace began to shovel in her soup. They had to finish and get out of there before…before…

"I'm just crazy about him, but I'm afraid he might be interested in another girl. He spent a lot of time with her at that party I had to miss. He says he likes me more, but…" Jess's doubts were evident.

"If he says he likes you more, then why don't you believe him?"

"It's not that I don't believe him. It's just that he thinks we should do something to prove how much we care about each other. Do you know what I mean?"

Grace only wished she didn't. "Jess, that isn't—"

"I know what you're going to say. But if I don't, Grace, Karen will. And then I'll lose him." Jess sank back in her chair, looking miserable.

Grace was close to panic. Levi was right. She wasn't up to the task of dealing with a teenager. Fear of saying the wrong thing made her mute. She didn't want to alienate Jess, but neither did she want her to make a mistake she might regret for the rest of her life. Despite the pain it would cause Jess, she almost wished Neil *would* choose Karen. Then the entire problem would fade away.

"Anyway, it's not such a big deal, is it? Maybe I'd be better off just to get it over with."

"Jess, if you're saying what I think you're saying, I'm afraid you may be making a big mistake."

"Why? I told you I loved him. Isn't that all that matters?"

"But you're so young...."

Jess gave her a look of disdain. "That's what adults always say. But lots of my friends do it, you know. It's not that uncommon."

Grace had heard the statistics, but she'd always found them difficult to believe. "What's the big rush, Jess?"

"If you met Neil, you'd understand."

Grace thought about that for a minute. "Okay, then, let me meet Neil."

Jess's face broke out in a huge smile. "You mean it? You want to meet Neil?"

Yeah, and she'd look into running a marathon next weekend. "Well, sure I do."

"This is great! It's really great! I've told him all about you. He even helped me track you down, find your address and everything. You can come to dinner tonight. Neil's going to be there."

"Whoa. Wait a minute. I didn't mean to invite myself to dinner. I thought maybe the three of us could meet at a restaurant sometime."

Jess shook her head. "No. I can't wait that long. And Dad won't mind. We're having burgers, and he always makes too many anyway."

Dinner with Levi? It was the last thing either of them would want, Grace was sure. But how could she disappoint Jess when the girl was so excited? "You'd better ask your dad first. If he's trying to get to know Neil better, he may not want anyone else around." *Especially not me.*

"Okay, I'll ask, but I'm sure he won't mind."

And even if he did, what was he going to say? Grace knew she should have made some excuse, explained that she simply wasn't available to come to dinner. Jess would have been disappointed, but she would have accepted that. It was too late now to pretend to remember a previous engagement.

"Once you meet Neil, you'll understand how I feel," Jess predicted.

Grace stared at her half-eaten bowl of soup, her shredded bun. She'd never seen anything less appetizing in her life. Meeting Neil was just a delay tactic, she realized. "What about school, Jess? How's your algebra coming along?"

Jess wrinkled her nose.

"If you want, I could help you with your homework sometime. Math was always my best subject."

"Really? I like English and history."

Jess seemed disappointed by this difference between them.

But what about Jess's real mother? Had she been good at English or math? For the first time, Grace really empathized with Jess's driving need to find her birth mother. Would she ever be successful? Not if Levi had anything to say about it. Grace felt guilty for being relieved. Because if Jess had her real mother, what would she need Grace for?

"GUESS WHO'S COME to dinner." Grace stood on the landing of Levi's apartment, feeling slightly ridiculous. The door had been left open, so she'd just walked in, a bottle of wine in one hand and a plate of Rice Krispies dessert squares in the other. She was afraid

Jess and Neil were too old to like them, but it was the only thing she'd had time to prepare.

Levi came out from behind the kitchen counter. He was clean and freshly shaven, much different from the last time she'd seen him, running almost naked on the beach. Now he was wearing white pants that hung low on his hips and a dark blue shirt the color of his eyes.

"Yeah, I know. Jess told me."

"I hope it's okay."

"Sure, of course. It's great." His eyes almost, but not quite, met hers as he smiled. "Thanks." He took the plate out of her hands, then asked her what she wanted to drink. "Jess has gone to get Neil. They'll be back in about fifteen minutes, I think. The grill's heating. I hope Jess explained that we aren't having anything fancy, just burgers."

"Burgers are great." Grace thanked him for the glass of wine, then followed him out to the patio, where a small wrought iron table was set for four, condiments arranged neatly in the center. Levi opened the lid to the barbecue, then carefully slid eight raw patties onto the very hot grill. Immediately, the air was filled with the sound of sizzling beef and a distinctive barbecue aroma. Grace followed the trail of pale gray smoke, avoiding eye contact with Levi while she searched for something innocuous to say.

Where was the poise that had seen her through important board meetings, presentations to financiers and complex labor negotiations? Why couldn't she think of something to talk about? Instead, she just stood there, unable to forget the humiliation of Levi's rejection of her in the dark of the night, the shame of knowing she'd stalked him that morning. Of course, he wasn't aware she'd been following him, but he sure as hell must be remembering the way she'd flung herself at him.

Maybe that was why he was acting so tense.

"Don't worry," she said. "I'm not planning any lunges or anything."

That choked a smile out of him.

"This is damned awkward, isn't it? Trust Jess to set this up, then not bother to be around when you arrive."

He stretched his arm out along the wrought-iron railing, and Grace's eyes traced the length of his tanned forearm.

"I wonder if she didn't plan it this way." The second she'd said it, Grace wished she hadn't. Maybe Levi hadn't figured out that Jess was trying to set them up. Even if he had, it might be better for both of them to pretend she hadn't.

But of course he had. "I'll have to have a talk with that kid."

That's right, Levi. Explain to her how I'm the last person in the world you'd ever be interested in. How you'd rather stand with your back to a hot barbecue than get too close to me.

"How was your lunch?"

"What?"

"With Jess. Didn't the two of you—"

"Oh, yes. We had a nice time." Nice? The bland word was not very descriptive. Did Levi realize how seriously Jess felt about Neil? That his daughter was actually contemplating.... Grace couldn't even think the word, not in the context of Jess and her boyfriend. Somehow she was quite sure Levi *didn't* know, and she wished the same could be said for her.

Why had Jess had a need to confide in her? And

now that she had, was Grace obligated to warn Levi
what his daughter was contemplating? Jess would be
furious; she would see such an action as a breach of
confidence. But the girl was only fourteen years old.
Too young for—

"What is it, Grace?"

Levi's expression had sharpened, as if he sensed she
had something important to say. But then, he'd always
been able to read her moods perfectly.

Oh, Lord. She knew she couldn't stay silent. "Well,
during our lunch, Jess and I talked about her...
relationship with her boyfriend." Levi's face grew
pale. Grace found she couldn't continue until she
looked away from him. She focused on the black metal
lid of the barbecue and cleared her throat. "And other
things."

"What sort of other things?"

"Well..." Grace stared into her wineglass. "Things
to do with sexuality, I guess." Lord, if the conversation was awkward before, the word just didn't begin
to cover it now.

"Sexuality," Levi repeated with solemn finality, as
if he'd just been handed the death penalty. "Why
would—"

The door slammed, startling them both. For a second, there was silence, then came the sound of footsteps, Jess's laughter.

Levi extracted a promise. "Later?"

Grace nodded, seeing no way out.

"On the patio, kids," Levi called. "Grab a drink
and join us."

"Okay, Dad."

Grace stared at the view from the balcony, not daring to look at Levi. She sensed he was seething at the

interruption, but she felt only relief. Obviously, she'd been naive, but when she'd first thought of the role she might play in Jess's life, she'd thought of influencing her choice of university, shopping together, discussing movies.

Not nitty-gritty stuff like losing her virginity.

Assuming Jess still was a virgin, of course.

Oh, Lord. Grace leaned over the railing, making a point of admiring the blooming cherry trees in the street below them. "Nice view."

Levi grunted.

A second later, the kids were there, filling the small space to capacity. Jess made the introductions animatedly, obviously happy to have the four of them together. Neil hung back, neither smiling nor making eye contact with any of them. His hair was cut close to the scalp, leaving his rather large ears open to inspection. Grace followed the line of silver studs that began at his earlobe and traveled along the curve of his outer ear. His dark T-shirt had short sleeves, which revealed a gruesome reptilian tattoo on his upper arm. And his face, which was otherwise quite attractive, took on a sinister aspect due to several rings in his nostrils.

In short, he looked like someone Grace would cross the street to avoid.

The very idea of his dating Jess made her want to shudder. She could well imagine how Levi must feel. Surely Jess didn't want her first sexual experience to be with this character.

But the look on Jess's face, the way she continued to hold Neil's hand even when they'd all sat down on the patio chairs and how she self-consciously kept pushing her hair behind one ear, indicated that she thought he was the greatest.

Grace could see her own dismay mirrored in Levi's face. Along with a couple of other emotions that were a little too violent for her liking. The group had suddenly fallen silent and Grace felt a nervous compulsion to get the conversation rolling. But what did you talk about with a sixteen-year-old boy who looked like a juvenile delinquent? *Vandalized any school property lately?*

"So, Neil, do you live around here?" she asked.

"Eight blocks that way." He spoke in a monotone, nodding to point out the direction.

Grace caught a desperate glance from Jess and remembered that Neil lived with a brother. It seemed that Levi had a right to know this, but Jess was already steering the subject to what she probably considered safer ground.

"Neil's a big hockey fan, Dad. Maybe we could use your tickets some night and go see the Canucks."

"A play-off game." Neil swayed to the beat of an unheard song. "That would be cool."

"I suppose we could arrange something," Levi said, but he didn't sound pleased.

He was trying. Grace wondered if Jess had any idea of the effort her father was making right now.

"So what do you like to do, Neil?" Grace asked. "Do you play any sports or—" this was a long shot "—musical instruments?"

Neil yawned. Widely. Without bothering to cover his mouth with his hand. "Hang out with friends. Mostly." He gave Jess a proprietary look, pulling her hand closer to his body. "Hey, Jay?"

"He calls me Jay," Jess explained. From her expression, Grace could imagine how she felt. Like wrapping ribbon pulled taut, then scraped with a knife so that it curled over and over on itself.

Grace herself felt slightly sick.

"The burgers are ready," Levi announced. "Jess, could you get the tray of buns and salads from the kitchen, please?"

Neil went with her.

"Do you suppose they'll come out holding one end of the tray each so they don't have to let go hands?" Grace whispered.

Levi almost smiled. "That would require a modicum of cooperation and effort far beyond our young James Dean's capabilities, I'm afraid."

Grace wanted to disagree, but she couldn't. She'd come to dinner hoping to find something to admire in Jess's boyfriend, but unfortunately his behavior at the table didn't help. Neil reached over Jess's empty plate to grab the first hamburger, then took his second and third without asking if anyone else wanted one.

He ate sloppily, ravenously.

He never contributed to the conversation.

And Jess could still barely take her adoring eyes off him.

Grace couldn't finish her first burger. She had a little pasta salad. And drank three glasses of wine. She hoped no one noticed, but of course Levi did, since he was the one filling her glass. And his own.

"Brownies for dessert?" Levi asked. "Jess baked them this morning." He paused, then added, "And Grace brought some Rice Krispies squares."

Jess beamed at her. "I haven't had those in ages. Thanks, Grace."

Grace smiled back, feeling foolish at how pleased

Jess's thanks made her feel. "You're welcome. I'm afraid I haven't made anything as complicated as a brownie in ages, but I'd love to try one." In truth, however, Grace couldn't imagine eating another mouthful.

"As long as they don't have nuts," Neil said. "Hate nuts."

Jess's crestfallen expression gave them all the answer to that one. Grace fought an urge to reach over the table and throttle the young man. From the look on Levi's face before he turned around to help Jess serve dessert and coffee, he felt the same way.

Left alone with Neil for five minutes, Grace considered her options. She would either jump over the railing or make a mad dash for the stairs. Both had more appeal than drumming up conversation with this most exasperating young man.

"How long have you and Jess been seeing each other?"

He shrugged. "A while."

"Do you go to the same school?"

"Nah. I'm in high school. Not for long, though. If I land a good job this summer, I might not bother going back."

Not even finish high school? Grace was shocked. "Are you sure that's a good idea? I'd talk it over with a few people beforehand. I'm sure your parents and guidance counselor could give you some helpful advice."

"Parents. Right." Neil grinned as though it was all some big joke. Then, just as Jess stepped out on the patio with the brownies, Levi right behind her with the coffee, he said, "So you Jess's mom or what?"

Fortuitously, the refreshments did not end up down

his back. A stone-faced Levi sat down and poured coffee while Jess served Grace a brownie. Both acted as if they hadn't heard a thing, and Grace pretended she hadn't, either.

"Have some coffee, Grace," Levi said. "It'll go good with the brownie."

Got anything else to go with it? Like a stiff shot of brandy?

Grace took a bite of her dessert. "These are great, Jess."

"Thanks." Jess smiled politely at the compliment, but her eyes were on Neil. He'd taken several Rice Krispies squares and swallowed them whole. Now he abruptly stood up.

"Have to go," he said.

"I'll walk you home." Jess almost bounced out of her chair, but her father quashed that idea immediately.

"Don't you have schoolwork, Jess? I'm sure Neil can make it home on his own, can't you, Neil?"

Neil shrugged. "Whatever." Then, without a word of thanks or farewell, he left, Jess trailing behind him to say goodbye before going to her room to study.

Once Levi and Grace were alone, he looked at her as if defying her to say anything nice about Neil.

Grace had to think hard. "He had clean fingernails. I think."

"Only because he bites them to the quick."

"You don't miss a thing, do you?" Grace helped him clear the table, load the dishes and put away the leftovers—those few items of food Neil had not cared for. He'd devoured anything he liked. "Maybe he's not as bad as he seems. Maybe he just acts that way because he's nervous."

Grace put the condiments back in the neat, clean fridge, noticing that despite the compact galley kitchen's small size, it was well organized and spotless. She hoped Levi would never have occasion to see *her* kitchen. Not that she cooked often enough to get it very dirty, but it had an abandoned, disused atmosphere totally opposite to the one in this home.

"I wish he'd been nervous. It would have been a good sign. No, I'm afraid he acts that way because he just doesn't give a damn. About us, about life and, worst of all, about Jess." Levi leaned wearily back against the counter, and covered one eye with his hand. Shaking his head, he admitted, "I don't know what to do, Grace—I really don't. It tears me up to think of her with him. My only solace has been that she's so young she can't really be serious about him.... But maybe I've been fooling myself." He stopped Grace's nervous puttering by resting a hand on her shoulder.

"Grace, tell me what you began to say on the patio before they arrived."

If only Grace dared ask for another drink, or light up a cigarette. She hadn't been prepared for this kind of stress at business school. "Okay, Levi. It's about as bad as you can imagine. She's thinking of sleeping with him—mostly, I believe, because she's afraid to lose him if she doesn't."

"Oh, God." Levi groaned. "You told her not to, didn't you? Thank God she at least listens to you these days...." His voice trailed off when he sensed her hesitation. "Grace. You did tell her not to sleep with him, didn't you?"

She turned away, faced the range top and wondered if she could sneak down the exhaust pipe and crawl back to her office, where she almost always knew how to approach her problems.

"Of course I don't think she should sleep with him, Levi. Of course I'm trying to steer her in that direction—"

"Steer her?" He cursed. "This is all a game to you, isn't it, Grace? Never had a child, so you thought it might be fun to step in and play mom for a while. You may have convinced yourself your intentions are good, but have you thought about the consequences for Jess? At best this guy is going to use her, destroy her self-esteem, then toss her aside. At worst she could end up pregnant or even sick. Deadly sick."

Grace twisted to face him. She sympathized with his pain—she really did. But what did he expect from her? "Well, surely you've talked about contraceptives, the need to use a condom." Oh, God. Was she really standing here discussing safe sex with her ex-boyfriend?

"Of course. But only generally. I never told her how to get them, how to use them. Why would I? She's still so young...."

"Obviously not as young as you thought."

Levi walked out of the room. Grace could see him standing in the hall, staring at a painting on the wall, shoulders slumped, arms hanging limply at his sides. She doubted he was admiring the painting's strong, bold strokes, the inventive use of color.

"I'm sorry, Levi." She'd followed him and now allowed herself to gently place a hand on his shoulder. "I want to protect Jess, too—please believe me. But I also want her to keep feeling free to discuss things with me. If I come down too heavy, telling her what to do instead of trying to make her realize for herself the right course of action, I'll lose what little influence I have.''

''That sounds nice, Grace, but in reality it's a load of bull. Jess doesn't need sympathy from you. She needs advice. If she were your daughter, I guarantee you would have found some way to get your point across. You're just skirting the messy stuff, the way you always have when it comes to heavy emotional issues.''

''That's not true!''

''Oh, really? Then why don't you knock on Jess's door right now and talk the whole thing through with her? Explain all she has to lose if she makes the wrong decision? Answer all her questions—not sidestep a single one? What's the matter, Grace? Why is your face turning so pale?''

Grace tried to quash the growing panic within her. ''You're her father! Stop turning this all onto me.''

''Sure I can talk to her, as I have and I will. But like it or not, you're the one she's willing to listen to now. You're the mother she's always wanted and now finally has. And don't blame me for that. You had your chance to back away and you wouldn't do it. I warned you it wasn't going to be easy.''

''I'm trying.''

The words came out in a whisper. He was asking way too much of her; he had to know that. She had to get out of here, and she had to go now. She couldn't think straight with him glowering like that. Anger glittered in the sapphire depths of his eyes with a potency that seemed strong enough to kill. Did he hate her that much? Blame her that much?

''I have to leave now.'' She grabbed her purse and headed for the stairs.

''Don't I know it,'' came his mocking reply.

CHAPTER SEVEN

WASN'T IT JUST LIKE LEVI to blame her because his daughter was out of control?

Actually, no. It wasn't like him at all.

Grace pulled in behind a departing minivan and slid her BMW neatly into the hourly parking stall on Robson Street. She opened her door, exited from the driver's seat, then adjusted the line of her chartreuse linen suit.

He was overreacting, the way any normal father would. It was easier for him to blame her than himself. It wasn't as if she had done anything wrong. She certainly hadn't told Jess to sleep with Neil. She'd told her it was a big decision, that she was still a little young. Sure, she'd been uncomfortable, but she'd tried to gently point Jess in the right direction.

Could she have done more? Would she have done more if Jess really were her daughter?

On the sidewalk, Grace tilted back her head and openly admired the pale-oak-and-brass facade of her flagship store. Body and Soul. This was her baby, the way Jess was Levi's. Stepping over the threshold was like entering another world: visitors were greeted with the sound of a trickling stream, a sweet, woodsy smell and a plethora of attractively displayed beauty and health products. The two shop attendants looked like well-heeled medical assistants in their pale green jackets. They were trained to remain in the background until a customer had a chance to orient herself, but they both rushed forward when they saw Grace.

"Ms. Hamilton! We didn't know you were stopping by today."

The bright smile of the manager, Vanessa Green, belied the nervousness in her eyes. It was always this way, and Grace was used to it. It didn't mean anything was wrong. A visit from her was intended to keep the employees on their toes. Since they never knew when it would happen, they had to ensure the stores were impeccable at all times.

And they usually were.

"The store looks good. How were last week's sales?"

Vanessa rattled off the numbers confidently.

"How about bookings for the spa services?" Part of the unique package of beauty and relaxation products and services offered at Body and Soul included such delights as the aromatherapy makeover and body buffing and bronzing.

"Pretty steady." The manager pulled out a large, leather-bound book and with a metallic-purple fingernail traced the time slots for the upcoming week, most of them already filled.

"Very good." Grace nodded, then turned to inspect the shelves. She walked around the room, making sure they were clean and the merchandise was effectively presented. For a moment, she allowed herself the luxury of taking a deep breath and thinking, *This store is here only because of me.* Me.

It was still hard to believe. There were fifteen more stores just like this one, all in western Canada. And if she had her way at the board meeting that afternoon, soon Body and Soul would break into the central Canadian market, as well.

"Good job, ladies," she said on her way out the door.

She got into her car, waiting for the flush of exhilaration that always buoyed her after a trip to one of her stores. The sense of pride and accomplishment gave her momentum to approach the next hurdle.

This time, all she could see was the disappointment on Levi's face. And all she had was a sinking feeling that somehow she'd let him down. Him and Jess. If she'd been smarter, more experienced with teenagers, she'd have known the right thing to say to Jess. She wouldn't have felt so nervous, would have approached the subject head-on instead of avoiding it at every turn.

Jess had looked to her for straight talk, but all Grace would deliver were a few stock answers: *You're so young. You may be making a big mistake.* What kid was going to listen to advice like that?

Driving through traffic, Grace found herself speeding and changing lanes frequently to avoid the slower vehicles as she focused her thoughts on the presentation she'd make at the emergency board meeting slated to begin in thirty minutes. She had to stop thinking about Levi and Jess; today of all days she needed to concentrate on her job one hundred percent. After all, her entire business empire was in jeopardy.

Back in the office, Grace picked up her overhead transparencies and the notes for her talk, then stopped by Douglas's office on her way to the boardroom.

"Everything ready to go, Douglas?"

He looked up, blinking as if she'd turned on a bright light. "What? Oh, yes, of course." He tapped a pile of papers into a neat package. "My secretary made a copy of those numbers for you."

Grace held out her hand and he passed the papers to her. A glance confirmed these were indeed the same schedules she'd seen on his desk the other day. "Looks good," she said, feeling relieved. If there'd been a problem, she would have had precious little time to correct it—the meeting was scheduled to begin in ten minutes. "Let's get this show on the road, shall we?"

"Why don't you go ahead? I just need to finish up something. I'll be right behind you."

In the boardroom, Grace settled her papers at the head of the table, then went to the door to greet the board members as they arrived. Adrenaline buzzed in her veins; she couldn't sit still. This meeting was crucial. Had she prepared thoroughly enough? Could anything go wrong?

Her own presentation was thorough and error-free. Both she and Jackie had reviewed it ad nauseam. The only possible weak link was Douglas. But she'd seen copies of his overheads and everything looked right.

So why did she have this nagging unease?

Roberta was one of the first board members to arrive. Dressed in a black suit, her dark hair immaculate, she pushed serious-looking, black-rimmed glasses up her straight, long nose as she approached Grace.

"Show us what you've got," she said, squeezing Grace's upper arm as she passed by on her way to her seat.

"You bet." Grace smiled, hoping to project her normal confidence, even though today that was a stretch. She was always pumped for these meeting, feeling, she imagined, the way a runner might at the beginning of a race. But she was way past pumped now. The slightest jolt to her system and she would fly out of control like a popped balloon careering madly in a blue summer sky.

She took in a lungful of air and held it for a few seconds. As she exhaled, she glanced around the room, meeting the eyes of the familiar board members. She smiled and nodded at each person, signaling her intent to begin the meeting. Then, suddenly, she experienced an unaccustomed weariness that frightened her. She'd done this so many times before; what was the sense in going through the whole exercise yet again?

Because it was necessary to save her business. What was the matter with her? Where was her drive, her ambition? Attitude was everything—Grace was firmly convinced of that. If she believed in her expansion proposal, then the people around this table would, too.

Grace took a sip of water from the glass in front of her. All the chairs were occupied now save one— Douglas's. Her vague sense of unease sharpened, and she dug her fingers into the papers in her hands.

"I see Douglas isn't here yet, but as it's already five minutes after the hour, I think we'd better start," she said, straightening her back.

"As you know, Jarvis Enterprises filed their official takeover bid this morning. This gives them twenty-one days to buy the remaining shares they need to gain control of Body and Soul."

Expressions around the table were serious as Douglas slipped into his chair a full ten minutes late. He avoided Grace's eyes as he settled his papers. The muscles in her chest tightened, making it hard for her to catch her next breath. She just knew something was up. But she couldn't stop now.

"As a board," she continued, "we need to advise our shareholders how to proceed. My strong preference, as you all know, is to recommend that they reject Jarvis's offer."

"On what basis, Grace?" Roberta asked, tilting her head down so she could look above her reading glasses.

Grace nodded in Roberta's direction. "I believe shareholders will maximize their return if they support current management and our plans for expansion. Douglas, could you put up the transparencies showing the financial projections for the flagship store on Bloor Street?"

She planned to outdo even her Vancouver store with this new venture. If she was going to take on the lucrative Toronto market, she would have to do it in style.

Besides the new store, her expansion plans included an investment in a large warehouse in Islington. Within five years, she intended to be servicing at least twenty-five new franchise outlets for Body and Soul in southern Ontario alone. Each of these stores was identified with a little sticker of the company's logo on a large map of Canada that Jackie had taped to the front wall. On a separate chart was an outline of the time frame for the expansion.

Douglas didn't apologize for being late; he just nodded and picked up his folder of transparencies.

"As I've previously explained to you all individually," Grace said, watching Douglas shuffle his transparencies with what seemed to her deliberate slowness, "the numbers Douglas developed for our last meeting were unduly conservative. Even factoring in an unfavorable interest rate and a below-expectation growth factor, we expect the new Toronto store to earn positive cash flows right from the first year.''

''Yes, that was our optimistic scenario,'' Douglas agreed, flicking on the light for the overhead projector.

All eyes flew to the chart now reflected on the large white board at the front of the room. The three columns of numbers had the headings Optimistic, Realistic, Pessimistic. In the Optimistic column were the numbers she'd seen on Douglas's desk. The Realistic column showed numbers marginally higher than Douglas's initial projection, but they still showed massive losses in the first three years. The Pessimistic numbers were devastating.

Grace grabbed at the edge of her table, swallowing the fury that made her want to hurl something, anything, in the direction of Douglas's triumphant face. He looked at her with a purposefully blank expression, then turned back to the board members.

''I know my views on the probable outcome of Grace's proposed expansion differ from hers. She would have you believe that my optimistic forecast should, in fact, be considered the most realistic.

''I feel, however, a sense of responsibility after my many years with this company, and in all good conscience, I'm compelled to point out the varying ranges of probabilities associated with this project.''

He sounded so bloody reasonable Grace couldn't blame the directors for nodding at him in agreement. But, damn it, he was wrong!

''I appreciate your *loyalty* to the company, Douglas,'' she said. ''However, I think you should have discussed your opinions on this matter with me privately, *before* the meeting. As I've said many times, the assumptions you've used to come up with your

realistic and pessimistic scenarios are so conservative
as to have no actual merit.''

Carefully, she assessed the reaction of the people
around the table. Many of them were confused. She
didn't blame them. It was unbelievably unprofessional
to have the company's top executives so fundamentally divided.

''That's your opinion, Grace,'' Douglas said firmly.
''I stand by my numbers. Body and Soul just isn't
large enough to secure the favorable financing terms
we'll need for the large-scale expansion you're planning. My own recommendation would be that we en-
courage our shareholders to sell to Jarvis.''

Around the room, a few people nodded. Grace could
have kicked herself for not getting rid of Douglas before he had a chance to do this to her. He was just
lining the path to the Jarvis takeover with gold, making it appear irresistible, almost unavoidable.

Grace placed a hand on her abdomen, aware of a
dull ache. It was time for her to face the obvious.
Douglas was hell-bent on destroying her business, and
her along with it. Belatedly, she saw the things she
should have done to discredit him. She could have
asked for letters of intent from the banks, proving she
could get the interest rates she wanted. She should
have summarized the market research that supported
her sales projections. She should have compiled detailed charts showing production costs and how they
would eventually be lower with the new warehouse in
Islington, and the suppliers they'd identified in the Ni-
agara Peninsula.

But it was too late now. In the end, Grace felt fortunate to persuade the board to delay their decision
about the Jarvis takeover, pending more research. It

was hardly the blanket vote of support she'd hoped to end the day with. In fact, it was damned discouraging.

No doubt about it—board opinion was definitely against her. For the first time, Grace had to admit the possibility that Body and Soul might soon be controlled by Jarvis Enterprises. Even Roberta Paxton had avoided Grace's eyes as she left the room.

IT WAS PAST SEVEN and at the Jolt they were getting the evening strollers, the most casual and relaxed crowd of the day. The slow but steady business provided an opportunity for the staff to catch their breaths before the after-movie rush. Usually this was Levi's favorite time of day, but today he was too wound up about his daughter to allow his mind to relax and go with the easy flow of his patrons.

After Grace had left Saturday night, he'd knocked on Jess's bedroom door and the two of them had had a long talk. It had gone okay, but not once had Jess opened up to him on the level she had with Grace. He had to admit it would be a pretty unusual daughter who would want to discuss with her father the possibility of having sex with her boyfriend. Or even discussing it with her mother, for that matter.

Unless her mother was new on the scene. A glamorous beauty who lived a sophisticated life that, up until then, Jess had seen only on television.

Levi tried not to give in to jealousy. It wasn't fair that after years of devoted parenting, it should be Grace whom Jess turned to, not him. But that didn't matter. This wasn't about him and his hurt feelings. It was about Jess and her future.

Was it possible Grace had somehow got it wrong?

That Jess wasn't really thinking of doing anything so drastic as sleeping with Neil?

Could he take that chance?

For the first time since he'd held his bawling, red-faced baby in his arms, Levi felt a complete lack of control over her future. He didn't want to think about his daughter's first sexual experience, but he knew that when it happened, he wanted it to be tender and sweet, with a man who thought the world of her.

The way he had felt about Grace. The way it had been between them.

Levi hoarded the memory of the first time he and Grace had made love, bringing it out rarely, usually when he was out late at night strolling the beach by himself. It had been her first time—something she'd been reluctant to admit and he'd been surprised to discover. Grace's veneer even back then was of a confident beauty that belied the vulnerability within.

Because her parents had been so strict, her experiences while she lived at home were limited. Most kids in that situation might be expected to go wild once they had their freedom, but not Grace. Even after she'd left home to continue her education, she'd kept herself in check, had focused entirely on her studies.

Until those last few months with him.

He knew her parents' deaths in a car crash shortly before he met her had something to do with it. Somehow that tragedy had pierced a hole in Grace's armor, and he'd happened along at just the right time to see the woman inside. From that first night, she'd let him know her intimately, something she'd never permitted another living soul to do. She'd told him so quite bluntly.

And having received this gift from her, he'd had no

choice but to respond equally. He'd revealed his thoughts, his dreams, his hopes, to her, as she'd shared the insecurities he could see driving her in a never-ending quest for success and perfection.

At the time, he'd thought his love could show her another route to happiness, but in the end he hadn't succeeded and he'd lost his heart in the process.

No, he hadn't come out very well from his affair with Grace. The only thing he was left with was his pride, and now, fifteen years later, it seemed that was still all he had.

"Well, I did it, buddy." Phil sat down at the counter and grinned.

Levi blinked. He hadn't even seen his friend walk in. "You did?"

"A For Sale sign is swinging on my front lawn as we speak." Phil rapped his knuckles on the counter, agitated and nervous. "All I need is one bite and I'm outta here, sailing the ocean blue. Coming?"

"You going on a sailing trip?"

A feminine voice, Grace's, reached them from the side.

Levi straightened. She was dressed to the nines as usual, but the light stripes in her bright green suit seemed slightly off-kilter, her strawberry-blond hair was tousled more than was fashionable, and there were faint smudges of eyeliner under her eyes. As if aware of his critical thoughts, Grace tugged at her skirt and brought it into line with her jacket.

She must have come to visit Jess. Levi was perversely glad his daughter was out. He was becoming increasingly certain that her seeing Grace Hamilton was not in Jess's best interests. It was obvious Grace was incapable of advising a young teen facing the harsh realities of life in the nineties.

But in the meantime, Grace had overheard his conversation with Phil. Now she was looking from him to Phil questioningly.

"I'm working on it," Phil said.

Grace's eyes narrowed. "Do I know you?"

"Grace. I'm wounded. How could you have forgotten? We went to university together, remember?"

Grace drew back visibly, her features settling into cool disdain. "Of course. Phil Trainer."

That his best friend and the woman he loved did not like each other had bothered Levi before. Now he was amused by the nasty vibes between them. "Phil's pulling up stakes to sail around the world and he's looking for a crew member." He raised his eyebrows at Grace wickedly. "Interested?"

She only raised her eyebrows higher, staring at him as if he were speaking another language.

Phil faked a shudder. "Don't say it even as a joke." He turned to Levi. "You know you want to go. Why won't you just admit it?"

"What about Jess?"

Grace appeared concerned—an emotion Levi resented. He'd done just fine up to the present without Grace's help. What made her think her intervention might be necessary now?

"Don't sound so worried." He swabbed the counter with a damp rag. "I'm not going, and Phil knows that."

"Jess could come, too. There is such a thing as home schooling, you know."

Phil kept glancing from Levi to Grace; Levi sensed

he was trying to provoke a confrontation between them.

"Come on, Phil. You don't need a fourteen-year-old girl on board. She would definitely cramp your style. And I don't intend to pull Jess from school or from her home. She's happy here and I want to keep things that way." Although it was tempting to think of ferrying his daughter miles and miles away from that creep she was dating—and any other red-blooded boys with the same inclination.

"Okay, okay." Phil held up a hand. "I know when to back off. But you can't blame me for trying, buddy. I understand how badly you really want to go."

Grace frowned at this, her pale brown brows knitted.

"How badly I *used* to want to go, you mean," Levi amended.

"You mean you don't want to travel anymore?" Grace asked.

Why was she looking at him so intently? Her concern was Jess, and he'd already made his aims clear.

"Come on, Levi," Phil said. "Traveling has always been your big dream."

Grace nodded, her eyes on Levi. "But he has a daughter. He has to put her needs first."

So he'd been right. She was only worried about Jess. "Speaking of whom, if you've come to see her, I'm afraid you're out of luck. She's over at her girlfriend's house." He hoped. These days, he was never sure if his trust in his daughter was misplaced or not. But short of chaperoning her every second she was away from the house, there wasn't much he could do about it. Basically, she was a good kid. He had to have faith in that or he would go crazy.

"I came for dinner, actually." Grace surveyed the list of specials on the chalkboard. "What do you recommend?"

For dinner? To the Jolt? "Come on, Grace. We have no white linen or fancy silverware at our tables."

"And you don't have a wine list, either," she said promptly. "The way I'm feeling tonight, I'm definitely safer without one."

Before Levi could decide what to do with that leading comment, Phil jumped in.

"Bad day at the office?" he asked, sounding as though nothing would make him happier.

"The very worst." Grace's eyes were still on the chalkboard, her calm expression belying the dull fatalism of her words. "How about the quiche?"

"Want a salad with that?"

She hesitated only a second. "Of course I want a salad." They exchanged a grim smile.

Phil stood up, shaking his head. "I have a feeling you two have things to discuss. Me, I'm going home to chart my route to South America. Remember, you're always welcome to join me, buddy. I'll reserve your spot right up to the day I leave."

"I see you're still friends with Phil after all these years," Grace remarked later, a forkful of smoked salmon quiche poised in her hand.

"Any reason I shouldn't be?"

"No. None." She bit into the pastry-and-egg mixture, chewing slowly and deliberately. Levi leaned over the counter to watch, following every movement of her mouth.

"I don't suppose you'd like to tell me what you're really doing here. Why you'd stop for dinner in an out-of-the-way local coffee shop?"

She wouldn't look at him. "I wondered if Jess was okay. I needed to eat. I—"

"Jess is fine. We had a little talk the other night, which wasn't very helpful, if you want the truth. But I'm hoping she won't do anything rash."

Hoping? Worrying himself sick was more like it. But Grace wouldn't understand that. To her, their life was like a case study in one of those management texts—an interesting problem, but nothing that involved her personally.

Why couldn't he view her and her life with that same detachment? Why did just having her near cause his skin to burn and his insides to ache? The fact that she'd made him aware in oh-so-subtle ways that she might not be averse to briefly resuming their physical relationship made things so much harder.

Realizing he wanted her so much and she was offering so little, he had to keep his distance.

"You know," she said, looking around the room, "every time I come here, the place is busy. You obviously do a very good business."

"Not bad."

"Do you rent or own the building?"

"Own."

"When did you buy?"

"Fourteen years ago. What is this, Grace? A financial survey? Are you checking me out for a bank loan? Would you like me to bring out the books so you can see everything down to the last nickel?"

"I'm sorry, Levi." She lowered her eyes to her dinner plate. "I guess I'm just naturally interested. The real estate in this area has skyrocketed in the past fourteen years, as I'm sure you're aware. If you wanted to sell this building as Phil suggested, it would yield a small fortune.''

''I've already said I'm not interested in selling.''

Grace looked relieved. Was she still concerned he might pull up stakes and take Jess away?

Noticing a line of customers at the till, he went to help his employees catch up with business. When he returned, Grace had pushed her plate away, food only half-eaten. Levi had to force himself not to push it back at her. She was so thin, at least ten pounds lighter than when he'd first known her. And tonight she had a faint tremor in her hands that made him nervous for her health.

''How do you survive on the amount of food you eat?'' At dinner the other night, he'd noticed she hadn't finished even one hamburger.

She didn't seem to hear him. ''You know, if you changed the arrangement of chairs in here, you could probably double your turnover.'' She pointed to the front of the shop. ''See how wide apart those are spaced? You could easily fit in another three tables.''

''And what would that do to the aisle? The mothers would have a heck of a time wielding their strollers in here. Besides, I have several students and one artist who come in here to work. They like those front tables with all the leg room and the natural light.''

Grace looked at him as if he were crazy. ''And your shelving displays…'' She waved a hand to indicate the rows of gourmet food items and coffee and tea accessories. ''If you wanted, I could get my merchandising experts over here to give you some advice on displaying your products more effectively.''

''Oh, really?''

She nodded, warming to her subject. ''What sort of

computer system are you using? Can you see which products are turning around the fastest, which ones are giving you the best margins? I could—''

"Enough." Levi fought the impulse to put his hand over her mouth. "You know, you're an intelligent woman, Grace, but at times you just don't get it."

He left the counter to clear tables, clanging the cutlery and banging the dishes just a little more than necessary. She was finished eating. Why didn't she just leave?

Grace analyzed everything according to one criterion: the bottom line. She couldn't understand, would never even begin to appreciate, that the Jolt was not about maximizing profits. He and Jess got enough income from it to live on. He set aside the earnings from his rental buildings for her university education. Squeezing in a couple of extra tables at the Jolt, selling a few more jars of mango chutney, just didn't matter. For him, running the Jolt was a labor of love.

He felt Grace's arm on his elbow.

"I'm sorry, Levi," she said softly. "I didn't mean to offend you."

He should have let the issue drop there, but he didn't. He twisted his arm so that he could take hold of her wrist. Then, leaving a tray of dirty dishes on an unwashed table, he led her outside and pointed up at the hand-painted sign that hung over the front door. Jolt O' Java. A friend had done it for him when he first opened the shop, and he'd resisted several later suggestions that a neon sign would be trendier and attract a bigger nighttime crowd.

"This place isn't about maximizing returns, Grace, and if I want your opinion on something, I'll ask for it. Next thing you know, you'll be suggesting I water down the coffee to increase my profit margins.''

· "Oh, Levi.''

Her expression was tinged with regret. He ignored it. Having Grace feel sorry for him was the last thing he wanted. "I know I'll never make the Fortune 500, but that was never my aim. Half my customers are my friends. That's why I'm in this business. My rewards go far beyond earning a comfortable living for Jess and me. And if you're worried about Jess's future, stop right now. I've set up a trust fund for her and have saved enough already that she can have her pick of universities.''

"I didn't mean to imply you couldn't take care of yourself or Jess. I just thought—''

"You thought that because you're so damned successful, some of your wonder dust might rub off on me. But you forget one thing, Grace. I'm not interested in your brand of success and I never was.''

Levi took a deep breath, his anger spent. Beside him, Grace's face appeared pale in the wash of streetlights. He'd expected his words would make her angry, but she looked sad more than anything else.

"I don't blame you, Levi. My success doesn't seem that great to me right now, either.''

The admission, the sound of defeat it held, didn't fit his image of Grace. He remembered what he'd noticed when she first walked in that evening—that she wasn't quite herself. "I don't get it. Last time I checked, your share price was going through the roof. What's the problem?''

"The reason the share price is so high is that Jarvis Enterprises is bidding up the shares in an effort to take over the company.''

"Yeah, I think I read something about that in the paper."

Grace made a bitter sound. "They launched a formal takeover bid today, and I called an emergency board meeting. Let's just say it didn't go well—thanks to my vice president of finance, Douglas Eberhart. He made me look like a fool."

"Why would he do something like that?"

"Funny, your daughter asked the same question, and the answer is, I don't know. I guess loyalty has gone out of fashion for some people."

"So what? It's your company, right? It's not like Jarvis Enterprises can take it away from you."

"I wish it were that simple."

"Why isn't it?"

"I only own thirty-five percent of the company's shares. If Jarvis can get more than fifty percent, I won't be controlling the company anymore even though I'll still own a large chunk of it. Jarvis already owns ten percent. Basically, it comes down to whether I can count on the support of my board members, who are also shareholders. Especially Roberta. The others tend to follow her leadership."

The despair in her face, in her manner and voice, shocked him. Grace was the proverbial dog with a bone. She never gave up. "Why wouldn't Roberta support you?"

"You wouldn't be asking that if you'd been at the meeting today. I tried to call her to sound her out, but her secretary said she wasn't available. It's been five hours and she still hasn't phoned me back. It doesn't take a genius to figure out she doesn't want to talk to me. Damn it. The truth is I don't blame her. I blew it at the meeting today, Levi. I trusted Douglas when I ought to have known better.''

''Well, what if the worst happens, Grace? What if you lose control of your company? Do you have a backup plan?''

''Oh, Lord.'' Grace swayed on her feet. ''I can't stand to think about that.''

He steadied her with a hand on each shoulder. ''Well, maybe you should. It's only a company, Grace, a business. In the final analysis, there are much more important things in your life.''

She pulled back from him, steady now, but somehow looking smaller than usual.

''Maybe there's more to your life than business, Levi. But there isn't to mine.''

CHAPTER EIGHT

"SO WHAT DID YOU THINK of Neil?"

Jess had asked Grace to meet her at the downtown library during her lunch break to help her research a school project on women's changing roles in the twentieth century. But so far, the girl was not having much success in concentrating on the subject at hand.

"Look at this list of articles," Grace said, pointing to the display on the computer monitor. "Why don't you write down the ones that seem most interesting, then we'll get copies for you to take home."

Reluctantly, Jess pulled up a chair beside her and started running her finger down the list. After a few minutes, she paused. "Don't you think he's the greatest-looking guy you've ever seen? Isn't his tattoo the coolest? None of my friends have ever dated a guy with a tattoo before."

"I'm sorry, Jess, but I have to admit that tattoos leave me cold. I guess it's a generational thing. Like this article here. See? A comparison of women's roles in one family structure. Maybe you should read that one."

"Okay." Jess made some notations on the pad beside her. Giving up her discussion of Neil's attributes—for the time being, at least—she allowed Grace to lead her through the entire list. A half hour later, they had copies of five of the more pertinent articles.

"That should be enough to get you started," Grace said, satisfied, as they left the building and headed for her parked car. "Do you want me to drive you back to school?"

"Sure." Jess pulled a sandwich out of her knapsack. "Mind if I eat in your car?"

Grace put a hand on the buttery soft leather of her seat and steeled herself. "Uh-huh, go ahead."

"Want half?" Jess offered a triangular piece of tuna and sprouts on whole wheat.

"Looks great, but no, thanks. I'll stop for something after I drop you off." Anything to postpone returning to the office. Grace was still feeling demoralized because of her ignominious performance at yesterday's board meeting. Frustrated and confused, she wasn't at all certain what her next step should be, and she had no idea how to answer the questions her staff were asking with their eyes, if not their mouths.

Then there was Douglas. She knew she had to sack him, but somehow she'd lost the fire that had always driven her to make tough decisions. This morning she'd put in a call to one of her lawyers, Ben Ryan. Removing an executive-level employee like Douglas was never easy, and she didn't want to risk a wrongful-dismissal suit on top of everything else.

Ben had promised her a memo. Then he'd asked if she was free for dinner that evening. Grace had put him off. She was barely eating these days, plus she knew she'd be terrible company.

"You didn't like him, did you?"

Jess was staring out the passenger window when she asked the question. It took Grace a few seconds to absorb its meaning.

"Neil?" Oh, Lord, how was she going to deal with

NO RISK, NO OBLIGATION TO BUY...NOW OR EVER!

GUARANTEED

PLAY "ROLL A DOUBLE" AND YOU GET FREE GIFTS! HERE'S HOW TO PLAY:

1. Peel off label from front cover. Place it in space provided at right. With a coin, carefully scratch off the silver dice. Then check the claim chart to see what we have for you – TWO FREE BOOKS and a mystery gift – ALL YOURS! ALL FREE!

2. Send back this card and you'll receive brand-new Harlequin Superromance® novels. These books have a cover price of $4.25 each in the U.S. and $4.75 each in Canada, but they are yours to keep absolutely free.

3. There's no catch. You're under no obligation to buy anything. We charge nothing – ZERO – for your first shipment. And you don't have to make any minimum number of purchases – not even one!

4. The fact is, thousands of readers enjoy receiving books by mail from the Harlequin Reader Service®. They like the convenience of home delivery...they like getting the best new novels BEFORE they're available in stores...and they love our discount prices!

5. We hope that after receiving your free books you'll want to remain a subscriber. But the choice is yours – to continue or cancel any time at all! So why not take us up on our invitation, with no risk of any kind. You'll be glad you did!

THIS MYSTERY BONUS GIFT
WILL BE YOURS __FREE__ WHEN
YOU PLAY "ROLL A DOUBLE"

"ROLL A DOUBLE!"

Place label here

SCRATCH HERE

?

SEE CLAIM CHART BELOW

336 HDL CQV2

135 HDL CQVG
(H-SR-07/99)

YES! I have placed my label from the front cover into the space provided above and scratched off the silver dice to reveal a double. Please send me all the gifts for which I qualify. I understand that I am under no obligation to purchase any books, as explained on the back and on the opposite page.

Name: _____
(PLEASE PRINT)

Address: _____ Apt.#: _____

City: _____ State/Prov.: _____ Postal Zip/ Code: _____

CLAIM CHART

2 FREE BOOKS PLUS MYSTERY BONUS GIFT

2 FREE BOOKS

1 FREE BOOK

CLAIM NO.37-829

PRINTED IN U.S.A.

Offer limited to one per household and not valid to current Harlequin Superromance® subscribers. All orders subject to approval.

The Harlequin Reader Service® — Here's how it works:

Accepting your 2 free books and mystery gift places you under no obligation to buy anything. You may keep the books and gift and return the shipping statement marked "cancel." If you do not cancel, about a month later we'll send you 6 additional novels and bill you just $3.57 each in the U.S., or $3.96 each in Canada, plus 25¢ delivery per book and applicable taxes if any.* That's the complete price and — compared to the cover price of $4.25 in the U.S. and $4.75 in Canada — it's quite a bargain! You may cancel at any time, but if you choose to continue, every month we'll send you 6 more books, which you may either purchase at the discount price or return to us and cancel your subscription.

*Terms and prices subject to change without notice. Sales tax applicable in N.Y. Canadian residents will be charged applicable provincial taxes and GST.

this one? "He's not very talkative, is he? People like that can be difficult to get to know."

"My dad makes him nervous. I've begged and pleaded for him to be nicer, but he won't listen." Jess sighed.

"I think it's pretty natural for your dad to be suspicious of any guy you're dating. You have to remember it wasn't so long ago that your father was the only man in your life."

Jess looked at her wonderingly. "I never thought of it that way."

Grace stopped in front of the school. "Call me after you've read the articles. I'd be happy to help you work on an outline."

"Thanks, Grace." Jess hopped out of the car, hauling her backpack behind her.

Grace felt a void watching Jess stride confidently up the walk toward the main school doors. The car seemed so empty without her. The trace of fish smell in the air was the only evidence she'd ever been there. That plus a few bread crumbs. Grace picked them up and tossed them out the window. Jess was out of sight now, swallowed up by the sprawling building, and Grace had no choice but to pull away.

And go back to the office? Grace's knotted stomach said no.

She wasn't hungry, but stopping for a bite to eat was the only excuse that would allow her to continue avoiding her work. Ten minutes later, she drove up beside the Jolt O' Java. Now why had she come here?

LEVI KNEW HE HAD a busy afternoon ahead of him. One of his two scheduled staff members had phoned in just half an hour ago, pleading for some time off to finish a term paper due the next morning. That left Sally, the university student he'd hired only a few days ago. She, however, was not working out nearly as well as he'd hoped. She was personable enough but somewhat scatterbrained.

"Here, let me help you," he said, stepping up to the espresso machine beside the uncoordinated, fuzzy-haired girl. "You have to twist it like this to get it to stay." He inserted the espresso holder in the slot, then pressed the switch. "Don't run it too long or the espresso tastes bitter. The coffee should be a rich brown color and foamy on the top." He watched as the liquid swirled into the bottom of the aluminum pitcher he held in his other hand. "See?"

Clearly she didn't.

The young woman flushed. "I'm sorry. Do you think I could work the till so I could watch you for a while?"

"Okay. Sure." Over the years, Levi had learned to spot the ones who would never quite catch on or who were too flustered to handle the job. It took a certain type of person to remain calm when a line of customers waited impatiently, or not get confused when a customer gave long, detailed orders.

Levi watched as the girl rang in another order incorrectly. Unobtrusively, he stepped forward to straighten things out.

"I'm sorry, Levi."

"That's okay," he said, although it was an effort to keep his tone neutral. "Why don't you clear some tables? The dishcloth is over there." He pointed to the stainless-steel sink.

Not thirty seconds later, he heard the sound of

something smashing and glanced up to see the girl standing in a pool of broken green glass.

"Don't move." He could just imagine her stabbing her foot with a shard of the broken mug. He quickly swept up the mess around her, then asked her to step aside while he got out the vacuum. In her attempt to stay out of his way, she managed to tangle herself around the long accordion hose.

"This isn't working out, is it?" she asked as she tried to free her legs from the hose.

"Not particularly."

"Would you prefer that I finish the day or just go now?"

Levi swallowed. Hard. "Maybe just go now."

She nodded, then promptly stepped backward into a display and sent a couple of pounds of whole coffee beans scattering over the floor.

That was when Grace Hamilton entered through the open front door. Wearing a tailored pantsuit, her hair pulled up from her face, she stood in the doorway, taking it all in. She finally raised a hand to her mouth, probably to hide a smile. For the moment, he ignored her as he picked up the broom again and handed it to the girl—she couldn't hurt herself on coffee beans, could she?

"I'm so sorry, Levi," the girl was saying. It had become something of a refrain with her.

He tried to smile but couldn't. Finally, he turned to face the woman in the doorway.

"Grace." Coffee beans crunched underfoot as he walked toward her.

"Having a bad day?" she asked.

"It looks that way, doesn't it? I guess I'm going to be a single-man operation today."

"Your assistant?" Grace nodded toward the girl. She was on all fours, trying to pry out some beans that had fallen between the cracks of the hardwood floor.

"She's on her way out. Thank heavens." He rolled his eyes.

"I could give you a hand, if you wanted."

He took in her toffee-colored suit, the fine cream silk of her blouse. "Thanks for the offer, but I know you have your own work to do."

"I guess I do, but somehow I'm not ready to face it right now. If you accept my offer, you'll be doing me a favor. Otherwise I have no excuse not to go back and face the music."

He noticed now the tiredness in her eyes, the tension lines around her mouth—flaws her expertly applied makeup had hidden from a distance. "This has to do with that board meeting you were telling me about yesterday, doesn't it?"

"Yes. I was up all night, but I still haven't decided what to do next. I didn't go to work at all this morning, just made some calls from home. Then Jess phoned me, wondering if I could meet her at the library. I just finished dropping her back at school."

She had? "Which library?"

"Downtown. I guess her class is working on a special project. I was happy to help her."

Levi compressed his lips. Jess usually asked *him* to help her with any special projects. Just another example of her growing away from him. He supposed he'd have to get used to this feeling.

"I'm done, Levi." The girl came up beside them. "I think I got them all. If you want to deduct the cost of the beans from my morning salary…"

Her morning salary wouldn't begin to cover the cost

of five pounds of coffee beans, but Levi decided against telling her that. "I'll cut you a check and send it in the mail," he told her. "There's no need for you to return."

"I'm sorry it didn't work out," she said, backing out the door.

"That's all right. Just do me one favor, Sally."

"Yeah?"

He cringed as she bumped into an old man leaning over a walking stick.

"Watch where you're going, okay?" He turned away, not able to stand looking at her anymore, and saw that Grace was smiling again.

"My offer still stands."

He eyed her skeptically.

"You don't think I can do it, do you?"

The way she'd automatically planted her hands on her hips, determined to prove him wrong even though he'd said nothing to indicate he doubted her ability, amused him. "It's not like sitting at a desk, moving papers from one pile to another, you know. This is real work, although it may not seem like that at first. And the espresso machine takes just the right touch. Not everyone has the knack."

"Hah!" Grace clapped her hands. "Give me a couple of hours and you'll be calling me the Queen of the Foam."

"Well…" He pretended reluctance, rubbed the jaw he'd shaved smooth only that morning. "You couldn't be worse than Sally."

Grace hung her jacket on the back of a chair, then rolled up her sleeves. He handed her a green apron to protect her fine clothes.

"Let me start by putting this display back together."

Her background was in marketing, Levi reminded himself, when half an hour later, the display was finished and ten times more attractive than the original. Grace joined him behind the counter, smoothly asking the next customer in line what she wanted.

He watched Grace measure the freshly ground coffee beans, then tamp them gently before inserting the doser in the machine and flicking on the switch. Deftly, she placed a small aluminum holder under the spout, then began to foam the customer's skim milk. With her free hand, she selected a clean mug. First she poured the foamed milk, then the rich espresso to the point where the foam rose above the rim of the mug but just before it began to cascade down the side.

"That will be $2.50," she said. "Would you care for a muffin with that?"

Levi took advantage of her presence to clear off some of the tables. Her performance had been slick—he had to give her that. She'd obviously watched him while setting up that display. He should have known she'd catch on quickly, but he was still impressed. And more than a little amused. Three weeks ago, he couldn't have imagined her with her sleeves rolled up, standing behind a counter, serving people. It wasn't her style, yet she seemed completely at ease doing it.

"This is fun," she whispered when he came back, his hands full of dirty plates and mugs.

"We'll see what you say at the end of your shift."

"Come on, admit it. I'm not as bad as you thought."

"I'll give you adequate." He sought eye contact with the person next in line. "Yes?"

The young, university-aged man said, "I'd like a cappuccino and a chicken salad sandwich on brown, with mustard, mayo and lettuce. And a pickle on the side."

Levi picked up a pencil and a pad of paper, jotted down the request and handed it to Grace. "Would you handle this while I steam the coffee?"

Grace made the sandwich, then a few minutes later, passed him back the piece of paper after adding a line of her own: *Bagel with cream cheese for the help?*

He nodded, glad she was planning to eat for a change. *Make one for me, too,* he wrote in reply.

She received the note with a strange expression on her face. In a flash, he understood. Somehow they'd automatically slipped into the old habit. It was how they'd communicated when they'd studied together in the library in the old days. He'd kept many of those notes, which were, of course, the ones Jess had found, the ones that had given her the false impression Grace was her mother.

Some of the notes had been funny, but most were amorous, and now he had an urge to pull back his request for a bagel and add a line to the bottom: *I'll show you a stock transaction or two if you meet me in the back room in fifteen minutes.*

"Levi?"

"Yeah?"

"Whole wheat with sunflower seeds, or sun-dried tomato?" She held up both varieties of bagels for his selection.

"Whole wheat." He couldn't write her notes like that anymore, of course. But it seemed a damn shame.

Two hours and dozens of customers later, he went into the back room by himself and cut a crown out of cardboard, then snuck up behind her at the counter and placed it on her head.

"I crown you the Queen of the Foam," he whispered in her ear, enjoying the brush of her hair against his nose and the sweet scent of her perfume.

She nodded regally so as to not dislodge the cardboard. "I told you so." Then took another bite of the confection she held in her hand. Business had hit a momentary lull, but soon the after-work crowd would arrive. "These are delicious. Where did you get them?"

He looked at the pecan butterhorn in her hand. "I make them. My own secret recipe."

Her eyes sparkled. "Secret recipe? That sounds enticing. You shouldn't hide them in this basket behind the biscotti. Give them a place of honor. Promote them as your store specialty." She began to rearrange the countertop, then suddenly stopped. "I'm sorry. I shouldn't be doing this, should I?"

"You mean butting your nose—" her sweet, adorable nose "—into my business?"

"I can't help thinking like a marketer, Levi. That's what I am."

"I know. Don't sweat it. Rearrange my counter. Put up a twelve-foot sign promoting my butterhorns. I don't care one way or the other." And he didn't. All he wanted was the right to pull Grace into his arms, to kiss the tip of her nose, whenever he felt so inclined.

Wait a minute—what was he thinking? He was never going to pull Grace into his arms. Nor kiss her nose or anything else, for that matter. He had to remember she was only here because she was avoiding her problems at work.

He stepped away from her to put on a new pot of

decaffeinated French vanilla, while she picked a small display blackboard from his shelves and used it to do a write-up on the butterhorns. She placed the basket and the sign on the other side of the cash register, then moved the jar of biscotti farther down the counter.

She did have a knack for making things irresistible. He'd give her that.

"Looks great," he said, feeling a little guilty about all her effort on his behalf. "You must be getting tired. My evening staff should be in soon."

"Oh."

Had he said something wrong? "Thanks for the help. It would have been a crazy afternoon without you."

"Any time," she said.

But he knew she didn't mean it. She might be down right now, but she wasn't beaten. Soon she'd be back in the ring, where she belonged. Big business. Now she removed the silly cardboard crown and he took it from her and pushed it under the counter, not willing to throw it directly into the garbage. Not yet.

"Good luck with your expansion plans," he said.

She nodded, her head slightly lowered. "Yeah. Thanks."

She pulled off the apron and tugged on her jacket; he handed her the purse he'd stuffed under the counter for her.

"It's been fun, Levi."

Fun? Yeah, he guessed it had been.

"So you're sure you'll be okay now?" she pressed.

Define *okay,* he wanted to say. Instead, he nodded. "Get going, Grace. You've got a company to save."

She eyed him, her chin moving up an inch or so. "You're right. I'd better get busy."

He noticed a coffee stain on the counter and began to rub at it, not glancing up until she'd walked out the door. Through the window, he watched her disappear along the sidewalk, her back straight, her hair swinging.

No doubt about it—she was a remarkable lady. The Queen of the Foam indeed.

CHAPTER NINE

"ARE YOU FEELING okay, Dad?"

Levi opened his eyes. He was sitting on the recliner, relaxing after doing the dishes. Jess had come home at five, as promised, and made them a hearty vegetarian stew for dinner.

"Sure I'm okay. Why do you ask?"

"Because of the music you're listening to." She sat cross-legged on the floor beside him, resting her head against his knee. "Cat Stevens, right? You usually put him on when you're feeling sad. Like when Grandma died."

He touched the silken strands of Jess's fine hair. How had it happened? The changes had taken place so gradually he'd hardly noticed. When was the last time he'd washed this hair for her? Helped her with her shoelaces? Comforted her after she'd fallen and hurt herself?

Someone ought to hang out a warning sign for dads in big, bright neon letters: *Hold her tight. This is the last time she'll let you do this for her.*

And now she was picking up on *his* moods. Worrying about how *he* was feeling.

"You are definitely growing up too fast. Have I told you that lately?"

She lifted her head. "Is that why you're playing Cat Stevens?"

He smiled. "Sort of."

For years, there had been just the two of them, and it had always seemed enough. How could he explain, to her or even himself, why he felt so lonely this evening? More to the point, he didn't want to explain because he knew the answer damn well, just didn't want to admit it.

"Maybe we could go out to a movie. What do you think?"

"Can't, Dad. I have to work on this report for school." She wrapped her arms around her knees and tucked her head down. "Grace said she'd help me with the outline, but I phoned to see when we could get together and she said she was too busy."

Levi wasn't surprised. Watching Grace walk out of the Jolt yesterday, he'd suspected she was gathering her strength for a counterattack.

"Can I help?"

Jess shrugged. "It's not so much the report. I can do it on my own. I just wanted to see her."

Oh, man. Didn't he know exactly how she felt. He wondered if Grace had any idea of the impact she still had on him. When she was in a room, it was impossible for him to look at anyone else or listen to others speak. She became his focus the way she had so many years ago.

And he still wanted her in a very real, very physical sense he didn't want to confuse with love. In that and so many other ways, her presence was a torment.

Most heartrending of all had been seeing how vulnerable she was at the threat of losing her business. He'd thought Grace had become hard. Now he realized that simply wasn't true.

"I have four tickets to the Friday night hockey

game," he said. "Maybe Grace would like to come with us…and Neil, too."

"Really, Dad?" Jess stood up, her cheeks reddening with pleasure. "Can I phone and invite them right now?"

"Why not?"

She called Neil first and confirmed that he could come. Then she tried Grace.

"I guess she's not at home yet," Jess said, her hand over the receiver. "I'll leave a message, then try her at work."

Levi closed his eyes. He didn't want to admit how desperately he hoped she would come. He selected a CD and tried to concentrate on the music, but his daughter's voice came in loud and clear.

"Hi, Grace, Dad and I were wondering if you could come to a hockey game with us on Friday…seven o'clock…. I see. Every night? Past midnight? So lunch…" Jess paused, listening. "In a few weeks. Yeah, sure. That'd be fine."

There was nothing fine, however, about the way Jess looked when she hung up the phone. Levi forgot his own disappointment at seeing the downcast expression on his daughter's face.

"I'm going to work in my room."

"Okay, Jess." *Damn it, Grace.* He was surprised how angry he felt. Hadn't he known from the beginning it would end with Jess getting herself too attached and Grace letting her down?

The inevitability didn't make the rejection any easier to accept. Jess had had enough disappointments in her life. Hadn't he warned Grace time and time again she couldn't treat a kid this way?

IT WAS PAST MIDNIGHT when Grace fumbled with her umbrella and her briefcase as she tried to free her right hand so she could unlock the front door. In the end, the umbrella clattered to the landing, leaving her unprotected from the gentle evening shower. Dimly she registered the sound of a car door slamming, then footsteps on the sidewalk. It wasn't until she'd opened the door and stepped inside that she realized those footsteps were getting louder, coming up *her* walkway, toward *her* house. Panicking momentarily, she whirled around, about to slam the door shut and dial 911.

Then she froze, gripping the door with her free hand, transfixed by the man on the threshold.

"Levi." She stepped back to let him enter, then shut the door behind her and leaned against it as if battling a strong winter wind.

"Did I frighten you?"

His blue eyes glowed eerily in the faint light from the hall, giving Grace the absurd impression he was glad he'd startled her. He handed her the umbrella she'd dropped at the door.

"Thanks." Grace propped it on the floor next to her briefcase, then shrugged off her navy trench coat. "What are you doing here?"

He didn't answer, just locked eyes with her, until she felt compelled to look away.

"Is it Jess? Is she...?" She paused, then looked back at him. A tiny muscle twitched at the side of his jaw, and now she knew it was condemnation she saw in his eyes. She reached a hand to the ever-present pounding in her forehead and pressed hard. He had every right to be angry at her. "I'm sorry," she began, then didn't know what else to say.

"Headache?" Levi asked almost grudgingly.

She shrugged. She wasn't looking for sympathy and had no grounds to expect it from him, of all people. Still, his expression softened.

"Have you had dinner?" he inquired.

She shook her head. Just too much coffee and too many cigarettes. Somehow she'd gone from smoking one pack a week to almost two. She followed Levi to the kitchen and sank wearily into a chair while he opened the fridge door.

After a moment's consideration, he took out a couple of eggs, the remains of a block of cheddar cheese and an apple with crinkled skin around the stem. From the freezer he pulled out a couple of flour tortillas.

Grace watched him, bemused. The scene was not unfamiliar—he'd often cooked for her in the past— but it certainly was incongruous, given the years that had elapsed, the hour, even the place. This was, after all, the first time Levi had set foot in her home. And she could see he was still angry.

"Do you have any herbal tea?"

Levi was checking her cupboards now, and if Grace had had the energy to be embarrassed, she would have stood up to stop him. Compared with his kitchen, hers was a disaster. Even she had little idea where to find things.

"Here we go." Levi pulled out a small cellophane packet containing two tea bags. Grace remembered receiving them a couple of months ago in a mail promotion. As he put the kettle on to boil, she turned on the radio, then went into her bedroom to change out of her suit into jeans and a sweatshirt.

She paused in the doorway before reentering the kitchen. Something smelled marvelous. Then she saw the table, where, on one of her plain white dishes sat a burrito and beside it a cup of fragrant tea. "This looks delicious. Aren't you having any?"

He shook his head, so she sat down and picked up the burrito. Inside was a delicious combination of egg, cheese and apple. She never would have thought of putting the three together, but the burrito tasted like heaven. Most importantly, it sat easily in her stomach, which had felt like molten lava for at least a couple of weeks.

It seemed only seconds before the burrito was gone. She closed her eyes, savoring the feeling of being full, dry and comfortable, with no pressing matters to handle. When she opened her eyes, she saw that Levi had sat down beside her and was watching her as if he didn't quite know what to expect from her.

"Thank you," she said, finding the words inadequate. She couldn't remember the last time someone had taken care of her this way. It almost made her want to cry, which only proved how truly exhausted she was.

"You're welcome," he said. "Now, drink the tea."

They went into the living room. Levi stood in the center of the room, looking uneasily at her modern, white leather furniture.

"If you open that chest in the corner, I have a couple of blankets. I'll turn on the gas fireplace. Even on a warm day, rain adds a chill to the air."

The blankets helped soften the atmosphere. So did the fire. Grace switched on the radio. James Taylor was singing an old favorite.

Levi was sitting close to her. He reached out and touched a strand of her hair.

"I came here to give you a piece of my mind, you know," he said.

Grace took a deep breath. "I figured as much." She looked down at his other hand, which rested in his lap. She wanted to curl her fingers around it and pull him even closer. "If making me dinner constitutes giving me a piece of your mind, you can do it whenever you want."

One corner of his mouth lifted in a reluctant smile. "You're hopeless, Grace. Did you know you've got weevils in your flour?"

Grace acknowledged she ought to feel embarrassed by her slovenly kitchen, but she was too tired. She didn't like to cook, she rarely had time for it, and she couldn't recall the last occasion she'd opened her flour canister. Or did she even have a flour canister? She suspected she kept the flour in the bag.

"They're my pets," she said. "Every single person should have a pet so they don't have to come home to an empty house. Don't you think?"

"And weevils are such low maintenance," he agreed. "I'll have to remember to suggest them to Jess the next time the subject comes up."

Jess. The mention of his daughter made Grace's stomach tighten. She knew that was really why Levi was here. Not to take care of her, keep her company, help her relax and unwind from a dreadful day at work.

"I'm sorry I had to disappoint her, Levi. But you can see the state I'm in. I'm trying to develop support for the estimates and assumptions in my expansion plan, but I'm not a finance person. I'm trying to get one easily understandable package that I can send out to the board members. Maybe once they see the possibilities for profit, they'll agree to turn down the take-over offer. It's a long shot, I know."

"Seems to me you've built a career out of long shots."

"A career and a life," she reminded him, thinking of all the things he had that she did not. "The weevils are kind of cute, but they aren't much fun."

"I've heard they can be a little standoffish." He let go of her hair in order to stroke the side of her face with his finger.

Desire, hot and instant, burned in Grace's core. Her heart was racing, her breathing quickening. How amazing that his light touch could kindle such sensation. Or maybe it wasn't just his finger on her skin but also the look in his eyes, as if he were devouring her.

Grace had never wanted anything as much as she wanted him to kiss her right then, but she didn't move, didn't even blink, because she was afraid she might spoil the moment. She wasn't sure how it had happened, but a bond had formed between them. For all she knew, it could break as quickly as it had formed. And that was something she didn't think she could bear.

Their eyes locked. Time and space converged. There was no reality beyond the moment. Levi pulled her head closer. She went willingly, her eyes automatically fluttering shut, her lips parting, her heart yearning.

The gentle touch of his lips soon became more demanding. Pent-up desire made caution the last thought on her mind. Now her hands could get lost in the thick waves of his hair. She could press her skin next to his, taste the richness of his mouth. Her hands splayed against his chest, then traveled up to stroke his face. There was no part of him she didn't long to touch, no part of herself she wasn't willing to offer in return.

She heard him groan when she pulled her lips away to travel the length of his neck. He was wearing a thick, gray wool sweater and made no protest when she reached under it to clasp his back through the thin cotton of the T-shirt he had on.

"Gracie, you're driving me mad."

"Tell me what it was so I can do it again."

With a demonic grin, he pinned her arms back with one hand, then allowed the other to slip under her sweatshirt to stroke the cool skin of her stomach. "Let me show you instead." Slowly, he moved his hand up, his eyes fixed on hers. When he got to her bare breast, she saw his eyes narrow at her groan of desire.

With his palm, he brushed the tips of her erect nipples, and she longed to shuck the cotton garment, resenting the awkward barrier between them. He must have felt the same way because, in the next instant, he pulled the sweatshirt up over her head. Her hands were free now, and she removed his sweater and T-shirt together.

He stared at her for a moment, and she felt a flash of self-consciousness. It had been so many years. There was no way her body was as perfect as when she was in university. Would he be disappointed with the changes?

"Ah, Gracie." He lowered his head to kiss each of her breasts, tenderly, lovingly, then caught one dusty rose nipple in his teeth with just the perfect amount of intensity to bring her pleasure without pain.

She was conscious she'd lost weight, that she wasn't as voluptuous as before. But he made her feel beautiful, desirable. She held the back of his head, her fingers tracing circles in his scalp like the circles he was kissing into her skin. When he finally raised his head, her legs were already wrapped around his body. He stood up from the sofa, and she balanced her upper body so she wouldn't tumble but instead moved with him.

Just as they had done so many times before, he carried her off to bed, only this time he needed directions.

"Down the hall. Last door on the right."

There, they sank onto the bed together, gazing at each other in momentary pause. What was he thinking? He looked so intense, his eyes shining with desire, but behind the desire was a touch of sadness. Instinctively, she placed her mouth on his, trying to draw him closer with her kisses. She didn't want him to pull away from her now. How could she stand the pain if he left her bed?

With relief, she felt him return her kiss and the tense muscles in his back relax beneath her fingers. He ground his pelvis against her lower belly as he lowered his head to kiss and suck the hollow at the base of her neck. He knew all the pleasure zones, the rhythms and tricks that never failed to please her. And she knew his. Yet there was something different about this experience that set it apart from all the other times they'd been together. A sweetness, a poignancy that hadn't been there in their youth. It had been so long.

"Move over for a minute, Gracie."

She shifted against the comforter, watching as he unzipped her jeans. She lifted her hips so he could pull them off. All that money on lacy silk lingerie. It was worth it to see his eyes burn at the sight of her pale pink thong. She moved her hips suggestively as he slid the fine silk garment down her legs, then reached out to release him from whatever clothing he still had on.

Naked, they fell back together, old endearments, almost forgotten, springing from their mouths. Grace ran a hand over his chest, marveling at how fit and strong he was. She wanted to make this a night neither one of them would ever forget. She knew he wanted to do the same for her.

IN THE HEAT OF her passion, three words had come out of Grace's mouth.

"I love you."

She was profoundly embarrassed afterward.

Why had she said that, acted like an adolescent fool? Was it force of habit? She couldn't remember a time when she'd made love with Levi without saying those words. Or a time when he hadn't said them to her. Excepting this time, of course.

Not that he'd seemed at all taken aback. He'd merely covered her mouth with his and given her a soul-reaching kiss that had spanned several minutes. Was it possible he hadn't heard? That he understood her utterance had just been instinct?

Now, at three in the morning, he was getting ready to leave, explaining he never slept away from home. It was, as far as Grace was concerned, a very convenient policy. She propped herself up against the headboard and watched him dress.

"Cover your breasts at least, Grace. How can you expect me to have the strength to go home when you're looking like that?"

She smiled. "Cover them for me."

He picked up a pillow from the floor and tossed it at her. It landed perfectly on target.

"That wasn't exactly what I had in mind."

"God, Grace. You haven't changed. You know

that?'' As he zipped up his jeans, she felt a buzzing
in her ears. It wasn't fair for a man to have such a flat
belly. Or such a well-developed chest. He was even
more powerful-looking, more fit, than when they were
younger.

Her gaze dropped to the duvet, which bunched com-
fortingly around her, and she thought about how the
room would feel in five minutes. She might as well
curl up in her refrigerator for all the comfort she would
get from this bed once he left.

''What have we done?'' She looked back up at him.

Conflicting emotions played out in his expression.
For a moment, she thought he might come over to
comfort her, but he just reached down to pick up his
socks.

''I don't know, Grace. I guess this has been growing
between us since we first saw each other again. Maybe
it was inevitable that it happened.''

Those were not the words she wanted to hear. But
what did she expect? A declaration of love? A promise
there would be many more nights like this?

What did she have to give him? No man wanted his
love life squeezed into the wee hours of the morning.

And then there was Jess. Grace had already proven
she could never meet the needs of a teenager.

''Why do we have to grow up, Levi? Things were
never this complicated before.''

He sat on the bed and she'd never seen him so serious.

''Why ask me? You were always the one with the
answers. Remember?''

God, yes, she remembered. She'd been such a fool.
She hadn't valued her relationship with Levi, hadn't

realized what a rare individual he was or that what they shared didn't often happen between two people.

"Good luck with your board members, Grace." Levi leaned over to kiss her forehead, but before she could reach out for him, he was standing again. "I'll lock the door on my way out."

Grace stayed in bed, listening to him rustle through the clothing they'd discarded in the living room only hours before. She heard the front door close, his footsteps fade, then the growl of a car engine and tires squealing on the slick pavement.

Stretching out in the bed, Grace pulled the covers up under her chin. She held the pillow Levi had tossed at her against her chest and listened to the softly falling rain. She realized she'd been fighting for the wrong thing.

All this time, she'd thought that what she wanted was just one night with Levi in her bed. Now he was gone, and the dark, empty feeling she had inside, the feeling she'd hoped he could somehow banish, was bigger than ever.

Stay. She wondered what he would have said if she had pleaded. But Jess was at home by herself. He'd had to leave, and she knew it.

Alone again. Her and the weevils.

LEVI FELT LIKE a suspect in a B-grade mystery novel as he drove away from Grace's house. "Damn fool," he muttered as he turned up the speed of his windshield wipers. He wished he was at home reading about a man who'd just made a tremendous fool of himself, instead of living it. In a book, you could quickly turn the page on a mistake. In real life, the whole thing played out so much more slowly.

There was no point in asking himself why he'd done it. He knew why. He'd known what might happen the minute he got in his car to drive over to her house. What almost certainly would happen.

Just as he'd known what would happen later.

Heartbreak.

For him, anyway. As for Grace, that was difficult to say. Her protective armor was stronger than his. But the expression on her face as he was dressing to leave led him to believe he had at least penetrated it. One thing he was sure of: despite her success, the money, the fancy car, he didn't envy her. Her home had all too clearly shown how empty her life was outside the office. Did she see it, he wondered, the desolation and loneliness that no amount of expensive, tasteful furniture could hide?

Levi rubbed his tired eyes. Her scent was everywhere—on his hands, his clothing—the way her memory permeated his every thought. Fixing her dinner tonight, he'd realized that he still loved her. Which had made it even more impossible to avoid what happened later.

Did she know how he felt? How it had pained him to hear her utter those words in a moment of unthinking passion—words that would have meant the world to him had she really meant them?

No.

He was being a damn fool for the second time in his life. Only this time was worse because he had a daughter. A fourteen-year-old trying to come to terms with her own sexuality. And what kind of example was he setting for her?

Levi parked, then let himself in the back entrance to their apartment. He'd no sooner opened the door to the coatroom between the two bedrooms than he knew something was up. The hall light was on. There were noises from the kitchen. He stopped first to wash in his bathroom, then went to investigate.

"Hi, Daddy. I couldn't sleep."

She almost never called him that anymore. "Hi, sweetheart." He tousled her hair, smiling at the picture of innocence she made in her gray nightshirt with Winnie-the-Pooh on the front, her hair a shambles and her skin free of any makeup. "Mixing yourself some hot cocoa?"

"Yes. But mine never tastes as good as yours." She looked down at her mug, where lumps floated on the murky brown liquid.

"That's because you don't make it from scratch the way I do. Here—" he took the mug from her hand and dumped the contents down the sink "—let me show you." He got out the saucepan, the cocoa, milk and sugar. He knew that Jess could have made it in her sleep if she'd really wanted to, but the ritual was comforting. For him anyway. He did up enough for both of them, then sat across from her at the table to drink.

After a moment, he became aware of Jess's scrutiny.

"Were you with Grace tonight? Don't look at me that way, Dad. Did you think I wouldn't hear you when you left just before midnight?"

Man, talk about role reversal. "Yes, I went to see Grace. Satisfied?"

Jess nodded. "I'm glad. I think you two were made for each other."

Oh, God. How did he explain this? "Don't get your

hopes up, Jess. We're two very different people, and our priorities have never been the same.''

''Do you love her?''

Levi had always tried to be honest with Jess, but surely there was a limit. Looking into his daughter's trusting gray-blue eyes, however, he knew he couldn't waver now. ''Yes, I love her, Jess. But I don't know if I could live with her. And I don't know how she feels about me, either. I guess I never have.''

''How can you say that? I know I wasn't supposed to, but I did read the letters she wrote to you. How can you doubt that she loved you? And if she loved you once, I'm sure she can love you again.''

''Sweetheart, I don't want to rock your boat, but just think for a minute what life with Grace would be like. She might say she'd do something with you or me, but then a catastrophe would occur at her company and she'd have to back out. Do you have any idea of the hours she works? We'd barely see her.''

''But if she lived with us, she wouldn't have to work so hard. You make lots of money with the coffee shop.''

''It isn't the money, Jess. Grace works because she needs to. It's the only way she can feel good about herself.''

Jess eyed him quizzically. It was clear she didn't understand what he meant.

''Enough of that. Now, tell me why you couldn't sleep.''

Jess suddenly became guarded. ''Just problems with my friends. Nothing too serious.''

Ah. So the openness was to be entirely one-sided, was it? Teenagers. ''With your girlfriends? Or with Neil?''

The way Jess quickly looked down gave him his answer.

Oh, Jess. He wanted to help her, but he didn't know how. She'd changed so much this past year, grown up. Maybe if she hadn't been such a tomboy before, it wouldn't have come as such a shock. Even when she was twelve, she hadn't seemed to care what she wore to school, or how her hair was cut, or whether the other girls had their ears pierced once, twice or a dozen times.

Now she was obsessed with her appearance, even more so since Neil had come on the scene. Levi was aware that Neil's attention somehow elevated Jess's status among her friends. He wished she could understand that her feelings for Neil were all tied up with her longing to be grown-up and accepted by her peers, but at the same time he knew that was a lot to expect. The only way kids learned these things was by living through them. Hopefully without making too many serious mistakes along the way.

"Daddy? Is Grace my real mother?"

"Why do you ask when you're not prepared to believe my answer?"

His daughter fixed him with tired but serious eyes. "I'll believe you this time. I promise."

Would she? Was she really ready to hear the truth? Levi didn't know the answer to either question, but he knew he couldn't lie. "No, Jess. Grace is not your real mother."

Jess let out a long, trembling sigh.

"Do you believe me?"

She nodded. "If I met my real mother and asked you about her, would you tell me the truth?"

Levi swallowed. That was a hard one. He'd promised Casey. But there were limits to any promise. "I think I'd have to, Jess. In those circumstances."

She nodded again. "I'll try to go to sleep now, Daddy. Thanks for the cocoa—it was yummy."

She gave him a little hug and a peck on the cheek, then rinsed her mug and put it in the dishwasher before she went to bed. She was a good kid. Casey had missed out on so much.

CHAPTER TEN

FRIDAY AFTERNOON AT FIVE, Grace's desk was piled with papers, work sheets and financial reports. She was alone in the office. Douglas had been gone all week, on a holiday she'd insisted he take, and her staff were out enjoying a well-earned round of drinks at a bar down the street. Jackie had accepted the corporate credit card when Grace handed it to her, but she'd said, "Why don't you come, too, for a change?"

"I can't. Until this proposal is completed, I wouldn't be able to relax anyway. I'd rather keep working, okay? Tell the staff how much I appreciate the hours they've put in this week, though."

Grace stared at the column of sales figures in front of her, frowning as it split in two before her eyes and became blurry. She blinked once, then twice, wondering if her not being able to see was due simply to eyestrain or if she needed glasses. Maybe a break would help.

Standing up, she linked her fingers and raised her arms above her head to stretch her shoulder and neck muscles. Out her window, she noticed the late-afternoon sun glinting off the ocean. The view was spectacular, but how often did she take the time to enjoy it? She walked over to the glass wall and leaned her forehead against the cool surface.

What a week! Pulling together all the research had

been harder than she'd thought. That Douglas's records were in a complete shambles hadn't helped. She suspected he'd already gone through his papers and removed those she might have found useful. In preparation for being fired?

Thank heavens for Jackie. Together they'd tracked down the information Grace had needed, compiling their research findings from various sources, arranging meetings with several bankers. At times, giving up had been tempting. But this was her last chance, her only hope. Aware of this, the entire staff had kicked in to help. They were close to finishing; only a few more days would see them through. Then what?

Here she was on real rocky ground because she had no guarantee the board members would give her proposal still another shot. They were busy people; they had their own jobs and most sat on several other boards. By now, they had to be pretty annoyed with the way she'd wasted their time.

Thanks to Douglas Eberhart. Yet, even as her thoughts settled resentfully on the man who'd once been her closest adviser, she knew she was just making excuses. She was the president; ultimately Douglas's behavior was her responsibility. She should have figured out what he was up to earlier. She should have defused the situation before it ever reached the board.

Grace returned to her desk and picked up her pen. She wasn't going to berate herself for past errors. But she did intend to remedy them as soon as possible. Jotting some notes to herself, she noticed a slight tremor in her hand and remembered she'd skipped lunch and it was almost the dinner hour—she hadn't eaten in hours. Maybe she ought to take her papers home with her. She could order a pizza and work all night there as well as she could at the office.

Assuming being at home wouldn't remind her too much of her night with Levi.

She swallowed, forcing her mind off that subject, and loaded her documents into her briefcase. She had to keep busy every minute of every day or she might find herself thinking of things better left forgotten.

But not allowing herself to dwell on a certain topic didn't mean she could forget it. She hadn't forgotten a single one of her nights with Levi. Why would this last one, the most thrilling of all, be an exception?

From the moment she'd seen him again, the possibility of their making love had always been in her mind. And now it had finally happened. She'd gotten exactly what she wanted, and it had been even more wonderful than she could have imagined. So why wasn't she satisfied?

Was it possible that making love with Levi wasn't what she'd wanted after all? Or was it that she wanted so much more than she'd initially suspected? Grace had no idea, but she knew that the two of them had opened a Pandora's box and things could never be the same again.

Levi's power over her was too great, and to remain on the margin of his life would be too painful for her. She would have to stop seeing Jess. There was no other solution—

Grace's contemplations were interrupted by the sound of her office door opening. Douglas stormed in, his face red and angry, his mouth hard.

"I need to talk to you, Grace."

"Your holiday doesn't seem to have done you much

good, Douglas. You look as stressed out as you did last Friday when I suggested you needed a break.''

''And now I know why you made that recommendation. Holiday, my foot. You wanted me out of the way so you could go through my files.''

Grace folded her arms over her chest, feeling more in control than she would have expected. ''You have such a suspicious mind.''

''Now what are you planning?'' He eyed the closed briefcase on her desk.

Grace smiled, happy at seeing him sweat a little. She'd known word would eventually get back to him, and the fact of the matter was, she no longer gave a damn. ''Did you think the business would shut down in your absence? It may surprise you, but you're not quite as invaluable as you think.''

He pushed his glasses up his short nose and glared at her. ''Since when do you go behind my back and do my job for me?''

Grace found it easy to remain calm in the face of his anger. For way too long she'd felt powerless to confront him. But Ben Ryan, her lawyer, had given her the go-ahead, and now everything was out in the open. She didn't have to carry on the charade that she and Douglas were on the same side. ''Since you stopped doing it properly yourself.''

''Who says you're doing it properly? You have no accounting or financial training.''

Grace leaned up against her desk, picked up a gold pen and looked at it casually. ''I may not have your accounting background, Doug, but I know my business. And that crap you piled on the directors at the last meeting isn't it. It's one thing to disagree with me, quite another to stand up in front of the board and tell them out-and-out lies.''

"I don't know what you're talking about. You're losing it, Grace, all because you're scared of giving up control of your baby.''

Baby? It took Grace a second to realize he meant the company, not Jess. "I'm not losing it, Douglas, but you are. Your job, I mean. Not only have you failed to perform your stated duties, but you've purposely withheld information gathered on my time, with my resources.''

Douglas's flush developed into a brilliant shade of red. "You can't fire me. Think of the field day the newspapers will have. They'll say you're panicking, that you can't even control your own management team.''

"I'll admit that was my concern earlier. But I'm long past caring how this appears from the outside.'' She picked up the phone to dial security. "I'll escort you to your office, Douglas. You can collect your personal effects, then go home—leaving your pass card and the office key with me, of course.''

"You're going to pay for this, Grace,'' Douglas vowed. "You'll never be able to run this company without me.''

The hatred in his voice was chilling. This wasn't the same man she'd known for so many years. Greed and ambition had changed him.

"We've done well enough this past week,'' she pointed out calmly. "Amazing how much gets done when you don't have one of your employees working against you anymore.''

"I was never working against you, Grace.''

"Oh, really?''

"This takeover is the best thing that could happen to Body and Soul. To you, too, you know. You stand to make a lot of money if it goes through."

"You're welcome to your opinions, but since you're no longer my employee, I'm not obligated to listen to them." She opened the door to the hallway and waited politely for him to exit.

"You'll regret this, Grace. Whatever plans you're cooking up, the board will reject. Leaving the door open for Jarvis to buy out the rest of the shares they need. Then you'll be out on the street. And *I'm* going to have *your* job."

She moved forward, blocking him as he was about to go. "That's been your plan from the beginning, hasn't it? To be president."

Douglas's grin was one of pure self-satisfied vengeance. "Of course. I'm surprised, and a little disappointed, that it took you so long to figure that out. As soon as I learned Jarvis was trying to take us over, I gave them a call. I've been cooperating with them from the start."

For the first time in her life, Grace understood the impulse to punch someone in the face. She would remove Douglas's glasses first, she thought. Tossing the delicate wire frames to the floor and grinding them with her heel would be her first pleasure. Then, while he was looking down, she'd plant her fist in that insufferable smirk of his.

With a deep breath, Grace checked her temper and raised her chin. She wasn't going to sink to his level. "A year ago, I never would have believed this of you, Doug. And you know what's really sad? You actually sound proud that you've betrayed me."

"Grace." He placed a hand on her shoulder. "You shouldn't take this personally."

"Oh, is that right?" She brushed off his hand and stepped away from him. "And why is that?"

"Because it's only business. You, of all people, should understand that."

GRACE PUT AN ARM OUT to the briefcase sitting on the passenger seat beside her as she made an abrupt stop. She hadn't seen the utility van to her left until the last second. Now, as it swung around the front of her car, she drew in a deep breath, ignoring the shaking fist thrust out the window of the van.

The adrenaline jolt made her arms feel weak and her entire body tremble. She drove out of the intersection, keeping her speed well under the limit for a change. What would the guy in the van have done if she'd opened her window and shouted, "Don't take it personally. I just wasn't concentrating on my driving."

As she considered Douglas's admission, she wondered if she should have guessed he was in cahoots with Jarvis. His revelation hadn't come as a total shock. Perhaps subconsciously she'd already suspected he was a snake. He was about as different from Levi as it was possible for a man to be.

Levi. Since when was he the standard by which she measured other men?

Since the first day she'd met him. That was the truth, much as she hated to admit it....

The tall Douglas firs of Stanley Park rose up to meet her as she followed Lions Gate Bridge Road toward home. She'd headed in this direction automatically, not because it was where she wanted to go but because she had no alternative. A week ago, she might have turned south, not north, from Hastings toward the Jolt O' Java, but not any longer. It was time she faced reality and accepted that she had no business in either Levi's life or Jess's.

At home, Grace changed into a sweat suit and ordered a pizza. She opened a bottle of red wine and drank a glass before the delivery man arrived. The phone rang just after she finished the first slice.

Could it be Levi? She pushed the traitorous thought aside as she reached for the receiver. Why would Levi be calling? He hadn't said he would, hadn't made a single promise. They'd both known their night together wasn't about starting but about finishing.

"Hello." She sounded too breathless.

"Is Mr. or Mrs. Hamilton there, please?"

Disappointment made her stomach ache. She sank onto the sofa and closed the pizza box. Her mind in a fog, she heard herself pledge fifty dollars to support the Kidney Foundation. Then she lay down, trying not to think of the last time she'd been on this sofa. With Levi.

She shut her eyes and wished she could relax. A briefcase full of work beckoned, but her head ached as she thought of having to concentrate on those rows of numbers. If only she could sleep. But she knew she was still too uptight. Maybe she should play with the weevils.

Slowly, Grace stood and made her way to the kitchen. Staring at the bleached-oak cupboards and the white countertops flecked with pink and mauve, she remembered the day she'd moved into the house, shortly after her company had gone public. The real-estate agent had walked her through each room, stopping in the kitchen to point out the state-of-the-art appliances, the plentiful countertops, the efficient triangle of sink, fridge and stove.

The week after the move, Grace had gone grocery shopping. She'd bought all the staples of the well-stocked kitchen—flour, sugar, baking powder, corn syrup, different types of cooking oil and specialty vinegars, a whole basket of herbs and spices. Now, opening cupboard door after cupboard door, she saw that most of the stuff was still in there, unopened, unused.

What about the dinner parties she'd imagined herself having in the elegant dining room she'd decorated with a marble-slab table and richly upholstered straight-backed chairs? Going to a restaurant or someone's club always seemed easier. As for breakfast and lunch, those meals she always ate at work.

It wasn't that Grace didn't know how to cook. Oh, she knew all right. Her mother had made sure of that. She'd also made sure Grace knew how much more important the work the men on the farm did was, compared with the work the women did.

"Then let me go out in the fields to work, and my brother can do the cooking for a change."

Her mother had slapped her face for that one.

Grace slid to the floor, propping her back against a kitchen cupboard. She felt a tickle on her cheek and when she reached up to scratch was surprised to feel something damp. Oh, please, she wasn't becoming maudlin about her childhood, was she?

So what if it hadn't been idyllic? Whose was? *Get over it,* she chided herself. *Your parents are dead. You never see your brother. Case closed.* And she'd done all right for herself, hadn't she? She'd proven she could do whatever she wanted. She didn't need a man to provide for her; she could make out just fine on her own.

Grace pulled herself to her feet, opened a plastic garbage bag and began to discard supplies—the brown sugar, the extra virgin olive oil, the tins of tomato sauce and paste. Each landed in the garbage with a satisfying *thunk*.

A momentary guilt pang assailed her. She could have taken the supplies to a food bank. But they were so old, many probably past their expiry date.

Baked beans, tuna, pasta—she would never eat this, never use that. Fast and furious, she emptied almost every single item from her cupboards, filling first one garbage bag, then another.

As she worked, she pictured her mother's kitchen on the farm. Its perfect order and cleanliness. The way her mother had taught her to wipe the lid of the cocoa tin clean after each use. The shiny stainless-steel canisters faithfully filled with flour, sugar, salt and coffee, then sealed tight to prevent contamination.

From things like weevils.

Grace picked up the unsealed yellow bag of flour with one hand, not daring to peek inside to see the insects Levi had told her about. With one toss, they were gone.

"So long, pals," she muttered, then turned to the fridge.

Very little was inside, other than bottles of unused condiments the same vintage as the stuff she'd thrown out. Once she'd added them to the garbage bag, all that was left was the carton from which Levi had taken some eggs to make her dinner the other night. Grace picked up the cardboard container and looked at the

Best Before date stamped in black ink, noting that it was well over a week ago.

Levi had fed her expired eggs. Probably he'd been trying to kill her. Grace almost laughed at the insane thought, but a choked sob came out instead.

God, but her life was pathetic. Why hadn't she seen it before?

"IT WAS A GOOD GAME, LEVI," Marian said. "Thanks for inviting me."

"Come on, you hate hockey, Marian." It was nearly dark in the coffee shop. Levi could make a cappuccino blindfolded if he needed to and he hadn't wanted to turn on the lights in case passersby thought he might be open.

He'd invited Marian to the game because she'd seemed depressed the last time he'd seen her and he did have a spare ticket, but the truth was, all night long he'd wished Grace, not Marian, were in the seat beside him. "The truth shall set you free," the saying went, but Levi felt ensnared by the truth. The painful ache from missing Grace was all too familiar.

"Well, it took my mind off my troubles for a while." Marian accepted her coffee, arching her eyebrows at him.

Levi sat up on the counter and sipped from his mug. "What exactly happened between the two of you anyway? It sounded like it was going so well."

"'Sounded' is right." Marian's short laugh was bitter. "He sure had me fooled. Remember how excited I was at the beginning? I really figured things were finally going my way. Just a coincidence, I thought— finding out about an inheritance and getting a date with a man I'd been interested in both on the same day.''

He nodded. He remembered hoping that this Richard Craig would turn out to be a decent sort of guy for her.

''Hah! Some coincidence. Apparently, Richard had overheard my conversation with the lawyer and knew about the inheritance. And I'd assumed it was my good looks and personality.'' She shrugged her slender shoulders. ''I'm such a fool, Levi. Even though he asked me lots of questions about my uncle's farm, land values and that sort of stuff, it never occurred to me until last week that he was really interested in the dollars, not the girl.''

''What happened last week?''

''Well, the lawyer discovered an unregistered but legal debt. Seems my uncle had borrowed money from a neighbor with the understanding that he would get the land when my uncle died.''

''Does that mean there's nothing left?''

''Well, fifty thousand dollars, which is nothing to sneeze at, but I guess Richard had something much larger in mind.''

Marian pushed her stool away from the counter. Her dark eyes gleamed, and in the dull light from the street, Levi couldn't tell if it was from tears or something else.

''What's wrong with me, Levi? Why do I attract such awful men?''

She stood up and held out her arms as if asking him to inspect her. Levi didn't need to look. She'd been his friend for a long time. Sliding down from the counter, he gave her a hug instead.

"Marian, I swear things will work out eventually. It's not you."

"Oh, Levi."

He stepped back and patted her shoulder. "If it gives you any comfort, you're not the only one who's made a few bad choices where love is concerned. At least you learn from your mistakes. I don't seem to be bright enough for that."

Marian dropped her arms, but her gaze lingered on his face with an expression he couldn't read. "Is it that woman I met here the other day? The one Jess thinks is her mother?"

Levi shrugged, embarrassed now that he'd brought up the subject. He couldn't discuss his feelings about Grace with someone else, especially not another woman. Hell, he couldn't even explain to himself how he felt. Grace was probably the least appropriate woman he could have picked to fall in love with; he'd known that from the first moment he'd met her. But that had never seemed to make an iota of difference where his emotions were concerned.

His life would have been so much easier if he'd fallen for someone not so complicated. Someone attractive, pleasant to be with, easy to talk to...

"Shit, Marian, why couldn't we have had a thing for each other? Wouldn't that have been nice and easy?" He rinsed out his empty mug, then reached for hers, shifting his grip when he accidentally brushed her fingers.

"Yeah, that would have been nice all right."

There was something funny in her voice, and Levi turned off the tap to concentrate on his friend. An expression, a secret longing in her eyes, though quickly masked, sent a shock of understanding through his body.

God, he'd had no idea. What an idiot he was.

"G'NIGHT, NEIL." Jess hung up the phone, then clicked off the bedside lamp and snuggled under her covers even though she knew she was never going to fall asleep. There was too much stuff bouncing around in her head. In just one week, she would be fifteen years old—halfway to thirty!—and her life was such a mess.

Neil. Oh, man, she was so crazy about him she hardly thought of anything else these days. They'd had fun at the hockey game. Her dad had brought Marian, who always claimed she loved hockey, but Jess suspected she said that only because she liked being asked to go somewhere with her dad. He couldn't see it, of course, but then, he never knew when a woman was interested in him. Her dad had stared at her like she was crazy when she told him the young painter who hung around the shop all last winter had a crush on him.

In a way, Jess was glad her dad was oblivious to that sort of stuff. It would have been embarrassing to have the kind of father who ogled other women and always flirted like her girlfriend Lisa's father had after he divorced Lisa's mother. Yuk!

All in all, Jess had had a pretty good night with Marian, Neil and her dad. Until the end, when her father casually said he would drop Neil off on their way home.

"Don't bother," Neil had replied.

But her dad had insisted, not only on driving him

home but also on knocking on the door to meet his brother.

The brother wasn't there, though, and Jess had seen the look of disapproval on her father's face. As if Neil needed someone to look after him. He was sixteen after all—a fact her father just couldn't seem to appreciate. Jess had felt her mood dampen as her father glared at her from the rearview mirror after they left Neil behind.

Worst of all, of course, was that again she and Neil didn't have the chance for so much as one quick kiss.

It was almost as though her father was purposely trying to keep them from being alone. He was always telling her to invite Neil over; or, if they wanted to go out, offering to drive them to the movie or the party or whatever. In almost two weeks, she and Neil had had little opportunity to do more than share the briefest of kisses—which in one way was kind of a relief. But in another...

Jess rolled over in bed. It was wondrous to her how she felt when Neil kissed her or when his hands touched her breasts and even more intimate places. Those places tingled now with just her thinking about it. For the millionth time, she wondered how much more fabulous going all the way must feel if touching felt this great.

When she was in Neil's arms, she felt like another person. Besides her own physical pleasure, she loved what touching her did to Neil. The power she seemed to wield over him, the way she and her body became all he cared about, amazed and fascinated her. Sometimes she felt he would promise her anything if only she would let him make love to her completely. She knew, for sure, that he would never give any other girl, not even Karen, another look once they took that big step together.

And yet, something inside her was holding her back. She felt uncertain and more than a little afraid.

She wished she could talk to someone about it. Not her girlfriends, who seemed to know as little about the subject as she did, but someone older and more experienced. Someone like Grace. Only, it was clear Grace found the subject way too embarrassing. Maybe because she'd never had kids and didn't know how to handle their questions.

Never had kids. Jess was now ready to accept that Grace wasn't her mother. Her father hadn't lied the other night; the truth was, she couldn't remember him ever lying to her. Even when she'd figured out there was no Santa Claus but had secretly hoped he would tell her she was wrong, he'd told the truth.

Grace wasn't perfect, but Jess had noticed that she, too, tried to tell the truth about things, and when she had a problem, she faced it head-on. Would Grace have walked away from her own baby? Despite her longing for a career, Jess didn't think so. She would have hired a nanny; she would have managed somehow.

And if she *had* walked away from her baby, would she have denied it fifteen years later when that kid came searching for her mother? Again, Jess couldn't see it. Grace didn't pull her punches. She wasn't made that way.

Which meant that Jess was approaching her fifteenth birthday and she still didn't know who her mother was.

There had to be some way of finding out, but what? She'd already been through her father's personal papers, which was where she'd discovered the love letters in the first place. The really important documents she knew he kept in the safe-deposit box at the bank. So what options did that leave?

Not many. But she'd had precious little to go on last time, too, she reminded herself, and still she'd found Grace. She would find her mother. She just had to develop a plan.

Undercover agent Shanahan was back in business.

CHAPTER ELEVEN

WHAT TO DO ABOUT JESS? After yet another restless night, Grace sat at the kitchen table with her third cup of coffee, wishing she could lose herself in the work she'd brought home in her briefcase, but she couldn't concentrate on her work until she'd resolved this situation. She couldn't let Jess keep making plans and wanting to see her when she'd decided that their friendship had to end.

Levi was right. She'd screwed this up royally. And the worst thing was, she would miss Jess even more than the teenage girl would miss her.

And yet, making that final break was going to be difficult. Grace stared at the sleek gray portable telephone lying on the table beside her mug. The easy thing would be to wait until her business crisis was over.

But that wasn't fair to Jess. She had a right to know. And it wouldn't take long—just a couple of hours. She could invite her over for lunch, explain the situation....

Taking a deep breath, Grace picked up the phone and punched in the now familiar number.

"Hello?"

Levi's voice conjured up memories of his presence in her kitchen only days ago. She cleared her throat. "It's Grace, Levi. May I talk to Jess?"

The digital clock on the stove clicked as the numbers changed from 9:59 to 10:00. Grace was aware not only of the silence on the other end of the line but of the silence in her own home, as well. She stood up to pour what remained of her coffee down the kitchen sink, then put the empty cup into the dishwasher.

''She's in her bedroom. Just a minute.''

When Jess came on the line a few seconds later, Grace asked her to lunch. The girl sounded achingly pleased at the invitation. After she'd turned off the phone, Grace considered her recently purged kitchen and decided to buy prepared sandwiches and some fruit salad at a nearby deli. When she came back, she set the table, put some tulips in a vase and wished it wasn't too early to have some wine from the bottle she'd opened last night.

Jess arrived at twelve-thirty, looking young and vulnerable in baggy overalls and a sporty ponytail. She also looked tired, maybe even a little depressed.

''Is everything okay?''

''Sure.'' Jess nodded, but there was no spark in her eyes. ''Thanks for inviting me over. I've missed you.''

Oh, Jessie. Guilt and pain crushed up under Grace's ribs. When was the last time someone had said those words? Why was it that every time she got close to anyone, something had to happen to make it all go wrong?

''How was the hockey game last night? I'm sorry I couldn't come.'' Sorrier than Jess could possibly understand.

''It was great. Vancouver won, three to two. Neil thought it was so cool—he'd never been to a game before. And Dad brought Marian along.''

Marian? The name dropped through the air like cold ice in an empty glass. Grace remembered meeting the woman at the Jolt. She and Levi were just friends. Weren't they?

"And did Marian enjoy the game?" She hated herself for fishing for more information.

"Not really." Jess sat at the table and watched as Grace took out the prepared luncheon tray from the fridge and set it on the counter. "She hates hockey. But she likes my dad."

"No kidding."

"Sure. They're really good friends. But I think Marian would like to be more than just friends."

The scamp was trying to make her jealous. Grace determined not to let her know how well it was working.

She pulled the plastic wrap off the tray of sandwiches, trying to recall the little speech she'd rehearsed while waiting for Jess to arrive, but now the words seemed artificial.

"I want to apologize for this past week, Jess. I realize I let you down and—"

"That's okay. You warned me from the beginning about your work, and it's not like you're my mother or anything."

Grace sank onto a chair. "I'm not? I mean, I know I'm not, but you finally accept that?" She couldn't believe how devastated she felt when Jess slowly nodded.

"Yeah. Finally."

"What…? How…?"

"I just figured you were too cool a person to lie about something like that." Jess shrugged. "Same with my dad. I asked him flat out the other night if you were my mother. He said no. I guess I should have believed you both the first time, but maybe I wasn't ready. I liked thinking you were my mother 'cause it meant that when I grew up I might be beautiful and smart just like you.''

"Dear Jess. You *will* be both those things, and a whole lot more besides.''

Jess was unconvinced. ''I should have known it was too good to be true, though.''

"Oh, Jess.'' The bubble had burst, and as unhappy as Jess appeared, and as desolate as Grace felt, surely it was the best thing.

What had she done for Jess except avoid her embarrassing questions and been absent when she was needed? As Levi had pointed out, work had always been her priority, and it was too late for her to change now. Besides, she and Levi would never be free to go on with their lives as long as they had any ties between them.

Grace got up to get the sandwiches and fruit salad. "Do you want tuna or ham?''

"Both, please.''

Grace handed her the tray. Jess's low mood obviously hadn't affected her appetite. There certainly were things to be said for the teenage years.

"Maybe we could go shopping after lunch,'' Grace suggested. "We never did find that dress for graduation.''

"I've already bought one, remember? I asked you last week if you wanted to see it.''

"Right.'' Grace swallowed and looked away. How could she have forgotten?

"Anyway, Dad'll be by in fifteen minutes to pick me up.''

Grace froze at the prospect of Levi's coming to her place again. "Did he drop you off?''

"No, I took the bus." Jess's face flushed a little. "Really, this time."

Grace hid her smile. "I believe you, Jess. That's okay." So this was it. She'd prepared her little good-bye speech only to discover that Jess had beat her to the punch. Like father, like daughter, she supposed. Grace took one of the triangular sandwiches off the tray even though she didn't feel the least bit hungry.

She ought to be thankful it had worked out like this, that Jess had finally accepted on her own that Grace wasn't her mother. This way, Jess wouldn't feel rejected. And Levi, she was certain, would be more than pleased the whole charade had ended.

After lunch, Grace showed Jess the computer she kept in her spare bedroom.

"Wow! We don't even have CD-ROM at home," Jess said. "Do you have any games?"

"A ton. Want to try some?" Grace opened the games icon and allowed Jess her choice. In a moment, she was lost to the world of Myst and didn't even notice when the doorbell rang.

Grace did. Her heart hammered as she opened the door. Levi was there, dressed in jeans and a soft wool sweater the same blue as his eyes. His hair was pulled back in his usual ponytail, and he sported a two-day growth of beard.

Grace stood still, not saying anything. At first, he didn't even realize that she'd answered the door, his attention apparently riveted by some kids playing street hockey in the driveway next to hers. He looked, she decided, as though he'd rather be anywhere in the world but on her doorstep.

"Hi, Levi." He turned toward her and for a second their eyes connected. But only for a second. She focused on a piece of lint on his shoulder. "Come on in. Jess is playing computer games. I'll go—"

"No rush." He shoved his hands into the pockets of his jeans and gave her an assessing look. "Let her finish the game. Unless you're in a hurry to get her out of here."

"No. Of course not." Grace moved aside for him to enter, then shut the door behind him, still not knowing where to look. How could he be so calm after what had happened between them? Didn't he remember that the last time he'd seen her she was lying naked on her bed? What if she tore off her sweater right now and reminded him? Would he still be so cool and collected?

"You look nice, Grace."

Oh, Levi. Don't tell me I look nice. Tell me this past week has been hell, that you haven't been able to get me off your mind. "Thanks," she said simply.

It was amazing how plain good manners could help in the most awkward of situations.

Let's just pretend we're polite strangers, and we can get through this. "Would you like a sandwich?"

He cocked his head. "I don't know, Grace. Have you shopped since the last time I saw your kitchen?"

He *would* say something funny. As if melting the ice between them were that easy. "Come and see. I think you'll be impressed."

He picked up one of the ham-and-tomato sandwiches and peeked under the bread. "The meat hasn't even gone gray yet. What gives, Grace?"

"I bought everything fresh after the little housecleaning party I had the other day. I even got rid of the weevils."

"Poor devils." He sat down and demolished half

the sandwich in one bite. "So, did you and Jess have a chance to talk? She was glad you called this morning. She had something she wanted to tell you."

"You mean that she accepts I'm not her mother now?" She couldn't face him as she said it. Damn, but she wanted to cry.

"I'm not too sure what finally convinced her."

"What does it matter? The important thing is that everything is straightened out and we can both start living our separate lives again—which is all you ever wanted anyway."

He pushed the rest of his sandwich away. "What do you know about all I've ever wanted, Grace?"

"Don't tell me you didn't object to the time I spent with Jess?"

"What time? All I can recall of the past few weeks is her phoning you only to be told you were too busy to see her. Isn't that right?"

It hurt to hear him say it, even though she knew what he said was true. "I'm sorry, but I've been a little busy, okay? I've been up till midnight most nights working on the revised projection numbers. Yesterday," she added, "I fired Douglas."

"From what you've told me, that's probably for the best."

"I should have done it earlier," she admitted. "Before all the damage was done."

"You'll turn it around. You always do. And now that this thing with Jess is settled, you won't have anything to distract you."

"Yeah, no kidding. Those personal lives can really get in the way, can't they?" With a short laugh, Grace pushed her chair from the table and went to stand by the patio doors that led to the backyard. In a few seconds, she could sense Levi standing behind her.

"I want you to know I appreciate how you handled things with Jess. You could have kicked her out of your office right from the start. You were under no obligation to be kind to her, but you tried."

She nodded. She didn't want him to say anything nice to her. She didn't deserve it. She'd wanted to be Jess's mother almost as much as Jess had wanted it. The whole situation had done nothing if not open Grace's eyes to the sorry state of her personal life. What she was going to do now, without Jess or Levi in her life, she had no idea.

"What's the matter, Grace? I'd have thought you'd be relieved to have all this behind you."

He was leaning against the kitchen wall, arms crossed over his chest. She could bear no more than the briefest of glances in his direction. Her throat felt choked, her chest compressed. This was proving much harder than she'd expected.

"Is it about the other night?" he asked, his voice low. "Are you regretting what happened?"

"I don't know. To be honest, I don't think it's making the situation between us any easier. At least not for me." And that had been the point after all. To get it out of their systems. Then why hadn't it worked?

She closed her eyes as he squeezed her shoulders. If she'd realized sleeping with him would hurt this much, would she still have done it? She knew the answer was yes. Would always be yes. What in the world was she going to do?

WORK WAS GRACE'S PANACEA, and somehow it got her through the rest of the weekend. Monday morning,

uncharacteristically, she cowered in bed. She didn't
feel ready to go out and face the real world. Not yet.
She lay there listening to the radio, only half-
concentrating on the talk show. Finally, by eight-
thirty, she knew she had no choice but to get moving.
If she didn't show up soon, Jackie would send out a
search party. She bypassed most of her normal groom-
ing routine, but it still took her longer than usual before she was ready to leave the house.

A glance in the hall mirror as she stooped to pick
up her briefcase confirmed she looked awful—beyond
the reach of what a little concealer and blush could do
for a woman. And, most unusually, she didn't care.
When she got in the car, she noticed the shade of her
panty hose was entirely wrong for the suit she was
wearing. She didn't care about that, either. Or that, for
the first time in her memory, she was starting the day
with chips in her nail polish.

The image was shattering.

As soon as she arrived at work, Jackie was at her
door.

"Have a minute, Grace?"

Grace peered up from the franchise contract she'd
pulled off the top of her In basket. There was something comforting in seeing Jackie standing in the doorway. With her prematurely gray hair, immaculately
tailored suit and customary business decorum, she was
a familiar, trusted colleague. One of few these days.
"Sure."

"I wanted to give back your credit card. And tell
you that everyone had a great time Friday night."

Grace tucked the card into a drawer. "Do you think
they're rejuvenated enough to face another hard
week?"

"Most of them would do anything for you," Jackie said bluntly. "But isn't Douglas back from his holiday today?"

Grace's lips curled upward. "Douglas won't ever be coming back from that particular holiday. I fired him on Friday, after hours."

"Really?" Jackie's eyes glinted. "That's fabulous. He hasn't seemed like part of the team for a long time."

"I know." Grace tented her fingers and contemplated her executive assistant's face. Jackie had been very discreet about Grace and Douglas's affair. Even now, she was saying nothing, and Grace appreciated her tact. "But that's old news. Now there's nothing to stop us from barreling ahead with our future plans."

"Yes. I think I'll start by having Douglas's nameplate taken off the wall this morning."

"While you're at it, why don't you have your own name put on to replace it."

"What?"

"I want to promote you to VP status, Jackie. We'll still need to hire another finance person, but I want to acknowledge the role you've played and, I hope, will continue to play in this company."

Jackie seemed overwhelmed. "I never expected—"

Grace raised her hand, not wanting any gratitude. "I only recently came to appreciate just how much I rely on you. And you've done a fabulous job on the expansion report." She looked down at the contract, wanting to prevent this scene from getting too emotional. But she couldn't focus. Her eyes burned from lack of sleep, from too many tears the night before.... She wanted to rub them, but that would only smear her mascara.

"I appreciate this opportunity. I won't let you down."

"Well, you've earned it, Jackie." Grace's eyes strayed back to the contract—a matter of some urgency pushed to the back burner while she'd worked on the expansion plans.

Untypically, Jackie didn't seem to take the hint to leave. "We missed you on Friday night. I'm sorry you were too tired to attend. The staff would've enjoyed your company."

"Pardon me?"

"I said, the staff would've enjoyed your company."

Grace blinked as the meaning meandered through the maze of inventory-count methods she was considering. Why hadn't she joined the staff for drinks? She couldn't remember. The truth was, while she often rewarded her staff for performance above and beyond the call of duty, she rarely joined them. Maybe that was a mistake. Maybe a more hands-on approach was what Jackie was suggesting.

"You've been working far too hard."

"I always work far too hard. What's different about this time?"

"I don't want to overstep Grace, but it *is* different this time. I can tell by looking at you. No matter how hard you used to work, how much pressure you faced, you never seemed to be so—"

"I see." Grace sighed, pushing aside the contract. "I know I'm not at my best today."

"Perhaps it's my imagination. Excuse me if I've offended." Jackie exited with her usual quiet yet brisk step.

Grace stared at the closed door, trying to remember the last time Jackie had made even the slightest personal comment to her. She couldn't recall a single instance.

So why had she spoken up today? Was she genuinely concerned? If so, on what grounds?

They'd worked together for many years, but always on a strictly professional level. That was one of the things Grace most appreciated about Jackie. She wasn't one of those people who felt the need to fill you in on every detail of their personal lives. Grace was aware Jackie was married and had a grown daughter, but that was it.

And she knew she'd never told Jackie anything about herself unless it related to work. Even during the time Grace and Douglas were seeing each other.

And now Jackie thought Grace was working too hard. Of course that was the explanation she would find for the circles under Grace's eyes, the lines of tension around her mouth.

It would never occur to her that Grace was suffering from a broken heart.

Maybe not broken. Maybe just bruised. After all, she'd gotten along just fine without Levi for the past fifteen years; surely she could continue in the same fashion now that he was out of her life again.

Grace wanted desperately to believe that but knew it was impossible. Whatever the future held for her, she could not go back to the way things had been earlier. Hadn't she always known there was no going back to what she'd had with Levi when they were younger, or to how she'd lived before Jess brought them together again?

Grace was unable to concentrate on the franchise contract in front of her. Maybe a break from the office

would help. She had a few errands to run, then she'd
pick up a bite of food. She hadn't eaten yet today.

The tourists were out on Robson Street, enjoying
the sunny spring morning, and Grace found it comfortable to blend in with the crowd and stroll along
without any real sense of purpose. She stopped in at
a drugstore, then had her shoes polished at a small,
dingy shop a few buildings down. She was considering
having a coffee and pastry when she noticed a couple
of men sitting at an outdoor terrace. The thinning hair
on the back of one man's head was suspiciously familiar. Douglas.

And seated across from him was none other than
Stephen P. Vanderburg, chief executive officer for Jarvis. Douglas certainly wasn't wasting any time secur-
ing his future.

Grace moved to the window display two stores
down and furtively studied them. Vanderburg was a
tall, beefy man in his mid-fifties. Generally well re-
spected in the business community, he owned a big
chunk of the Canadian retail market, including the Jarvis department-store chain.

What were he and Douglas discussing? Now that
Douglas no longer worked at Body and Soul, his value
as a corporate spy was limited. She wondered if he'd
already given Vanderburg the details about her proposed expansion plans. Not that there was much Vanderburg could do to stop her.

Grace moved to the next store window, where
smooth Italian leather shoes gleamed in the afternoon
sun. During lulls in the noise from the traffic, she
could hear snippets of their conversation.

"...can still do it, of course." Vanderburg's deep,
gruff voice sounded confident.

"Of course we can. If Grace Hamilton thinks—"

The mention of her name had Grace's full attention, but the rest of the sentence was obliterated when a bus squealed to a stop just a few yards from the restaurant.

"…always had a Plan B. But then…" Douglas's voice trailed off when he noticed Grace walking toward them. "Well, well, well." He tugged at the knot in his tie, his eyes flashing to those of his luncheon companion's.

"Good morning, gentlemen," Grace said. "Mind if I join you for a moment?" Not paying any heed to their reaction, which was hardly positive, she pulled over a chair from another table.

Vanderburg had risen awkwardly to his feet and remained there until Grace was seated. Douglas, openly glowering at his former boss, didn't move.

"Mr. Vanderburg." She turned to the older man. "You wouldn't be discussing a certain takeover bid this afternoon, would you?"

"Precisely, Ms. Hamilton."

"I suppose I should thank you for pushing our share price so high. It will make further share purchases rather expensive, don't you think?"

Stephen Vanderburg looked amused. "But for such an excellent acquisition, the money will be well spent."

"I couldn't agree more. On the excellence of the target company, that is. But you may find the rest of our directors a little more loyal than Douglas has turned out to be."

"Oh, really?"

The cool disbelief in Vanderburg's voice chilled her, reminding her that Roberta still hadn't returned any of her calls. "So that's plan B, is it?"

Douglas choked on his drink, but Vanderburg just widened his smile.

"Exactly, Ms. Hamilton. I can't help but think it a pity you decided against that initial offer I made you."

"What offer was that?"

Both Grace and Vanderburg ignored Douglas's interruption.

"And I can't help remaining pleased that I did so." Grace stood. She wasn't going to learn anything more; that much was obvious. "Well, let me leave you gentlemen to your lunch."

"Good luck, Ms. Hamilton." Vanderburg had toned down his loud baritone to a purr. "You're going to need it."

She raised her chin. "We'll see about that. As for you, Douglas." She glanced at her former lover and colleague. "I wish you all the success you deserve."

JESS REACHED PAST the bundle of papers she knew contained the love letters Grace had sent her father and pulled out an old shoe box. Inside were a bunch of disorganized, unlabeled photographs. She'd come across them when she first found the letters, but they hadn't meant anything to her then. They probably wouldn't mean much to her now, either, but they were all she had to work with.

Jess climbed off the chair, returned it to the corner of her father's bedroom and went across the hall to her room, clutching the shoe box guiltily to her chest.

She shouldn't be doing this. It was an unforgivable invasion of her father's privacy. She thought about the long talk they'd had after she admitted to reading Grace's love letters, and her cheeks burned. If the situation were reversed, if she found her father going through her personal belongings... Well, she knew she'd be livid. Just as he would be to see her now.

But she couldn't stop herself. She just *had* to know her mother's name. Had to meet her, speak with her, if only just once.

"Here it is."

Neil was waiting for her, sprawled out on her bed. He was dressed in jeans and a black T-shirt, and his very male presence was incongruous in the feminine decor of her room. She opened the box and spilled the pictures on the patchwork quilt beside him. Neil shuffled them around, as if playing Fish with a deck of cards, then picked one up at random.

"Hey, cool. Look at this." He held up a picture of a young woman standing by a red convertible.

"That's Grace." Gosh, but she'd been pretty. No wonder her dad had flipped over her. Her hair was longer then, and in her shorts and tank top her figure was curvier than now.

"Forget the woman. I'm talking about the Mustang convertible. Your dad doesn't still own it, does he?"

"No. He sold it when I was just a kid—around grade one, I think. He said we needed something more practical, something he could haul a bunch of my friends around in."

"That's too bad." He gazed at the picture regretfully, until Jess had to finally pull it from his fingers.

"We're supposed to be looking for my mother."

"Right." Neil propped himself up on one elbow. "So what do we do?"

"Let's start by putting all the pictures of people we recognize in one pile, people we don't know in another." She placed a photo of her father and Phil on top of the picture of Grace by the car.

They were halfway through this process when Neil gave up with a sigh. "This is hopeless. Even when we get them sorted, you're still not going to know which one of these women is your mother. And even if you did know which face was hers, you still wouldn't know her name."

"Do you have any better ideas?"

"Yeah, as a matter of fact I do. You'd have to get these pictures off the bed for me to carry them out, though." He slid a hand under her hair to cup the back of her neck. Leaning toward her, he settled a light but promising kiss on her lips.

It felt nice. It felt more than nice. But she only had an hour until her father came upstairs expecting dinner since it was her turn to cook. She turned her attention back toward the photos. "I know it seems hopeless, Neil, but I have to try. You don't have to stay if you don't want to."

The mattress shifted as he sat up. She swallowed, warning herself not to be disappointed if he left. She'd given him the opportunity and could hardly expect him to be as keen on finding her mother as she was.

But he wasn't leaving. He was looking at the pictures again, at the pile of people she hadn't recognized. He passed one of them to her, a photo of a woman reclining on a sofa—Jess remembered the sofa was the one her father had had in university.

"There are lots of pictures of this woman. Are you sure you don't recognize her?"

Jess studied the woman's features. She'd noticed her before, had almost thought she was Grace until she looked closer. The two women had similar coloring, were tall and had the same elegant style about them. But their features were quite different; there really was no mistaking the two women.

"I have no idea." She spoke slowly, still concentrating on the picture he'd passed her. There was *something*...

"'Cause you resemble her a bit. Look at the shape of her face."

Jess swallowed. Was it possible? Had they finally found her mother? "Let me see the other pictures of her."

Quickly, they sorted through the photos, picking out several more of the same woman. Next to Grace, no other person figured as predominantly in Levi's collection. That had to be a sign they were on the right track, didn't it?

Jess turned each picture over carefully, hoping against hope for a name, a date, a place, any clue that would help them identify this woman. There was nothing. It was infuriating. Why couldn't her father have been a little better organized?

"What's that noise?" Neil asked suddenly. "Is that your dad coming up the stairs?"

Jess froze, recognizing the familiar pattern of creaking sounds. She'd been so caught up in the search she'd forgotten to be careful. "Quick, hide the pictures under my bed."

Their fingers scrambled over the fragile photos as they piled them back into the shoe box. Neil slid the box under the bed just as her bedroom door swung open.

CHAPTER TWELVE

"DA-AD!" JESS COMPLAINED, trying to sound offended rather than scared out of her wits. "You didn't knock." Had he seen Neil put the shoe box under the bed? Did he know what they were up to? It almost seemed he must have—she'd never seen him so angry. He gripped the door, his face red.

"What are you doing in here?"

Suddenly, Jess realized what her father was thinking, and it had nothing to do with old photographs. She felt her face grow warm as her father's eyes examined first her, then Neil, with white-hot precision. She knew what he was looking for—disheveled clothing, fast breathing, other telltale signs. An ugly, sick feeling welled up in her chest, making her want to dive for cover.

"It's not what you think, Dad." Boy, wasn't that the truth.

But he wasn't listening. He was standing absolutely still, arms crossed. All his attention was focused on Neil. To his credit, Neil didn't cower. He met her father's condemning gaze with an apparent lack of concern.

"Get out of here." The words came out staccato.

Jess saw her father flex his right hand as if resisting the urge to become physically violent. Thank heavens

Neil didn't argue but silently walked out of the room, then let himself out the back door.

Jess sat down on her bed and stared at her father's feet. That was as high as she dared allow her eyes to go. "Nothing happened, Dad. Not what you're thinking." She swallowed, suddenly close to tears. "I'm sorry, Daddy. I won't have him in here again."

Still Levi said nothing.

"I said I was sorry!" She flung herself around and buried her face in a pillow.

"Jessie."

He sounded as though he was about to start on a speech. Jess stiffened, preparing to block out the words she didn't need to hear. She was old enough to decide for herself whether to sleep with Neil. Why should she listen to her father? He didn't even trust her enough to tell her her mother's name.

"Oh, Jessie."

This time, he sounded sad. And instead of starting on that speech, he must have decided to leave her alone. She heard the click of her bedroom door closing.

After a few minutes, she finally raised her head to check. Sure enough, she was alone. She let her head fall back to her pillow and started to cry.

NEIL DIDN'T RETURN to the house for a week. And Levi noticed that Jess didn't ask to go over to his house, either. She seemed very busy with a school project that required her to spend long hours at the downtown library. As far as he was concerned, the timing was perfect.

He'd decided against lecturing her about the inappropriateness of a fourteen-year-old girl inviting her boyfriend into her bedroom. She'd known it was wrong and she'd promised not to do it again. For now, that would have to do.

So it was life as usual in the Shanahan household. Or as close to usual as either of them could muster. Levi loaded his mug and plate into the dishwasher, then wiped off the kitchen counter. He had to do payroll this morning—a job he hated but one that his new computer program made much easier. Only, he still had to write the damn checks. He went over to his desk, pulled the computer printout from the printer, then searched for his checks.

Jess came in and grabbed one of the honey bran muffins from a plate on the counter. "Daddy, did you remember my birthday is this weekend?"

"Haven't forgotten one yet, have I?" Where was the checkbook? Could he have left it downstairs in the back room after paying the bakery yesterday afternoon?

"I was wondering if I could have a party."

"A party?" She hadn't had a party in years. Ever since she'd turned ten, it was sleepovers and movies with just a couple of her closest friends. They would order in pizza and he would make her favorite chocolate tunnel cake.

"Yeah. I want it to be a family sort of thing. With Neil, too, of course."

He noticed the hint of trepidation when she mentioned Neil's name but decided to ignore it. After locating the checkbook underneath a stack of unpaid bills, he consulted the calendar. "That'll be a pretty small party. You, me and Neil." Since his mother's death, they had no other relatives in the city.

"What about Phil and Marian?" Jess perched on

the edge of his desk, sprinkling muffin crumbs over his papers.

Levi wrote out the first check. "Of course." Phil was her godfather after all. And Marian had known her since she was a toddler.

"And Grace."

Levi's pen froze over the signature line. "I thought we talked about that the other day."

"The mother thing? Yeah, I know. But she still sort of seems like family. Just because she isn't my real mom doesn't mean I can't ever see her again, does it?"

Well, actually, he'd kind of hoped that was exactly what it would mean. "Oh, Jess. I don't know."

"It's my birthday. Why shouldn't I get to pick who comes to my party?"

Why? Because she was tearing her father's heart to pieces each time she forced him to confront Grace Hamilton just one more time. Someday, when she was older, he might try to explain. At present, it seemed easier just to agree.

"Your pick," he agreed, scrawling his name. Maybe Grace would have the good sense to refuse the invitation. Maybe she'd be too busy.... "Shouldn't you be leaving for school?"

"Yeah, I guess." She tossed the paper muffin cup in the garbage, then finished the glass of juice he'd set out for her on the kitchen counter. "So, are we having the party?" She picked up her backpack from the floor and swung it over her shoulders.

"Sure."

Jess whooped. "Thanks, Dad."

He followed her downstairs, taking his checkbook and papers with him. He might as well work with a mug of fresh java in his hand. Settling himself at a front table, Levi watched from the window as his daughter walked toward her bus stop. He smiled at the way her flared jeans dragged on the ground, remembering the same style from his junior high school days. Then he noticed her backpack. It was bulging at the seams this morning. Must be that project she was working on.

UNDERCOVER AGENT Jess Shanahan got off the bus just three blocks from home and walked the rest of the distance to Neil's. The door opened immediately when she tapped.

"What took you so long?"

Neil stood on the threshold, his arms crossed over his chest. He must have just showered—she could smell the soap, and his T-shirt was clinging to his chest and arms.

"H-hi, Neil." Funny how she could be out of breath after such a short walk. "I was late because I was talking to Dad about my birthday. He said I could have the party."

"All right!"

Neil smiled, a slow, deliberate smile, the kind that always made her feel she had to sit down or lean against a wall or something.

"Did you remember all your stuff?" he asked.

Jess shrugged the backpack off her shoulders. "Uh-huh."

"Well, come on in, then."

As much as she liked Neil, Jess felt uncomfortable in his house. It was kind of dark and messy and had a peculiar smell she couldn't identify. Neither Neil nor his brother was much on housekeeping—or cooking, for that matter. They had a cleaning service in once every two weeks, but as far as Jess could tell, that wasn't quite often enough.

"Want to come in my room?"

Jess pressed her back against the door, a sudden fear making her forget her purpose. She'd never been in Neil's bedroom before. When she came over to study they usually sat in the living room in front of the television or sometimes at the kitchen table.

"Or do you want to change out there in the hall?"

Jess laughed and tried to act as if nothing was bothering her. "Why don't I change in the bathroom instead?"

"Fine. Have it your way." Neil shrugged as though he didn't care, but Jess got the impression she had hurt his feelings.

"Your room is fine, too. It doesn't matter."

"Whatever. I'll wait in the kitchen."

Jess was relieved to hear that. Given her choice, she opened the bathroom door and immediately wished she'd picked the bedroom. The sink was really gross, with clumps of toothpaste and curly dark hairs clinging to the white porcelain. She turned her back to it and quickly peeled out of her jeans and sweatshirt. Ten minutes later, she came out in the spandex running gear she'd borrowed from Mandy last night. The jogging shoes were a little snug, but hey, it was all for a good cause.

Neil watched her walk from the doorway to the kitchen, letting out a low whistle as she drew near.

"You look pretty hot in that outfit," he said, putting his arms around her bare waist. "Maybe you should take up running as a full-time hobby."

As always, having Neil touch her made it difficult

to think of anything else. She was very aware of how the skintight running shorts and sports bra accentuated her curves, and it gave her a thrill to see Neil react. He bent down to kiss her, and she parted her lips willingly. Neil was the first boy she'd ever kissed, but she would rather have died than let him find that out. She knew full well she wasn't the first girl he'd kissed.

"Thanks for skipping your morning class to help me," she said.

"No problem."

He ran his hand down the back of her shorts, and Jess felt an aching need deep inside her.

"What do you say we take a little detour this morning?"

Jess pulled back. "No, I can't. I have to be outside the nursery school at 9:25 sharp. Sometimes she drops them off early."

She and Neil had covered a lot of ground since they'd found the photo of the woman they believed was her mother. It was Neil who had the brilliant idea of taking the picture to the old neighborhood, where Jess had lived with her dad after she was born, to see if anyone remembered the woman's name. They'd struck pay dirt when they found the same old apartment building still standing, with the same old landlady still running it.

"Why, that's Casey," she'd said, remembering the name instantly. She'd had to check her old records to find the last name, though. "Allinson," she'd finally proclaimed, and Jess had thanked her profusely.

From there, they'd gone to the phone book, then called over a dozen numbers before locating an uncle who told them Casey had married, then gave them her new last name and her address.

They'd done it. They'd found her mother. Her name was Casey Booker and she lived in a suburban neighborhood in Richmond with her husband and twin boys, both enrolled in nursery school. Jess knew it was silly, but she was glad her mother hadn't had another daughter.

Now she swallowed, wondering how Casey Booker would react when she saw her firstborn again. "Come on, Neil, I have to get going."

"Okay, okay, calm down. You'll be there on time. You checked the bus route, right?"

She nodded.

"Okay, then, what can go wrong? By my estimate, we have an extra fifteen minutes." He tried to pull her into his arms once more, but Jess was suddenly reluctant.

"I'd better leave now. Just to make sure."

He sighed, digging his hands into the pockets of his ultrabaggy jeans. "When will I see you again?"

"I don't know. Before my birthday party, I hope."

"You're turning fifteen, right? I've been thinking about that. We should celebrate in a special way. Something private, just you and me." He gently took her hand, then squeezed her fingers.

"I don't know, Neil."

"Come on. What's the big deal? Most girls have done it by the time they're fifteen. You don't have to be scared."

But she was. Besides, most of her friends had *not* done it, although rumors abounded about plenty of other girls at school. She would just die if anyone talked about her that way. Of course, she and Neil would never tell another soul.

"I'll have to think about it."

"You been thinking a long time, babe."

Jess backed up toward the door. "I've got to go...the bus..."

"Right. Phone me later."

"I will." Once outside, she ran to the bus stop, praying everything would be on schedule. She didn't have time to think about Neil anymore or to wonder what she'd decide to do on her birthday.

She had to concentrate on her plan. In this instance she knew there was no mistake. Casey Booker was her mother. She'd confirmed this by going to Phil, her dad's oldest friend. She figured if anyone knew the truth about her mother, aside from her dad, it was Phil. She couldn't ask him directly, of course, so she'd shown him a bunch of the old photos, and when they'd come to the one she figured was her mother, she'd asked him if he'd known Casey Allinson when she and Dad were together.

He'd given her a funny look. "Yeah, I knew her. Why do you ask?"

"I was just going through Dad's pictures and I thought it was interesting how much this woman looks like Grace."

"Big coincidence, huh?"

Phil had grinned at her and she'd quickly shoved the snaps into her backpack before her father could see them. The next morning she'd returned the shoe box to her father's closet, and prayed he would never find out what she'd done.

Now the bus jerked to a stop just two blocks from the nursery school, where a certain dark blue-and-silver minivan would be pulling up in about ten minutes. Jess had seen the van parked in the Bookers' double garage the day she had checked out Casey's house. Neil had pressed her to knock on the door, but she'd decided to avoid a face-to-face confrontation right from the start. Better to set up a meeting with a note, give Casey a little time to adjust to the fact that her daughter wanted to get to know her.

But they couldn't leave the note at the house. What if the husband found it? Or one of the little boys.

Jess stepped off the bus, then began to jog. The nursery school was in the basement of a church, next to a small park. She circled the park five times before parents began to show up with their children. Soon the vehicle she'd been watching for pulled up to the curb. The woman driver got out and took her two boys out of their car seats.

Despite having tracked Casey Booker to her house and checked out her vehicle, this was the first time Jess had actually seen her mother. She was surprised she didn't feel some overwhelming emotion, an urge to run and throw herself in the woman's arms; she was actually able to view her mother dispassionately.

Casey had gained some weight since the years the photos were taken, but she looked nice, much more "momish" than Grace. Her hair was darker than in the photos, and she wore it in a straight, above-the-shoulder cut. Her clothes were conservative—a full navy skirt, a white blouse and flat navy shoes.

Once Casey had the two towheaded boys inside, Jess jogged toward the minivan. She snuck the envelope she'd prepared earlier out from the waistband of her shorts and slipped it under the windshield wiper on the driver's side. Then she jogged to the bus stop without looking back.

"I'M GLAD YOU'VE TAKEN care of that Douglas Eberhart situation," Ben Ryan said. "I hope my advice was of some use to you.''

"Yes. Thanks, Ben." Grace nodded at her lawyer, then glanced down at her watch. She'd phoned Ben this morning to tell him she'd fired Douglas. When Ben had suggested they go out for dinner and a movie, she'd agreed. But it hadn't taken long for her to realize this date wasn't a good idea.

At the time, she'd thought she couldn't face another evening alone at home; now she realized that a microwaved dinner and an evening of sitcoms would have been vastly superior to this. She was too tired to act as though she was having a nice time when in fact she was miserable and lonely in the way that no number of people could assuage, except the one right person.

Grace listened as Ben regaled her with a case he'd recently taken to court. She sipped the cappuccino she'd ordered after dinner, unable to stop herself from comparing it—unfavorably—with the ones Levi served at the Jolt. She'd had such fun that afternoon when she helped Levi. She'd especially enjoyed working on the displays and wished she could do the entire coffee shop. Not that the place didn't look good, but she'd had so many ideas while steaming milk and grinding beans.

Although not all of them had to do with the shop.

"I don't see the relevance, I said. Do you?"

Ben's loud voice snagged Grace's attention back to the present. Not sure how she was meant to respond, she shrugged noncommittally.

Ben nodded. "Exactly. After all, the evidence boiled down to one half-eaten sandwich.''

Grace pictured it as chicken salad. With mustard, mayo and lettuce. A pickle on the side. Which reminded her of the note she and Levi had passed back and forth while they were busy waiting on the customers. Did he know she'd stuffed the piece of paper in her pocket rather than throw it out?

She wished she'd saved at least a few of the other notes, too. The ones they'd written in the heat of their first romance.

Ben was leaning over the table now, reaching for her hand. "Perhaps we should just skip the movie, Grace. I have a hot tub on the balcony of my condominium...."

Grace removed her hand and raised it to signal for the bill. "But the movie has had such great reviews, Ben. I don't think we should miss it. No—" she stretched out her arm to prevent him from snatching the bill from the approaching server's hand "—you paid last time. It's my turn tonight."

They had to line up on the sidewalk to buy their movie tickets. Ben kept standing too close, and Grace's feeling of disquiet grew. Not that she couldn't handle the situation if worse came to worst. But Ben was a good lawyer. She didn't want to antagonize him. She almost laughed at the irony of the situation she'd gotten herself into. Thank heavens she'd insisted on meeting him at the restaurant and had brought her own car.

Just then, a teenage girl walking down the street toward them caught Grace's eye. She had straight, strawberry-blond hair and was wearing the long, flared jeans Jess favored.

"Grace!" The girl lifted an arm to wave at her.

It *was* Jess. Grace had spoken to her only that afternoon. Jess had called, saying she wanted to talk to her about a number of things, but Grace had felt it wasn't a good idea. They were supposed to be making a clean break, after all. But she *had* mentioned the movie she'd be seeing that night, and as it was playing in only one theater in town, Jess had obviously decided to track her down.

Of course, when she'd mentioned her plans, Grace had not passed on the information that she was going with a man. She saw Jess bristle at the sight of Ben Ryan hanging on to her arm.

"Ben, this is a friend of mine, Jess Shanahan. Jess, this is Ben Ryan." The intense young teenager and the sophisticated lawyer nodded at each other. Grace took advantage of Jess's arrival to work herself out of Ben's grasp. "This is unexpected, Jess."

Jess's face pinkened. "When you told me about the movie, it sounded so interesting I decided to see it myself. Mandy was coming with me, but she forgot she told her mom she'd baby-sit tonight."

"I'm surprised your father let you come downtown on your own." Beside her, Ben nodded his agreement.

Jess took a deep breath before answering. "Well, I did kind of mention I'd be meeting you here. And you'd give me a ride home." She smiled sheepishly.

Grace could feel Ben stiffen. "You should've cleared that with me first, don't you think?"

"Are you angry?"

"Not really. But what if we'd missed each other? I hate to think of you alone at this time of night."

Jess shrugged apologetically. "I'm sorry, Grace. I never thought you'd have a date."

Grace gave a short laugh. "Thanks a lot."

Jess smiled at her tentatively. "Do you want me to go home?"

Grace saw her opening. "Ben, you weren't all that interested in the movie in the first place, were you?"

He looked confused. "Not particularly."

"So maybe this is all working out for the best."

"It is?"

"I'll go to the movie with Jess, then I can drive her home after it's over. Leaving you free to go home to your hot tub, just as you wanted."

Ben seemed to appreciate the opportunity to escape. "I'll call you tomorrow," he said.

Grace turned her face so that his kiss fell on her cheek. "Why don't I call you?"

Once he was gone, Jess was apologetic. "I'm sorry if I wrecked your date."

"Are you really?"

Jess hesitated, checking Grace's face carefully for signs of disappointment. "Actually, no. I didn't like that guy."

"You only just met him."

"He looked like a geek."

Grace knew how a real mother would respond to a comment like that. A lecture on judging people on more than appearances would be in order. Thank heavens they were both clear that she wasn't Jess's mother.

"He *was* a bit of a geek. But the movie should be great. I'm glad you came to rescue me."

The movie was a tearjerker, and on the drive home they both agreed it was one of the best they'd seen that year. Then Jess admitted she had an ulterior motive in wanting to meet her.

"I'd like to invite you to my birthday party this Saturday. Dad makes the best ribs and—"

"Birthday party?" Grace had done the mental calculations the day she met Jess and figured Jess was born in the fall or early winter. "Are you celebrating early this year?"

"No. My birthday's this Saturday."

"Saturday?" This was only the end of April. But perhaps it was possible—if Levi had found someone else practically the day after she left, and if Jess had been born a couple of months early. "Um, Jess, how big were you when you were born? Do you know?"

"Sure. Dad kept a baby book. I was eight pounds two ounces and twenty-one inches long. He said I was a big, healthy baby with a great appetite right from the start."

"Really?" This wasn't making any sense. If Jess wasn't premature... Grace counted back the months...

"Anyway," Jess said, "it should be a great party, so I hope you can make it. I have a little surprise planned." The corners of Jess's mouth turned up smugly.

...and arrived at July. But she and Levi hadn't stopped seeing each other until September. Grace put a cold hand to her cheek. Mid-September, actually, a week before the first day of her new job. How could Jess have been conceived in July?

It was, it was...

Inconceivable.

Bad joke. Grace tried to laugh at herself, but there was no humor in this situation. Absolutely none.

"What's wrong? Can't you come?"

Grace looked at her passenger and tried to focus on the matter at hand. She *was* pleased that Jess still wanted her in her life even though she knew she wasn't her mother. "Yes, of course I'll come. I wouldn't miss it for the world."

"Or for a board meeting?"

Ouch. "Especially not for a board meeting."

THERE HAD TO BE an explanation, but by the time Grace had parked her car beside Levi's sedan, she still hadn't thought of one. If Jess was not born premature and her birthday really was in April, then Levi had to have been sleeping with her mother at the same time as he and Grace were having their affair.

Even with the facts staring her right in the face, Grace found it nearly impossible to believe. Levi was not that kind of a man. They'd shared so many intimacies beyond the physical. Their relationship had been a close one, extending far beyond the superficial. He couldn't have slept with another woman during that time.

And yet he had.

Perhaps it had been a one-night-stand sort of thing. A mistake he regretted and never felt worth mentioning. A mistake that resulted in a daughter nine months later.

Grace hated to think of Jess as a mistake.

But what else could she believe? That, while pretending to be madly, head over heels in love with her, Levi had actually been deeply devoted to another woman, Jess's mysterious biological mother?

That the great love of her life had been a sham?

"The lights are on, so I guess Dad's home. Thanks for the ride and the movie, Grace. It was great. And I'm glad you're coming to my party."

"Me, too." Grace followed Jess out of the car, her limbs as stiff as if she'd spent the day, not just the past twenty minutes, behind the wheel. She stopped short when the back door opened and Levi stood at the threshold.

"There you are, Jess. Go on up to bed, please."

Grace felt Jess move closer toward her. "You did see my note, didn't you, Dad?"

Note? Grace thought back to what Jess had told her earlier. She'd definitely gotten the impression Levi had given Jess his permission to go to the movie with her.

"Yes, I saw the note." Levi sounded tired. "I would rather have talked it over first, though."

"But you were out with—"

"Yeah, I know. So this time we'll let it pass, okay?"

Who had he been out with? Never mind. What did she care? Especially now.

After another quick thanks to Grace and a kiss for her dad, Jess went inside. Grace stepped back toward her car. "I'm sorry if you were worried, Levi. When Jess met me at the theater, I thought she had your permission."

"I wasn't worried. I knew she was with you."

Levi stepped out from the shadow of the back door. He seemed tense, but his movements were fluid and light. In a few seconds, he was beside her, resting a hand on the hood of her car.

Grace buttoned her suede jacket against the cool night air, but it did no good. The lining lay on her skin like a thin layer of ice. Probably the best thing for her would be to get in the car and drive away. Now.

But she lingered.

"Jess invited me to her birthday party," she said.

"Really?"

The challenge in his voice had no relation to her statement about the party, she decided.

"I hope you don't mind."

"Mind? Of course not. It's her party."

He leaned against the car just inches away from her, and she could smell the alcohol on his breath.

"You've been drinking."

"Only a few, Grace. Don't worry. I'm not drunk and disorderly."

Grace's curiosity deepened. Where had he been? And with whom? A woman? She hated the pangs of jealousy that ripped through her chest at the thought. Well, why not? He was a free agent.

"Don't expect too much. It'll be a small affair."

"Pardon?"

"Jess's party."

She should have left it at that. But avoiding confrontations had never been her style. "So Jess was born in April, was she?"

"The twenty-fourth."

He met her eyes squarely, and she could tell he knew what she was driving at. Still, she had to ask. "How could that be, Levi? You and I were still together in July."

Levi straightened. She could feel him stiffen and move ever so slightly away from her.

"I can't fault your math, Grace."

The smoldering hurt and betrayal flamed into anger. "How could you, Levi? I thought we were in love."

His face had hardened into that of a stranger's. "Why do you care, Grace? It was so many years ago. What difference does any of it make now?"

What difference? How could he even ask such a question? Maybe there was no hope for the two of them; maybe there never had been. But he held a place in her heart that no one ever had. If she could no longer believe in the love they'd once shared, then she would be left with nothing. Absolutely nothing.

She figured Levi would understand that.

Obviously he wasn't the man she'd thought he was.

How could she have been so mistaken about him? How could she have considered him so special? *Like your judgment in men has been so infallible,* she reminded herself, as Douglas's smug face came to mind. She'd believed she could trust him, too, but look what happened. Of course, his betrayal didn't hurt like Levi's.

"Maybe this is a fitting way to finally end things between us."

Levi's voice was harsh and Grace twisted away from him. She didn't want to feel the warmth of his breath on her cheek, not when his words were so cold.

"With the truth, you mean? Too bad it was so elusive fifteen years ago."

"Jess had nothing to do with what happened to you and me. It was your ambition that finished us off, Grace. I knew there was nothing left for me."

"I suppose that's how you justified your actions. But when we were together, I was yours complete—" She choked on the word. After what he had done, he deserved no explanations.

Levi's hands on her shoulders forced her to face him.

"Don't try to act the martyr. Did you ever stop to think how I felt the day you told me you'd decided to accept that job with Roberta Paxton and that our affair was terminated? You never once considered that I might be willing to stay with you. How do you suppose that made me feel?"

"What are you saying, Levi? You'd always made

it clear you planned to travel. Why would I assume you would do anything else? Besides, I distinctly recall your reaction when I gave you my news. You really didn't care one way or the other."

They'd been standing by a car then, too. His red Mustang. He'd been driving her home, and she'd been trying to work up her courage to tell him about Roberta's job offer and her decision to accept. The words hadn't come out until they stopped and he was about to walk her to her door.

They never made it that far.

Perhaps his cool acceptance of her decision had masked deeper feelings he'd never admitted to. If she hadn't assumed her new job necessitated the end of their relationship, would he have?

But what did any of that matter in light of what she'd learned today?

"You can think what you want."

He made it sound so subjective. "You can't deny the truth. Your daughter's very existence proves it. You slept with another woman."

"Yes, Grace, I think you're right. Let's stick to the facts here."

Why did he sound so angry, when she was the one who'd been betrayed? "I wish I never had to see you again."

He dropped his hands from her. "Nothing says you have to."

"Jess's birthday party." The irony was ruthless. She would be back in one week to celebrate the anniversary of the night Levi had cheated on her.

"So don't come. She'll get over it."

Like she's done all the other times. Grace heard the condemnation in his voice.

"I can't tell Jess I'm not coming after I've already accepted her invitation. But this will be the last time."

For an answer, Levi opened her car door. Grace glared at him, refusing to get in until his hand was no longer touching her car. Once he'd stepped back, she got behind the wheel and backed out quickly, changing gears before the car had even stopped, then ripping forward down the road.

Goodbye, Levi, and all my dreams that never were.

CHAPTER THIRTEEN

"DAD, CAN I DECORATE the house today? You know, with balloons and streamers and stuff?"

Levi nodded, then added a dash of cayenne pepper to his barbecue sauce. He hadn't seen Jess this excited about a birthday since she'd turned seven and he'd had a clown come to the house to entertain the fourteen screaming, excited children. Tonight's party was nothing in comparison. Just him and Jess, Neil, Marian, Phil—and Grace, of course.

If she came.

Despite her promise, Levi had expected a phone call from her all day, giving a very good reason for being unable to attend. The truth was, he was hoping for such a call. Jess would be disappointed, but in the long run it would be for the best. She had to learn to accept that Grace was completely unreliable. Besides, Grace's presence tonight would make things damn uncomfortable for him, and as the father, he thought he had a right to enjoy his own kid's birthday.

Although "enjoy" might be stretching things. He hadn't had much pleasure from anything since the scene between him and Grace. It had been ugly, and he knew now he'd been naive not to think that Jess's birth date would create such a rift between them.

If he'd known, maybe he'd have brought up the issue earlier. Because what he really needed—what they both really needed—was an end to whatever was, or had been, between them. He knew he'd never gotten over Grace, and as long as she kept popping up in his life, he never would.

So let her hate him. Let her vow never to see him again.

Except for this afternoon.

In just a few minutes...

"Dad, are you sure you're cooking enough ribs?"

Levi took the sauce off the stove. "Why do you keep asking that? Has a guest ever left this house hungry that you can remember?"

"I know. But your ribs are so good everyone's bound to eat more than usual."

"You wouldn't be trying to butter up the old man, would you? If you are, it's working." He reached out a hand to tousle her hair, then thought better of it. Jess had already spent the better part of an hour in the bathroom with a can of mousse and a hair dryer.

But his daughter didn't notice the aborted gesture. She opened the fridge and surprised him by picking up the bottle of white wine he'd put in to chill.

"I hope this is a good wine. Nothing too cheap or anything," she commented.

"What do you care? This is your fifteenth birthday, not your nineteenth."

"I know." She sighed. "I just want things to be perfect. For the guests."

"Guests" had to mean Grace. Jess had never made such a fuss when Phil or Marian were over for dinner. "You know, kid, Grace might not show. It wouldn't be the first time."

"Why do you keep saying that? She promised me she'd be here."

Which was precisely why he was concerned. Grace's promises were not exactly sterling.

Jess was now opening the lower bin of the fridge, where he'd put the vegetables he cleaned that morning. "Do we have enough salad?"

"Jess…" He held a wooden spoon over her head threateningly. "Get out of my kitchen. Now. Why don't you put some music on before the guests start arriving?"

Jess danced out of his reach. "Your music or mine?"

It was her party. He was the father, though. "Let's compromise on classical." He expected her to object, but she snapped her fingers at the suggestion.

"Perfect."

Perfect? Since when did his daughter think classical music was perfect for anything? Unless she figured it would impress Grace.

Grace. It all came back to her. When the doorbell rang, he found his gut tightening with anticipation. He felt like a kid again, and it scared him. Was he as prepared as he thought to have her walk out of his life once more?

Neil's voice, and Jess's giggle in response, restored his equilibrium. Grace wasn't here. Of course not. She wasn't going to come, remember?

"Hi, Neil," he said while Jess poured pop into tall, narrow glasses. As usual, he felt a chill of dislike when he saw his daughter's boyfriend. The kid was looking even sloppier than usual, if that was possible. Levi especially objected to the way his eyes kept steering toward the low neckline of Jess's blouse. Levi had planned to ask her to change earlier—the silky fabric of her top clung to every curve, and her skirt was much, much too short—but he hadn't wanted to start a fight on her birthday. So now he had to pay the price of watching her boyfriend leer at her all afternoon.

"Want some chips, Neil?" Jess passed the bowl, then turned to the table to rearrange the napkins she'd set out hours ago. He'd thought that once the guests began to arrive, especially Neil, Jess would start to relax, but if anything, the opposite was true. With every passing moment, she was becoming more and more uptight.

"Here, I'll get that, Jess," he said when she knocked over her half-full glass of pop in an uncharacteristically clumsy move.

"Sorry, Dad," she said, checking her outfit for signs of spillage, totally oblivious to the dark stain pooling on the hardwood floor. Fighting back a few well-chosen words about her priorities, Levi mopped up the excess with a rag.

Then the doorbell rang again, and Jess was out of her chair like a shot. She returned a few moments later with Phil and Marian, disappointment evident in her expression. Levi checked his watch. It was five o'clock. If Grace was planning to cancel, then she was being damn rude leaving it to the last minute like this. Jess was going to be crushed when she didn't show.

Then a bitter possibility occurred to him. Maybe she wasn't even going to call. Could even Grace stoop so low?

GRACE BALANCED a gift-wrapped box in one hand and a bouquet of flowers in the other. With the right toe of the new shoes she'd bought that afternoon, she kicked the door of her car closed. She was late. Almost half an hour. She'd considered calling but had lost her nerve. What if Levi picked up the phone?

She'd been tempted not to come, but how could she do that to Jess? The answer was, she couldn't. So she'd spent the day shopping for a new outfit in the hope that moss-green suede pants, matching leather shoes and a silk sweater would mask her nervousness, even insecurity—emotions she was not at all used to dealing with.

Grace hurried across the street and up the flight of stairs to the separate entrance behind the store, where she discovered she wasn't the only late guest. Another woman was standing by the door. She appeared hesitant, as if unsure she had the right place, but in her left hand she carried a colorful gift bag.

"Hi," Grace said. "Are you going to Jess's birthday party?"

She wondered who the woman could be. A distant relative, an old family friend? She looked about Grace's age, pretty, with ginger-colored hair just a shade darker than Grace's. Her square-cut black suit was matronly and hung loosely from her shoulders, and her shiny black pumps seemed stiff and uncomfortable. The woman eyed her suspiciously.

"Do I know you?"

"I don't think so." Grace rang the buzzer.

"You look so familiar." The woman's gray eyes narrowed.

"Grace Hamilton. I'd shake your hand, but as you can see—"

"Grace Hamilton," she repeated slowly. "I think I remember now. You're the one—"

The door flew open and Jess was before them, her cheeks flushed pink, her eyes unnaturally bright. "You

came," she said as if she couldn't believe it. "You
actually came."

"Happy birthday, Jess." Grace moved to hand her
the flowers, then realized that Jess hadn't even noticed
her. Her attention was riveted on the other woman, the
woman who hadn't yet told Grace her name and who
now was so pale she appeared ready to collapse at any
second. The woman shrank back when Jess reached to
pull them both inside the apartment.

"Come on in," Jess said. "Everybody's waiting. I
can't believe you're really here."

Grace got the distinct impression Jess was still
speaking solely to the other woman. Curious and feeling strangely left out, Grace followed Jess inside. She
saw Neil right away, sitting with his shod feet up on
the recliner. Marian and Phil were standing together,
sipping wine. All three stared openly at the newcomer;
Grace again felt her presence was completely inciden-
tal.

Levi was in the kitchen, pouring white wine into
elegant glass flutes. He was dressed in his black jeans,
with a thin knit black sweater. The dark color lent a
dangerous edge to his good looks, drawing the blue
from his eyes and emphasizing the jet streaks in his
hair. He seemed as aware of her as she was of him
and their eyes locked for several seconds before his
glance shifted to the other guest. Grace knew instantly
by his reaction that something was wrong.

His eyes widened and the glass he was filling over-
flowed onto the counter. He didn't appear to notice.
Setting down the bottle, he strode toward them just as
Jess began her introductions.

"Excuse me, everybody," Jess said in a high, unsteady voice. "I'd like you all to meet my mother. Casey Booker."

Mother? The room turned completely silent. Grace stepped back, colliding into a wall. Was it possible? Jess looked so happy, yet a certain anxiety marred her excitement. Grace noticed she avoided her father's eyes when he walked up to her.

"What the hell is going on?" He turned to the woman herself. "Casey? What in God's name are you doing here?"

"That's what I'd like you to tell me," Casey said, wrenching her arm away from Jess, running her hands down the sides of her skirt. "We had an agreement…" She set down her gift bag and pulled an envelope out of her purse, waving it in Levi's direction. "And attending fifteenth-year birthday parties was definitely not part of it."

Levi took the invitation and glanced at the contents. "Jess?"

"If this is some attempt at blackmail," Casey said, "you might as well forget it. We're comfortably—"

"Stop!" Levi held up his hand. "Whatever this is about, it isn't money."

The smile had faded from Jess's face by now, but Grace recognized the determined angle of her chin. "I decided I would give myself a present this birthday. I was going to find my real mother."

Grace felt both admiration and sympathy for the girl. She remembered the bravado Jess had displayed when she'd broken into her board meeting, so convinced Grace was her mother. No question that Jess had a flair for the dramatic. But was this just another mistake? The woman certainly didn't look very happy about the situation. However, Grace noticed, she wasn't denying anything, either.

So was this, after all, the woman whom Levi had cheated on her with? Grace turned more critical eyes on Casey Booker. The woman's reaction puzzled her. As far as Grace could tell, there was no sign of residual feelings between Casey and Levi. No hint of the kind of awareness Grace herself always felt when he was in the same room with her.

As for Jess, Grace could detect no tenderness, or even curiosity, on Casey's part for the daughter she had not seen since she was an infant. It was a most peculiar situation.

Casey pointed a finger at Levi's chest. "You promised you wouldn't tell her."

"And I didn't."

"Oh my God," Phil croaked. "I've been duped, haven't I, kid?"

He sounded as though he'd just sunk his sailboat in rocky waters.

Jess was apologetic. "I had to know."

Phil turned to Levi. "She had Casey's picture, but it was mixed in with a bunch of others. And she knew her name. I meant to tell you about it. I mean, I assumed you let her see the pictures for a reason, but I still meant to talk to you. I can't believe I forgot."

Levi's face had paled, and Grace couldn't help but feel sorry for him he was so obviously distressed. "You were going through my pictures, Jess? After our talk about privacy? How did you find out her name? None of those pictures are labeled."

"Dad, I know I did some things I shouldn't have. But I had to know who my mother was. I just had to know."

"Jess, you kept saying all you wanted was to find out your mother's name, but you don't really believe that, do you? Deep inside, you were hoping for a reconciliation between the two of you, maybe even including me. But that just isn't going to happen, and I knew it never would. That's part of the reason I never told you her name and part of the reason I wish you would have left this alone."

Jess backed away from her father and turned to Neil, who put an arm over her shoulder protectively. Grace could see how the intimate gesture drew a frown from Levi.

"You don't understand," Jess said, her voice carrying both anger and sadness. "You've never understood. I had no choice. I had to know."

"But why?" Casey's voice cracked. "Levi's been a good father, hasn't he?"

Jess's face softened. "The best." Then she turned back to Casey. "Weren't you ever curious about me? Didn't you ever wonder what would happen if we met, maybe accidentally, walking down the street...?"

"Oh, God." Casey put a hand up to her face. "I should have realized this would all come out one day."

Jess wet her lips. "I'm not going to cause you any trouble. I just wanted to know who you were. I thought maybe we could spend some time together..."

It was all so familiar. So painfully familiar. Grace's heart ached for Jess as Casey reacted to the suggestion with horror.

"No! Absolutely not. I can't ever see you again. You have to promise me, just as Levi did all those years ago."

"But why?" Jess's voice came out in a whisper.

Casey shook her head. "My husband doesn't know I had a baby before I met him. He's a very traditional, conservative man. I don't think he would understand why I had to give you up. I was so young—I wasn't ready for that sort of responsibility. It was the best thing for you and for me."

"He doesn't have to find out, does he?" Jess sounded desperate. "I just want to get acquainted. Aren't you even a little curious about me?"

Casey closed her eyes. "I can't allow myself to be. Don't you see? I have to think of my husband and my two little boys."

Jess's face flooded with color and she stepped back from her mother. Grace could feel the girl's tears; tears were welling up in her, too. She watched Levi step toward his daughter, saw the anguish on his face when she shrank from him, as well. Grace dropped the flowers and gift she was holding and began to move forward, but she was too slow.

One harsh sob choked out of Jess before she covered her mouth and ran to the door. She and Neil left before anyone realized what was happening.

"Jessie! Please come back!"

Levi's voice was raw as he called out after his daughter. For a moment, it seemed he would run after her, but then he slowly retreated into the room. Grace saw him clench and unclench his hands in helpless frustration. How could this Casey be so uncaring and unfeeling? As far as Grace was concerned, Jess was better off without her, but she knew Jess wouldn't see it that way.

"She'll be back soon," Phil said hopefully.

Grace just shook her head when Levi glanced at her. She knew he wasn't so sure, and neither was she.

"POOR KID." PHIL'S WORDS rang clearly in the silent room.

No one looked at Casey. Grace wondered if the woman had any idea what she'd given up. Jess was such a treasure. Brave and funny, smart and sweet. How could Casey have left her little baby? How could she have turned her back on the young woman that baby had grown up to be?

After a long, uncomfortable pause, Phil spoke again. "I'm sorry I was such an idiot, Levi. I should have talked to you first before I said anything to Jess, but she was a damned good actor, let me tell you."

"It doesn't matter. She was bound to find out sooner or later." Levi's flat voice matched the deadened expression on his face. "I should never have promised Casey in the first place. What kind of father keeps his kid's mother's name a secret for so many years?"

Grace wanted to cry. An honorable man, that's what kind. A man who would pick up the pieces after a young, confused woman walked out on her child. Not only that, a man with enough compassion left over that he could respect her wish to have no further contact with that child.

"I better go," Phil said. "I feel like a real shit, Levi. You'll call if I can do anything?"

"Me, too," Marian quickly added.

Levi nodded at them both as they left.

Grace picked up her purse, aware she should leave, as well, but she was reluctant to go without first finding out if Jess was okay. She looked over at Levi. He was slouched against a wall, his head bowed in defeat and exhaustion.

''Do you think they might have gone to Neil's?''
Grace asked.

Levi raised his head. ''It's possible. I'll give them
a few minutes, let Jess have a chance to sort herself
out, then go there and see. In the meantime, anyone
besides me need a drink?'' He went to the kitchen,
ignored the open bottle of white wine and reached for
the scotch in a cupboard over the fridge.

''My husband thinks I'm at a funeral,'' Casey said.
''But I suppose one glass won't hurt.''

The three of them collapsed into seats.

''Why did she have to track me down? If my husband finds out...'' Casey began to rock like a woman
keening.

''It's only natural a girl would want to know about
her mother,'' Grace said, unable to believe this
woman's ability to stay so firmly fixed on herself and
her own problems. Didn't she realize she'd just shat-
tered the soul of the young woman who was her
daughter, however much Casey wanted to ignore that
fact?

Grace wished with all her heart she were Jess's
mother. It wasn't fair this way—it really wasn't.

''But we had an agreement.'' Casey held her empty
glass on her lap, her rocking movements intensifying.
''This can't be happening. It can't.'' She looked over
at Levi. ''You have to tell her there's been a mistake,
that I'm not her real mother. You have to make her
be-believe...'' Casey covered her mouth with a hand
and shook her head. Tears shone in her eyes and her
entire body began to tremble.

Levi moved to sit beside her. Putting an arm over
her shoulder, he bent his head next to hers. ''It's okay,

Casey," he said. "Jess is going to be okay, and so are you."

Casey's shoulders heaved with sobs.

"It's okay," he repeated. He nodded at Grace. "Make her a cup of sweet tea, would you?" Then to Casey, "Have you eaten anything today?"

"I c-couldn't. I've barely eaten since I got the letter...."

Grace turned on the stove and popped a piece of bread in the toaster, unable to believe they were going to all this effort for the woman who had just wounded Jess so profoundly she would likely carry the scar all her life. Didn't Levi understand what this rejection would do to Jess? Or were his old feelings for Casey impairing his judgment?

A few minutes later, she carried a cup of tea and a plate with buttered toast into the living room. They clattered against the glass tabletop when she set them down.

Casey was unaware of the food, but Levi handed her the cup and forced her to start eating. Grace, unable to stand watching the spectacle of him helping the unraveled woman, carried their empty glasses back to the kitchen and washed and dried them. By the time she'd put them back in the cupboard, Casey was finished.

"I'm walking her to the car," Levi said. His voice, so tender toward the other woman, sounded harsh when he spoke to Grace. "Would you mind sticking around a few minutes longer?"

Grace nodded. She didn't say goodbye to Casey as they left, and the other woman didn't even seem to notice her as she passed by.

Unbelievable.

Grace picked up the gift she'd dropped to the floor earlier, then stuck the flowers in some water in the sink. Spotting Casey's gift bag still on the tiles by the entry, Grace went to place it on the table. It was very light. A glance inside revealed a classical CD, no card. Grace shook her head, thinking of the hard rock she'd heard pounding from behind Jess's bedroom door the first day she'd come over.

For the first time, she noticed that pink and burgundy balloons were tied to the light fixture on the ceiling and streamers had been twisted and strung to each corner of the living room.

Not wanting Levi or Jess to have to deal with any reminders of the party that wasn't, Grace dismantled the decorations, then tucked them away in a corner. When Levi finally walked in, she had covered the birthday cake and was putting it in the fridge.

"So she's gone?"

"She's gone."

Grace shut the fridge and stared at the white door, hating the desolate sound of his voice. "How could you do it? How could you be so nice to her after what she did to Jess?"

"Does it really look so black and white to you?"

She felt him standing behind her and turned. Her back was pressed against the fridge door with only mere inches between them. "You can't mean to blame Jess for what happened."

"Of course not."

"Then who?"

Levi moved away to pour himself a second scotch. "When Casey found out she was pregnant, she wanted to get an abortion. I'm the one who convinced her to have the baby. I told her she could put it up for adoption if she felt the same way after it was born. Then, when Jess made her grand entrance, I convinced her to bring the baby home for a few days before making the final decision.'' He held up the bottle of scotch. ''Want one?''

Grace shook her head. ''But she didn't change her mind?''

''No. She didn't want the baby. She couldn't even bring herself to feed or change Jess, so I did all that. After a week went by, she insisted we give the child up, but I couldn't let her go.'' Levi took a swallow of his drink. ''So you see, if it hadn't been for me, Casey wouldn't have had to go through any of this.''

''That's the past, Levi. That doesn't excuse how she behaved today. Even if she didn't want to tell her husband the truth, she could have been more understanding.''

''Could she, though? Think about it. How can she accept Jess now without admitting she made a terrible mistake fifteen years ago? If the baby had been taken away at birth and given to adoptive parents, the chances are Casey would never have been put in this position in the first place.''

Grace acknowledged what he was saying, but that still didn't make it right as far as she was concerned. Casey ought to have understood that Jess's feelings had to come before her own. ''I still don't understand how you can be so forgiving.''

''That's simple.'' He leaned against the kitchen counter, shoving one hand into the pocket of his jeans. ''Because I have Jess, and that's what's important to me. It's a wild feeling, Grace, to hold a helpless baby in your arms and know she's counting on you for everything—food, shelter, love. You have no idea how protective you become in a situation like that.''

"Didn't it scare you—raising a daughter from infancy on your own?"

"I guess I didn't know enough to be scared. Somehow we muddled through."

"And Casey?"

"She left the day I persuaded her I was serious about keeping the baby."

Grace couldn't imagine it. "That must have hurt."

Levi looked her squarely in the eye. "I never loved her, Grace, and she never loved me. Not really. I stayed with her to help her through the pregnancy, and she stayed with me because she had nowhere else to go. That was all there was to it."

Oh, Lord, how she wanted to believe him. But Jess had been conceived in July.

"She looked a little like you. I think that's what attracted me to her in the first place."

Did he have any idea what those words meant to her? How badly she needed to believe he had once loved her as much as she'd loved him. Once had and still did. Grace closed her eyes as the admission forced its way to consciousness. Yes, she still loved Levi.

The power of the emotion swept over her, making her feel both weak and strong in the same instant. It was better that she finally accept what she'd tried to deny. Her first love had been the real thing, and her emotions now were genuine, not a lingering yearning for the way things used to be.

Whenever she looked at Levi, she saw a man of integrity, a man who thought of others before himself, a man who found strength and confidence from within. How could she ever have thought it possible she didn't love him?

CHAPTER FOURTEEN

LEVI NOTICED GRACE was looking at him with a strange, bemused expression. He should have known better than to try to explain Casey's motivations to her. To her, Casey must seem selfish and cruel, while the truth was simply that Casey hadn't been strong enough to handle what life had dealt. She hadn't had the maturity to handle motherhood when she was twenty, and she couldn't handle the emotional baggage of a daughter she hadn't seen in fifteen years now. He wasn't surprised that Grace judged her so harshly—she had never been able to understand that not everyone in the world was as strong as her.

In truth, hardly anyone was. Grace flowered under adversity. She was like a tough desert plant—the less water there was, the deeper she dug her roots. How could he expect her to relate to someone like Casey, who always looked for the easy way out?

He hadn't seen that fatal flaw in Casey at first, of course, or their relationship would never have progressed as far as it had. The truth was, he'd been attracted to Casey because she looked like Grace, and then, a month later when he'd realized how wrong they were for each other, it was too late. One package from the drugstore, and they knew she was pregnant. He could hardly have left her to deal with that on her own, even though he was aware from the start the baby wasn't his.

Maybe it was because he'd been there from the moment Casey found out she was expecting. Or maybe it was because he'd witnessed the birth from first contraction to that final, gut-wrenching push. Possibly it was holding that little slip of pink skin and blond hair and knowing she had absolutely no one in the world to look after her except him.

Whatever the reason, Jess had felt like his daughter. And for him that had always been enough. He wished Jess had felt *he* was enough for her and not been so determined to find her mother. Now that she'd found her, where had she gone? He'd hoped that if he gave her a little space, she'd come home when she was ready. But how much space could he give her? She was only just fifteen, hurt and vulnerable, and she was with Neil. The possibilities in that combination weren't too hopeful from Levi's perspective.

After downing the rest of his scotch, he glanced at his watch. "She's been gone for an hour. I think I'd better go hunt for her."

"Let me help." Grace reached over to take the empty glass from his hand. "I'll drive."

"Two drinks will hardly put me under the table, Grace."

She lifted her chin. "But they might put you over the legal limit."

He thought about arguing, but what was the point? Somehow she'd developed a bond with his daughter. If she wanted to help find Jess, so much the better. As for what would happen later, well, they'd deal with that when they had to.

"Fine, Grace." He stepped forward, eyes locked

onto hers, effectively pinning her back against the fridge. There was nothing he wanted more than to find his daughter, yet at the same time he longed to know the secrets hiding behind those serious gray eyes of Grace's. He imagined she might look at an annual report the way she was looking at him now. Speed-reading to find the information she needed.

What was it about him she found so compelling? Had she guessed how he felt about her? Did it amuse her to think she'd held his heart captive for so long? He stared down at her, glad at least that he had the advantage of height. And strength. He rested an arm against the fridge, locking her in tighter, and had the satisfaction of seeing her gaze falter.

What was he doing? Any minute now he'd be beating his chest, yelling out a jungle chant. If there was any woman that sort of macho display wouldn't impress, it was Grace. Yet he didn't want to impress her. He just wanted to claim her. To see the pillar of strength waver. To see her reach out for help and let him be the one to catch her when she fell.

She put a hand against his chest as though to push him back, but instead her fingers curled, digging past the hard muscle to the bone as if she wanted to rip out his heart.

Of course she already had.

Then her hand flattened and moved outward, spanning his shoulder. He hadn't kissed her since the night they'd made love, but there'd been times that he'd wanted to, and never more than now. One small step forward brought him close enough that her breasts just rubbed up against his chest, and when he lowered his head, he heard the whisper of his rough skin against the silk strands of her hair.

Levi shuddered, then drew in a sharp breath. He had to regain his sanity. To find his daughter.

"Where do you think they went?"

Her sigh warmed the skin of his throat. "What?"

He could hear the hammering of her heart, feel its rhythm blending with his own. It was gratifying that he had at least this small power over her. He knew he shouldn't take advantage of it, but hell, he'd never claimed to be a saint.

But he had to find Jess. Another deep breath, then he dropped his hands and turned to the counter. "Maybe they went to Neil's. I suppose we should check there first."

He heard the clink as Grace set his drink on the counter beside him.

"Right. I've got my keys. Let's go."

Levi sat next to her in the BMW, staring silently out the window as she drove to Neil's. He didn't know what to hope for. That Jess would be there? But then he was afraid of what might have happened in the past hour. Hurt and vulnerable after her mother's rejection, Jess would have been in no condition to choose rationally if Neil decided to press her to make love with him. To her, it might have seemed the logical way to fill the void she must feel inside.

Grace had no sooner parked than Levi was out the door. He rang the doorbell once, tried to peer in the transom, then buzzed again. He'd know just by looking at her if something had happened. And then he'd kill the punk. Or at least pierce a few body parts Neil hadn't gotten around to yet. Like his head.

At the sound of footsteps approaching the door, Levi forced himself to calm down, to think maturely. Beside him, Grace was quiet. Did she, like him, fear the worst? As the door opened, he felt her hand on his arm, as if she thought she needed to hold him back.

A man in his mid-twenties, dressed in suit pants, white shirt and a loosely knotted tie, stood in the doorway.

"Can I help you?"

Neil's brother. Levi didn't like to judge a man by his clothes, but he had to admit the respectable business attire he saw gave him a small measure of comfort. When he heard Neil was living with a brother, he'd assumed the worst. Maybe, just maybe, he'd been wrong about the guy.

"I'm Levi Shanahan. My daughter, Jess, is a friend of Neil's. This is Grace Hamilton."

"Peter Lambert."

The young man stepped forward to shake first Grace's hand, then Levi's. His slender good looks suggested that, cleaned up, Neil would also be an attractive man one day.

"Is something wrong? I thought Neil was supposed to be at your place, celebrating Jess's birthday tonight."

Peter knew where Neil was supposed to be. That, too, was a good sign. "Yes, well, there was a problem," Levi said. "Jess got upset and the two of them left together. I thought they might have come here."

Peter appeared worried. "How long ago was that?"

"Over an hour now. We have a list of Jess's friends to check with." Levi pulled it out of his pocket to show the young man. "Do you have any idea where they might have gone?"

"Neil's car is here, but they could be anywhere, really." Peter opened the door wider to allow them to enter.

Levi stepped over a pair of track shoes and a discarded sweatshirt. After waiting for Grace to precede him, he followed his host into the living room, then waited again while Peter removed a big empty bowl from one chair and a football from another.

"Please sit down," Peter said. "Sorry about the mess."

Between them, the two brothers obviously didn't have much in the way of homemaking skills. The furniture appeared to be thrift-shop castoffs. They'd tried to add some homey touches, but the two baseball posters were hung too high on the walls and the token houseplant was so dusty it didn't even look green anymore.

"Maybe we should try phoning Jess's friends," Grace said.

Levi nodded, then turned to Peter. "Do you have any other suggestions?"

"Neil works at the video store around the corner. We could try there." Peter picked up the cordless phone sitting on a side table and began to dial.

Neil had a job. Another surprise. Did Jess know? She must. Why hadn't she ever mentioned it to him?

"No luck." Peter handed the phone to Levi. "Want to try that list of friends you have?"

Levi's concern grew with each number he rang. No one had seen them. Grace had risen from her chair and was pacing the room. Peter was flipping through an address book, trying to come up with new angles. After the last call, Levi handed the phone back to Peter.

"No one's seen or heard from them." He was beginning to wonder if he should call the police.

Peter had closed the address book and was tapping it on his knee. "Sometimes when Neil's in trouble or thinks he's about to be, he goes to visit our grand-mother. He's never taken any of his friends with him before, but I suppose it's possible...."

Levi nodded. "Can you phone and check?"

As Peter dialed, Grace came and perched on the arm of his chair. "What if they aren't there?"

Levi rubbed the side of his neck. He was trying not to overreact, but it was hard. Jess was his daughter and he ought to have some idea where she might have gone. But the truth was, he didn't have a clue. For the first time, it occurred to him that there were even worse possibilities to worry about than Jess and Neil's sleeping together. What if they had decided to run away? The very thought made him feel physically ill.

Grace squeezed his shoulder. "Maybe they're back home already. We should have left a note."

"I did. While you were getting your purse." He knew Grace's touch was meant to be comforting, but he found it quite the opposite. He couldn't afford to let his guard down around her now. He stood up from the chair and began to pace the room, too, tracing the path that Grace had taken only minutes earlier.

Of course, there were dozens of reasonable places Jess and Neil could be right now. They could have gone to grab a burger or see a movie. Dropped in on friends he didn't know about.

Behind him, he heard Peter snap his fingers.

"It's okay. They're at our grandmother's."

Levi whirled around. "You're sure?" It seemed too good to be true.

Peter nodded. "They took the bus. I told Grandma to keep them there, that we'd come and pick them up." As he spoke, he reached for a jacket hanging over the back of a chair, then pulled some keys out of the pocket.

"Perfect," Levi assured him.

"What's the address?" Grace asked. "We'll follow you." She was at the door already, impatient to get started.

Levi went to stand beside her. "No sense in us taking up even more of your evening, Grace. I thought I might ride with Peter, if that's okay with him."

"No problem," Peter said. "If you guys don't mind stepping outside, I'll lock up the house and back my car out of the garage."

On the front step, Grace turned to him. "I don't have anything else to do. I don't mind driving."

"It's not that." He headed for the driveway, needing to keep distance between them. "I've said it before, but this time I mean it. I don't think it's good for Jess to start depending on you. You saw how Casey hurt her tonight. I can't let a woman hurt her like that again."

Grace couldn't have looked more wounded if he'd slapped her. And maybe, in a way, he had.

"I know my track record hasn't been great—"

He shook his head. "This thing between us, Grace—it has to be over. I thought that night at your place we'd be able to get things into perspective, but it hasn't really worked. As long as you're around, my life's in limbo. I need to move on and I think Jess needs that, too."

Grace didn't say a word. She just stared at him from the landing, and he thought she'd never looked more beautiful or more remote. She could have been a model in a fashion magazine, posing in expensive clothes, with perfectly styled hair and flawlessly made-up face.

He knew he was hurting her, but what were his choices? If he went to Neil's grandmother's with Grace, what message would that give Jess? If he expected his daughter to face reality, then he ought to expect the same of himself. And of Grace.

"I'm sorry, Grace. I appreciate your help today." His words sounded cold and flat even to him.

"Platitudes I do not need. Thanks anyway." Her voice was sarcastic, bitter. As if suddenly released from a trance, she began to move, her high heels clacking on the pavement as she walked briskly toward her car. She paused at the driver's door. "I know you didn't want me at the party today. I came only because of Jess. And that's why I'm here right now. Because of Jess. I thought I might be able to help somehow."

"Jess can't pretend you're her mother anymore. She found out the truth today and now she has to learn to deal with it."

"I know what you're saying, but why today? Hasn't she dealt with enough already? My being there might help, just a little. Or maybe you don't want to admit that."

"Maybe I don't. Do you want me to say this is mostly about me? Okay. I admit it. I don't want to have my ex-girlfriend hanging around my daughter. I don't think it's healthy. For any of us."

"Don't mince words, Levi. Why don't you just say what you really think." Grace glared at him, then climbed into her car and slammed the door. She started the engine; then, as she was pulling into the street, she lowered a window. "You know, if you'd just thrown those stupid notes of mine away in the first place, none of this would have happened.''

And before he could say a word in return, she was gone.

"THANKS FOR TAKING ME HERE, Neil," Jess said. "Your grandma's really sweet."

''She's great, isn't she? I used to visit a lot just after my brother and I moved away from home.''

Jess felt her eyes fill with tears. Neil never referred to his life with his parents, who still lived in Vancouver, but she knew it must have been pretty awful for him to have left to stay with his brother. Neil had physical scars, too—on his back. He never talked about that, either. Her imagination had supplied a likely explanation for them.

She took her last sip of tea, then placed her cup in the saucer. The china was so delicate—nothing like the thick green glass mugs they used in the coffee shop and at home. Neil's grandma had insisted on giving them a special tea when she'd heard it was Jess's birthday. They'd had fancy cucumber and cream cheese sandwiches, delicate little butter tarts and, of course, numerous cups of freshly brewed Earl Grey tea.

Jess carried her cup into the kitchen, where Neil's grandmother was elbow-deep in steamy, sudsy water. "Everything was so delicious," she said. "Please let me dry the dishes at least."

"Absolutely not." There was a trace of an English accent in the old woman's speech. "It's your birthday, dear. You mustn't spend it in the kitchen. And I can tell my Neil is eager to have a few minutes alone with you."

Jess didn't argue any further because she was equally eager to be alone with Neil. She found him sitting on the sofa in his grandmother's very tidy living room. He patted the cushion beside him, held out his arm, then wrapped it around her shoulders when she sat down.

"Feeling better?" he asked.

She nodded. "Much." She rested her head on his shoulder. "This day has turned out so different from what I planned."

"I know. I'm sorry about that."

"It's okay. Really. When we left my house, I thought I was going to die, but it doesn't seem so awful anymore. I mean, it's not as if I ever knew Casey. I guess I was never meant to have a mother."

"You've got your dad."

"Yeah. And I've got you." As she shot him a glance, she was surprised to see his ears redden.

In the kitchen, the phone rang. Jess heard Neil's grandmother. "Yes, they're here."

Jess tuned out the conversation. Neil was leaning over her now, moving his mouth slowly in her direction. She immersed herself in his kiss, in the warmth, the pleasure, the tingle of excitement. When he paused, his lips a fraction of an inch from hers, she said, "You know, you're a much nicer guy than you like people to think."

He laughed, then nuzzled her ear. "Do me a favor, Jay," he said. "Don't tell anyone."

GRACE SCREECHED TO A STOP in her garage, got out of the car and slammed the door, then went in the house and pitched her purse down the hallway. It hit the wall with a thud, the metal clasp marring the pale-colored walls.

Grace swore. She noticed the blinking red light on her answering machine but chose to ignore it, heading instead to her freshly stocked liquor cabinet. "Another scotch? Don't mind if I do, Levi." She poured with a liberal hand, then retrieved her purse from the floor, passing the damn flashing light again. She lit a cigarette.

Another business emergency? It could wait, she decided, feeling the burn of the scotch, the hit from her cigarette.

How dared he humiliate her like that? In front of Neil's brother, no less. As if it had been her idea to insinuate herself into their lives. Did he forget that it was Jess who'd tracked her down? Jess who kept phoning and wanting to see her. She'd only tried to be kind.

Grace paced. She pulled at her hair. Kind? Was she being honest with herself? She marched to the kitchen, yanked open the cupboard doors. Newly cleaned, practically empty, they mocked her. *Now what, Grace?* they seemed to ask.

Now what indeed. Her motivation had not been selfless. Yes, she'd cared about Jess; yes, she hadn't wanted to hurt her. But hadn't she needed Jess just as much as Jess had needed her? And hadn't she used every excuse she could find to see Levi?

Levi. Did he know she was still in love with him? Was that why he'd sent her away? Strange how things had worked out. She'd pursued her dreams and made them all come true. Behind her lay a trail of successes, each one bigger than the last.

So why did her life feel so empty?

Her first rush of anger drained, Grace walked slowly through the rooms of her house, trying to remember how she had occupied her time before Jess and Levi came into her life. Had it always been work? Was that all there was?

She rinsed her glass, stubbed her cigarette. Finally, with a sigh, she pressed the playback button on her answering machine.

"Hello, Grace. This is Shelby Taylor, Roberta Paxton's secretary. Roberta's had a heart attack. She's at Vancouver Hospital and would like you to come see her as soon as possible."

CHAPTER FIFTEEN

GRACE HAD NEVER BEEN in a hospital before. Odd, at her age, but there it was. She'd never had children, never needed an operation, never had any sick relatives. Now she felt fortunate. The atmosphere was oppressive, the attitude of the receptionists and nurses authoritarian and the faint but pervasive chemical smell in the air nauseating.

Her shoes sounded loud as she walked along the linoleum hallway that led from the emergency department doors.

She was out of her element and she knew it. Fear, an unfamiliar emotion, bubbled in her stomach, and all the deep breathing in the world couldn't keep her from trembling. A right turn took her to the cardiac care unit, where a tired-looking receptionist directed her down one of the curtained aisles to where Roberta lay. There, another nurse spoke to her sharply.

"Are you Grace Hamilton?"

She nodded.

"Good. The patient has been very anxious to see you. Dr. Baxter will explain the situation to you."

Grace hung back. "Did she really have a heart attack?"

Grace could tell from nurse's expression that she obviously found the question strange.

"Yes, she did."

"But she's only in her late forties. And she's a woman. I thought—"

A male voice cut in. "Heart disease is the number-one killer of women."

The doctor stepped up beside the nurse. He appeared to be in his mid-fifties, with thinning gray hair and a grim expression, intensified by deep furrows that ran down either side of his small, stern mouth.

"Smoking, drinking, improper diet, lack of exercise, too much stress..." He ticked off the infractions with his fingers. "Sound like anyone you know?" He snapped the pen he was carrying shut and tucked it in the breast pocket of his lab coat. "With her family history of heart disease, she's lucky it wasn't worse."

Grace took a shaky breath and wished there were something solid she could lean against. "What happened?"

"Massive myocardial infarct, that's what happened," the doctor said impatiently.

"Pardon?"

"Ms. Paxton has had a serious heart attack, caused by clogged arteries, that has damaged the inferior part of her heart."

"Will she be okay?" To Grace's ear, her own voice sounded like a little girl's—thin and higher-pitched than usual.

"Probably." The doctor did not look as though he thought this was particularly good news. "We'll monitor her for the next twenty-four hours, schedule her for angioplasty, and then she can go home in a couple of days."

Angioplasty. That was a procedure to repair blocked blood vessels. Grace nodded. At least there was no suggestion of more major surgery at this point.

"You can see her now if you want," he said. "Just keep it short—she needs her rest."

Grace nodded and took a tentative step over the threshold. Roberta lay on the bed, her complexion gray, her hair pushed up away from her face. She looked like the central plug-in for a host of appliances, what with all the cords that led from her body to various kinds of apparatus alongside the bed. Grace found some room to stand beside her and gazed down at her longtime mentor.

As if sensing her presence, Roberta slowly raised her eyelids. She was obviously exhausted and frail, but by the way her eyes darted from Grace's face to the cardiac monitor positioned on the other side of the bed, she knew what was going on.

"Roberta." Grace delicately placed a hand on a section of arm with nothing attached to it. "How are you feeling?"

"Like hell."

Grace smiled. Or tried to. The corners of her mouth quivered, and she had to blink rapidly to keep back tears.

"Thanks for coming, Grace. I need to talk to you about a few things."

"Of course." Grace patted Roberta's arm reassuringly.

"I wanted you to know I've made you the executor of my will. You can get the name and number of my lawyer from my secretary if it comes to that."

Grace shook her head. "But, Roberta, the doctor says you're—"

Roberta held up her hand. "Let me finish, Grace. I've left most of my assets to a trust fund. I want to help young women make careers in business. The details are in the will, and I'm hoping you'll agree to administer the fund.''

''Of course, Roberta, but I don't think this is the right time—''

''It's exactly the right time.'' Roberta was as authoritarian as ever. ''Of course I have no intention of dying. But I must prepare for all eventualities. So you'll do it?''

''Yes. Certainly.''

Roberta relaxed visibly, her eyelids fluttering, her shoulders sinking deeper into the pillow beneath her. ''Good. Good.''

''Anything else I can do for you? People who need to be contacted?''

''Shelby's taking care of that. Rescheduling my appointments.'' Suddenly, each word cost an effort. ''Notifying my associates.'' Her eyelids drooped, her breathing slowed.

Grace withdrew her hand. ''I think I'd better go now.''

No reply. Roberta was asleep. The steady rhythm on the heart monitor was reassuring. Grace backed out of the room and headed down the hall. There was no sign of either the doctor or the nurse she'd spoken to earlier. The hallway was almost spookily vacant and pinpricks of anxiety played on the back of her neck. Without thinking, Grace broke into a run.

''SO JESS IS OKAY?'' Phil asked. He was reclining in the leather chair in Levi's living room, cradling a beer in one hand while he clicked the remote control with the other, looking for the hockey scores.

''Seems to be.'' Levi had his feet up on the sofa. It

had been a bloody long day. "Stop. There. The Canucks lost. Five to two."

"Damn." Phil clicked off the television. "So much
for my hockey pool at work." He leaned his head back
comfortably. "You found her at the boyfriend's
grandma's?"

"That's right." Levi was beginning, reluctantly, to
revise his opinion of Neil. Taking Jess to see his
grandmother had been just the right move. Being the
center of the affectionate older woman's attention was
probably the best remedy for Casey's coldhearted rejection. And he'd been impressed with Peter and the
handle he seemed to have on his younger brother's
life. Neil was actually holding down a part-time job.
And his marks, according to Peter, weren't nearly as
bad as he liked his friends to think.

The important thing was, of course, that Jess was
going to be all right. She would get over Casey's rejection. They'd talked about it for over an hour before
Phil arrived. Levi tried to explain that Casey just
wasn't a very strong person. It didn't mean she was a
bad person, any more than it meant Jess wasn't worthy
of her mother's love.

In the end, he thought Jess would accept it. The way
she would eventually accept that Grace no longer belonged in their lives. Oddly enough, that had upset
Jess the most. It made him wonder if he was being
selfish by denying his daughter Grace's friendship.
Wasn't he really only trying to protect himself? Was
that fair to Jess?

"I was surprised that Grace turned up at the party,"
Phil said.

Levi let out a long breath. Trust Phil to find the
open wound.

"So are you seeing her again or what?"

"She came because Jess wanted her to."

Phil snapped his chair into the upright position, settled his arms on his knees and leaned forward. "While you, of course, didn't care one way or the other."

"Damn you, Phil—"

"Hey! Watch the language. Don't blame me because you're still crazy about her."

Levi stared at his hands, thinking that at times a friend could know you too well.

"Have you told her how you feel?"

"How can I, Phil? Nothing's changed. She's still on the short track to success. I was never interested in being on any woman's back burner. Especially when I've got Jess to consider. Bad enough that her own mother washed her hands of her."

The doorbell rang, then the unlocked door opened and Marian came in.

"Hi. I figured I'd find you over here," she said to Phil. "Mind if I grab myself a beer?" She raised her eyebrows at Levi.

Levi ignored the rhetorical question. A few seconds later, Marian joined him on the sofa.

"How's Jess?"

"She's fine." Levi stood up suddenly and went to stand by the window. What was the matter with him tonight? A guy's friends dropped by to make sure he was okay, and all he wanted was to get rid of them. It didn't make sense.

"How about you, Marian?" Phil asked. "Levi told me about that jerk, Richard."

"Par for the course these days, I'm afraid." Marian sounded more than a little despondent.

Levi turned and propped himself on the windowsill.

"Just forget about him and move on, Marian. You'll find someone better."

"Yeah, maybe." She toyed with the can in her hands a few seconds, then looked at Phil. "You found someone to sail with you yet?"

Phil glanced at Levi. "No. Not yet."

"How about me?"

"What?" Levi exchanged a look of astonishment with Phil.

"I didn't know you sailed," Phil said.

"I don't. But I could learn, couldn't I?"

"Are you serious?"

"I gave notice at work yesterday."

"You gave what?" Phil looked at her as if she'd lost her mind.

"Don't give me a hard time, guys. You can't say anything my supervisor didn't, believe me. I just don't give a damn anymore about seniority or my bloody pension plan. I'm sick of showing up at the same office day after day, pushing papers and having to see that creep Richard everywhere I go."

"Okay, fine. But there are other options besides going sailing, you know."

"What, Levi? Like find another job for another bank, or maybe an insurance company this time for a little variety? I'm forty-two years old..."

It was the first time Levi had ever heard her admit her real age. This had to be serious.

"...the clock is ticking, and I'm tired of waiting for things to happen. I want to start making them happen. My inheritance may not have been big enough to impress Richard Craig, but it's certainly big enough for me to take a year off work and see a bit of the world."

She faced Phil. "That is if you can put up with me, of course."

Phil wore a stunned expression, and Levi couldn't imagine what he was going to say. The three of them had been friends for years, but it was no secret that Marian's strong opinions sometimes grated on Phil's nerves. On the other hand, Phil was a social man, and the long hours alone ahead of him certainly had to have him nervous.

Punctuating the end of the drawn-out silence, Phil slapped his hand against his knee. "Why the hell not? If it doesn't work out, you can always grab a plane home." He raised his beer can in Marian's direction. "To my newest crew member. We'll have to get you started pronto on some heavy-duty sailing lessons."

Levi watched Marian return the salute. Part of him felt a twinge of envy that Marian was the one joining Phil in the adventure, and not him. But only a twinge. He was remembering Grace's face when he'd told her not to come with him to Neil's grandmother's. That final rejection had been brutal, and even knowing it was for the best didn't take away any of the pain.

"You're being awfully quiet, Levi," Marian remarked. "What do you think of all this?"

"You and Phil together on a forty-foot sailing craft for twelve months?" He raised his eyebrows. "It'll be damn interesting to read those postcards."

WHEN GRACE LEFT the hospital and got into her car, it was ten o'clock Saturday night. Instead of going home, she drove straight to her office, where she worked almost round the clock on the package she was putting together for the board. She didn't dare stop, not even for a nap on the love seat. She knew the minute she wasn't working she would start to ponder the terrifying events of the past twenty-four hours, and that was the one thing she simply couldn't stand.

Grace was panicked. She couldn't even admit to herself that what had happened to Roberta was real. Life was avalanching in on her, and the only way she could hope to avoid the rushing snow was with continuous forward momentum.

She smoked, drank innumerable cups of coffee and ate the crackers she found in the lunchroom as she consolidated the figures her staff had calculated, then compiled them into one final report. She'd thought it would take a week to complete everything, but by the time the sun rose Monday morning, the result was resting on her desk.

When Jackie knocked at her office door at eight-thirty, Grace realized it was her first human contact in over twenty-four hours. "Come in."

"Hi! How was your—" Jackie's smile froze, her eyes wide with shock. "Grace, what happened to you? You look like you've spent the whole night here." She waved her hand through the air as if trying to push back a heavy set of curtains, then dumped the contents of the ashtray on Grace's desk into the wastebasket and shook her head disapprovingly. "You did, didn't you?"

Grace nodded. It was two nights, actually, although she had napped on the couch. She avoided Jackie's eyes, not wanting to tell her the whole story, not sure she herself understood what the whole story was. She would fill Jackie in later about Roberta's heart attack. Right now, she didn't want to talk about it. She stood up, stretched her arms and felt the almost pleasant ache between her shoulders.

"You're obsessed. You know that, don't you?" Jackie picked up the pile of papers that constituted the completed report.

"Can you have those proofread? And check the numbers yourself. Make sure they're right. I don't want a single error, not so much as a misplaced comma."

"I'll take care of it," Jackie promised, heading for the door.

Grace smiled, although it was an effort. She knew she could count on Jackie.

"I hope you're planning to go home and rest now," Jackie said. "I don't mean to be rude, but you look like hell."

Grace ran a hand through her hair, knowing it was a mess and the style she'd blow-dried into it on Saturday morning had long gone. She still didn't want to go home, but of course she had to. All her clean clothes were there, and her new moss-green outfit was ready for the laundry.

Maybe home would be easier to face in the daylight.

GRACE FELT LIKE SHE'D seen the Ghost of Christmas Future. She stood in the entranceway of her too large, too empty house. The music and banter from a local morning radio program, playing automatically from her alarm clock in the bedroom, should have cheered her. But it couldn't begin to reach the cold, lonely corners of her heart. She dropped her purse and briefcase to the floor and kicked off her shoes. Then she headed for her bedroom, discarding items of clothing as she went.

Grace picked up the phone and called the hospital for an update on Roberta. The patient was fine, she was told, sleeping peacefully. Had anyone else been to visit her? Grace wondered. Thinking back to what Roberta had said Saturday night, she doubted it, unless perhaps Roberta's secretary had stopped by. Was this what Roberta's life boiled down to? It still amazed Grace that the one thing on Roberta's mind as she faced death was ensuring that the arrangements described in her will would be carried out as she intended.

It seemed so bleak. So pointless. Shouldn't there have been others standing by that bed who cared about what happened to Roberta? Others who loved and needed Roberta the person, not just Roberta the business executive?

Grace slipped into her bathrobe, then stared out her bedroom window at the bright spring day. If Roberta had any regrets, she certainly never let on. Her single-mindedness appeared as strong as ever. *Focus,* Roberta had told her over and over again in her career. *You'll never get ahead if you allow yourself to be distracted from your goal.*

But what good was getting ahead if you died in your prime, alone in a sterile hospital room with no one but a disapproving doctor looking on. *Smoking, drinking, improper diet, lack of exercise, too much stress... Sound like anyone you know?*

Who would be standing by Grace's bedside if it happened to her?

Her new vice president, Jackie?

Grace sank onto the bed and closed her eyes, icy fear knifing her midsection. She imagined Levi and Jess standing by her bedside. Levi would hold her hand and promise with his eyes that he would never forget her, that he would love her always.

But why should she have something in death she'd never had in life?

No, not never. She'd had it once. For a few short months that hot golden summer. Driving along the beach in his red Mustang, listening to the radio, her hair blowing in the wind, touching his shoulder, the side of his face…

They'd park somewhere—he always found a private place to stop. Dusk would fall. They would lie on the woolen blanket, the one he kept in the trunk, feeding each other strawberries and cheese they'd bought at the market.

They'd read to each other, his philosophy, her management techniques. They'd kiss, and touch. It would always happen slowly; inch by inch the clothing would disappear. Cradled by the dark, they would make love, their rhythm matching the roaring of the waves. Then he'd pull the blanket over them, roll them up like sausages in dough, and they'd sleep, arms and legs entangled, hair in knots, skin salty from the sea air and sweat.

Grace stuck out her tongue, tasted the salt of her tears now. Remembering was driving her crazy. She had to stop. She wasn't the sort of person to live in the past, to refuse to confront the realities of a situation.

He'd loved her once, but he didn't love her anymore. How could he? Her executive position, high salary, luxury car and upscale address—none of these mattered to Levi. She knew he saw beneath the veneer of her success to the real woman within, the woman who'd sacrificed anything and anyone to meet her goals, who lived for that rush of adrenaline that always hit in the hours before a big presentation, an important meeting, a last-minute assignment.

He knew all her weaknesses. No wonder he wanted her out of his life, away from his daughter.

Grace started prowling. She poured herself a glass of juice, then forced herself to drink it. She washed the glass, wiped the counter, then moved through each room of her house as if searching for something she'd lost.

Without any forethought, she picked up the phone and dialed a number she still hadn't forgotten despite not having used it in over a decade.

Her brother answered. "Hello?"

She cleared her throat. "Billy? It's me, Grace."

A gravelly cough. "Grace? My sister?"

"None other."

"Shit, Grace. It's been a lot of years. Whaddaya want?"

She hadn't been home since their parents' funeral. She thought she remembered sending a card at Christmas for a couple of years. But he'd never written back.

"I wondered if you'd still be on the farm."

"Yeah. Never thought I was too good for it. Not like some people."

"Come on, Billy. Aren't we a little old to keep up this feud? So I went to live in the city. Is that such a crime?"

His laugh sounded reluctant. "Not exactly a crime, I guess. You're right about that." There was a pause. "Saw your picture in a magazine. Guess you're doing well for yourself."

"Not bad. Have you married, Billy? Do you have any children?"

"Expecting one real soon, me and Carrie. You remember her—she was in your grade at school."

Grace couldn't, actually. "Well, when the baby's born, you'll send me a picture, right?"

"Could do that," Billy said, speaking slowly. "Guess I'll need your address, though."

When the conversation was over, Grace broke the connection and stood in the kitchen, her arms wrapped around her. Her glance fell on the liquor cabinet, and for several long moments she stood there pondering those cold, hard words the doctor had barked out. He'd described Roberta's lifestyle, but it had sounded awfully familiar.

Finally, she reached for the cabinet door and pulled out the first bottle. First she uncapped it, then she held it upside down over the sink. The vodka gurgled from the bottle. She cleaned out the entire cabinet, and when she was done, she took the cigarettes out of her purse and the top drawer of her night table. She even ran out to the car in her bare feet to get the pack she kept in the glove compartment.

There it was—that adrenaline rush that always hit when she started a new project. That buzz of energy, that lightening of her spirit. Suddenly, it was so clear to her where she had to go, what she had to do.

After slipping out of her bathrobe, she put on a pair of shorts, a T-shirt and an old pair of running shoes she found in the basement. Then, once she'd tucked her wallet and keys into a pocket, she locked the front door behind her and started to run.

SHE WAS BACK on her street again by ten, her physical exhaustion finally a match for her mental fatigue. She'd jogged for only fifteen minutes before her burning lungs had made her slow to a walk, but she'd continued walking for an hour, only stopping once for a bagel and juice.

Now the familiar sight of the sloped roof of her house beckoned. She wanted nothing but to sink into her bed and sleep her life into oblivion. She was so tired she knew she wouldn't even dream. Her brain finally had gone numb.

Then she saw Jess sitting on her doorstep, dressed in a black T-shirt and baggy overalls, her hair pulled up in a ponytail high on her head.

"Grace? Is that you?"

Through her mind-numbing fatigue, Grace tried to collect her wits. Half of her was delighted to see the teenager; the other half wasn't sure if she was ready to handle this yet. Obviously, she didn't have a choice. She plopped down on the step below Jess's.

Jess was looking at her, fascinated. "I've never seen you without makeup."

Grace brushed her hair back with her fingers, feeling the accumulation of oil and grit. "I don't know how to tell you this, Jess, but you shouldn't be here. I promised your father we wouldn't see each other anymore."

"I know. He told me. Poor Dad. He feels so awful about what happened with Casey."

"How do you feel about it?"

"At first I thought I wanted to die. But finally I realized it had nothing to do with me, not really. I know Casey is my biological mother, but even when I met her, touched her, I didn't feel the connection, you know what I mean? The way I do with you..." She stared down at her shoes. "You'd think Dad would understand. After all, I can't imagine loving him more if he were my biological father.''

Grace blinked at Jess's last statement. She couldn't have heard that right. "Excuse me, Jess. It sounded like you were saying that Levi isn't your—''

"Yeah. That's right.'' She nodded. "I'm adopted. I don't tell a lot of people. Dad said it was up to me whether I wanted people to know.''

Grace accepted instantly the truth in what Jess was telling her. That Levi had slept with another woman while he was seeing her had always felt wrong to Grace. After all, here was a man who had honored, out of a sense of culpability for another person's pain, a promise made fifteen years ago. Was he the type of man who would cheat on a woman he professed to love deeply? With all her heart, Grace now believed it to be impossible.

Jess *was* conceived in July, but Levi *wasn't* the father. As preposterous as it was, that was the only possible truth. Which meant he had stuck by a pregnant woman when he wasn't the father and raised a child he had no legal obligation toward.

Now, didn't that sound more like the Levi she knew?

"Oh, Jess…''

"Dad says it isn't healthy for me to see you, but he's wrong.''

"Does he know where you are?''

Jess nodded. "He dropped me off at the bus stop, and I'm supposed to phone him to pick me up. He said I should have a chance to say goodbye.''

Grace straightened out her legs, feeling the ache from her morning's exercise already. The things Jess

had told her only made her more determined than ever
to stick with her plan.

"I'm glad you came by, Jess. I understand what
you're saying. I hope you won't take it the wrong way
if I tell you I wished almost from the beginning that
I really was your mother. I think you're a great kid. I
only wish I'd been a better surrogate mother."

"You were just fine."

Grace gazed at the cherry tree on her front lawn,
watching the white petals fall to the ground in the
gentle morning breeze. "A while ago, you asked me
some pretty important questions, but I cut you off because I was uncomfortable talking about them. That's
not the way a real mother would handle the situation."

"What do you mean?"

"Well, when you asked me about love, Jess, what
I should have told you was that you know you're in
love when you feel complete with the other person.
It's as if two pieces of a puzzle go together. You look
in his eyes and the pieces click into place. And once
they're interlocked, they're very hard to separate. You
know, even if you knock a puzzle onto the floor, most
of the pieces still end up together."

"Uh-huh, I think I know what you're saying."

Grace glanced at the girl. Jess was sitting still, her
attention rapt. "There's something even more important than knowing when you're in love, Jess. And
that's finding out enough about yourself that you don't
really need someone else to give you the answers. The
stronger you are as an individual, the stronger your
partnership can be when you finally find the right person."

Jess ground her toes into the concrete. Grace was

afraid she was being too preachy. Was she turning her off? Worse, embarrassing her?

"Does any of this make sense to you, Jess?"

"Yeah, it does."

Not sure whether to believe her, Grace swallowed and continued. "I know your feelings for Neil are really intense, and that sometimes they seem like the most important aspect of your life. But my advice to you is to hold off on the making-love part of your relationship. Wait until you really know yourself and you're sure of your partner's love for you. Then you'll find the experience will give you more joy and pleasure than anything you could imagine."

"Like how you felt with my dad?"

Grace stared at the ground, resting her face in the curves of her palms. What could she say? She couldn't lie. "Yes. I felt that way with your father."

Jess nodded. "But things change, right? Just because you love someone once doesn't mean you'll love him forever, does it?"

A gust of wind tumbled some petals up to the steps. Several clung to the sides of Jess's thick-soled shoes; one brushed up against Grace's bare leg. Grace bent to pick it off, then stroked the soft velvet with the tip of one finger.

"I don't know, Jess. Maybe the pieces hadn't fit quite right in the first place."

CHAPTER SIXTEEN

GRACE STOOD AT her living-room window and watched as Levi came for his daughter. He didn't even get out of his car, just pushed open the passenger door as she ran toward him. For a split second, she saw his face—grim and tired-looking—before Jess jumped inside; then the door closed and they were gone. Five minutes later, when the portable phone beside her rang, Grace was still standing there, staring at the empty road.

Without taking her eyes off the spot she'd last seen Levi's car, she lifted the phone.

"We've checked this thing over forward and backward and we think it's perfect," Jackie said. "I'm getting a rush print job done. Do you want me to send the report out to the board members now or wait until you're in?"

Grace let the curtain fall into place, then turned her back to the window. "Send it out now."

"You've also got several messages, a couple of them urgent."

"Just a sec while I grab a pen and paper." Grace went to the kitchen table and copied down the names and numbers. After hanging up, she went to the bathroom to shower.

She turned the water on hotter than usual, shampooed her hair, then stood under the jets, letting the soapy water stream down her body. She'd given up the idea of going to bed. Her talk with Jess and all too brief glimpse of Levi had unsettled her and made her anxious. She had to continue with her plan; she couldn't wait, not even another day.

Funny how just a few short months ago, she'd believed she was in control of her life. Now she knew she'd been wrong. Her life had controlled her.

But no longer.

She changed into jeans and a light sweater, then spent the next hour on the phone before driving to the hospital. Roberta had been moved out of the cardiac care unit to a private room and was no longer hooked up to anything except the telephone by her bed.

Amazingly, the final copy of Grace's revised proposal, printed and bound in an attractive navy folder, was sitting on the food tray in front of her.

"...no, I can still do that presentation, but you'd better cancel the one on Wednesday..." With her free hand, Roberta beckoned Grace into the room.

Grace set the vase of flowers she'd brought on the ledge by the window, alongside another bouquet with a card from Roberta's office, then took the empty chair at the foot of the bed.

"...okay, then, we'll do the staff meeting next week if you can get those slides ready for me in time. You can? Great. I'll call you tomorrow to see how it's going." The call over, Roberta turned her attention to her visitor. "Back already, Grace?"

"These hospitals are fun places."

"Tell me about it." Roberta drew in a long breath. "God, I wish they'd let me have a drink."

"Roberta—"

"Don't give me that look. I get enough of it from

the doctor.'' She put her hand on the package in front of her. ''I received your proposal fifteen minutes ago and I've already had a read through it.''

''Are you sure that was a good idea?'' Obviously, Roberta's secretary had rerouted the courier. ''Shouldn't you be relaxing instead of thinking about business?''

''Thinking about business *is* the way I relax,'' Roberta countered. ''And the proposal looks to me like quite a comeback, Hamilton. You've fired Douglas. That's a good first step.'' She patted the booklet in front of her. ''Your research proves his estimates were way off base. I see no reason the board shouldn't endorse your expansion plans. According to these numbers, you're going to make us all rich. Quite extraordinary.''

Grace knew she should feel exultant at this verdict, but all she could manage was a small measure of satisfaction. ''So you'll vote against the takeover bid?''

''No question. And so will the other board members if I have anything to say about it. And I usually do,'' she concluded with a throaty laugh. She began to look around the room as if searching for something. ''You don't happen to have a cigarette on you, do you?''

''As a matter of fact I don't. I quit this morning. And I'm surprised you aren't planning to do the same.''

''Oh, you can't let these doctors scare you.'' She peered at Grace pointedly. ''Something else on your mind?''

Grace nodded.

''I figured as much. It's written all over your face. What is it? Planning to take over my company while I'm temporarily out of commission?''

"You're incorrigible, you know that? No, the fact is I'm taking myself out of the picture. Temporarily."

"What?"

"I'm planning a leave of absence for a couple of months, although I'll keep tabs on the business, especially the expansion plans."

"Are you crazy? Why would you do that when you've finally got the approval you need?"

"Try to understand, Roberta. This job of mine has consumed my life. I want to get things back into perspective. I'm hiring myself another executive assistant—I've promoted Jackie to VP—and spreading the load a little. I don't have all the details worked out, but I think I can pull it off."

Roberta was shaking her head. "If you think you can manage without giving a hundred and ten percent, you're wrong. It isn't possible."

"I can't accept that, Roberta. Work will no longer be the only thing in my life. It's possible to strike a balance—I know it is—and I intend to find out exactly how to do it."

"You're deluding yourself, woman. And what about during your leave of absence? Your company could fall apart in two months, and Vanderburg will be the one to pick up the pieces."

"I'm not that indispensable. Jackie is stronger than you know, and I'll still spend some time in the office." It would work. Grace knew it. She felt the heady kick of a major adrenaline rush.

"At least take a few days to think this over. You're about to make the biggest mistake of your life."

No. The biggest mistake she could make would be to end up like Roberta. Grace thought the words, but of course she didn't speak them. Instead, she said,

"I'm giving the board notice of my intentions next Monday morning. It'll work out, Roberta. Just wait and see."

IT WAS DARK, PAST CLOSING, when Grace finally found the nerve to go to the Jolt O' Java. Levi's silhouette was outlined in the glow of a single light over the counter as he wiped down the espresso machine. She rapped her knuckles on the window to get his attention.

Sharp lines of disapproval etched his forehead as he unlocked the door. He turned his back to her as soon as she came in.

Grace followed him to the counter but remained on the customer side while he resumed his cleaning. "I know I'm not supposed to be here, but I needed to talk to you."

He started to unload the dishwasher, stacking the dark green mugs with reckless abandon. "Why? Grace, you know darn well there isn't anything left for either of us to say."

He sounded as exhausted as she felt. But he didn't ask her to leave.

The tiles were smooth and cool beneath her hands as she leaned forward to speak. "I think there might be a few things. Like the fact that Jess was conceived in July when you and I were still seeing each other."

Levi's eyes narrowed. "We've already discussed that as I recall."

"Yes, but you let me jump to the wrong conclusion, didn't you?"

He paused in his work. "What do you mean?"

"Just that I wish you'd told me you weren't Jess's biological father."

She saw a nerve ticking at the side of his jaw. "And why should I have done that? You believed what you wanted to believe."

She knew he was blaming her for thinking the worst of him, but that wasn't fair, since hers had been the most logical explanation. "If Jess knew you weren't her biological father, why did she assume her mother was someone you dated?"

Levi dropped his rag and rested a hand on one hip. "Because I told her her mother was a woman I used to date. It's not that complicated, really."

"But it is. At least to me. You gave up everything, Levi—all your dreams for the future—to raise a child who wasn't even yours."

"So what? What does that have to do with you?"

"I guess it shouldn't have anything to do with me. Except that I've come to care about Jess. And I think you deserve a chance to live your dream."

"Grace, you're not making any sense at all. What are you talking about?"

"I'm talking about Phil and his sailboat. I'm talking about your going with him. Selling the business if you have to."

"Hey, I must be missing something here."

She saw that his sarcasm masked a growing anger.

"You claim to care about Jess, but now you're telling me to desert her and my business and take off into the wild blue yonder."

"You wouldn't be deserting her. You'd be leaving her with me."

He stood completely still. Grace heard a drop of water fall into the stainless-steel sink, then another. And all the while, his eyes bored into hers, as if he thought he could pierce the very depths of her soul.

"With you?"

"Yes." In the act of raising her chin, she was struck by the memory of Jess behaving in just the same way when under attack. The similarity fueled her determination. "Jess can live with me while you're gone."

Levi was shaking his head in disbelief. "You must be crazy if you think I'd even consider—"

"Why?" Grace leaned farther over the counter. "Why won't you consider it?"

"Do I have to spell it out?"

"Yes, I think you do."

"Come on. You know you couldn't handle the responsibility. What about the nights you'd have to work late, the weekends? Who would drive her to her friends, be there to make sure she came home on time? Help with her homework and make sure she ate breakfast in the morning. Do you want me to go on? There are dentist appointments, annual medical checkups, shopping for clothes, figuring out when she needs to talk and when she wants to be left alone. Oh, God. It's a lot more complicated than it looks."

It did sound daunting, Grace was realistic enough to admit to herself. But she was determined that it could work. "I've taken a leave of absence from the business. I plan to completely revamp my schedule to fit in with her life."

"A leave of absence?" It was clear he didn't believe her.

Grace stared down at the counter, tracing a finger around the tile squares. "Roberta Paxton had a heart attack a few days ago. She almost died."

Levi settled back on his heels. "Roberta? She's not that old!"

"I know. It was quite a reality check. For her and

for me. It made me realize I was headed down the same path. But not anymore. I'm changing a lot of things in my life, Levi. I've quit smoking, and I'm trying to exercise, eat better. And I intend to restructure my work life, too. Roberta doesn't think it's possible, but I know I can do it.''

Levi lowered his head; she couldn't see his eyes or read his expression. Would he believe her? Would he allow her this chance she so desperately desired? He'd spent almost his whole adult life giving, putting himself and his needs last. She wanted him to have the chance to fulfill his dreams. And she wanted the opportunity to build a real relationship with Jess. She wanted to be the giver for a change.

''Well, Grace, when you set your sights, you rarely miss the target.''

His voice was deep and gravelly. The way she remembered it being in the morning.

''Does that mean you agree?''

''You're that eager to get me out of the country?''

''That's not it at all.''

''Really?'' One corner of his mouth turned up, and he raised his eyebrows mockingly.

Grace felt confused. Was he purposely misinterpreting her motives? ''Sailing around the world is what you've dreamed of for so many years. And it's within your grasp. All you have to do is say yes right now, and you can go do it. I don't understand why you're not jumping at the opportunity. Unless you don't trust me with Jess....''

''No, it's not that.'' He moved closer and rested a hand on the counter just a fraction of an inch from hers. ''You think you know me so well. But you've never understood what I really wanted, Grace. You haven't a clue.''

Grace's confidence—in herself, in her ability to make this work—faltered. She dropped her gaze to her hand and his and the minuscule space between them. "What do you mean, Levi?"

"I mean the dreams of a kid at twenty-one are not the same as those of a man of thirty-five."

He was leaning toward her now, his face little more than six inches from hers. Grace wanted to look at him, but she felt afraid. Afraid of what, she didn't know.

She licked her dry lips, struggling to find her voice. "You don't want to go?" The words came out in a whisper, but then, it wasn't necessary to speak more loudly. He was so close she could feel his breath against her hair, smell the faint espresso aroma that clung to his clothes and skin.

"I don't need to sail around the world to be happy."

Grace could feel her heart thumping against her rib cage; the sound filled her ears. Finally, she dared to raise her eyes to his, dark blue gems glittering in the pale light. He held her with the intensity of his gaze, the solemnity of his expression. The world around her faded into darkness until there was only Levi—his face, his voice.

"What do you need?" Could he even hear the words? She had to fight to get them out of a clenched throat, a dry mouth, parched lips. Just the barest shift, and her baby finger came into contact with his hand. The tiny connection, however, changed the meaning of her entire world. She could see he was watching her, gauging her reaction, trying to decide if he could trust her with what he was about to say.

"What I've always needed, Grace." He moved so that his mouth almost, but not quite, brushed up against her cheek. "You."

The last word stabbed her heart, cutting it into little pieces that floated through her body, alternately emitting exquisite pleasure and unbelievable pain. "Please mean it, Levi."

"Why would I lie?"

Grace closed her eyes and tipped back her head. As his mouth fell on hers, she parted her lips, bringing up her arms and clinging to him. She felt his strong hands on her waist, lifting her up to the counter, then he pulled her forward so her legs straddled his jean-clad hips. After a few more kisses, he pulled back, smoothing the hair from her face.

"That night we made love. When you said—"

She pressed a finger to his lips, seeing the question in his eyes. "I meant it then and I mean it now. I love you, Levi. I was too young to appreciate what we had before, but I understand now. I've never come close to feeling this way about any other man."

"You know you almost killed me when you told me about the job you had with Roberta, your casual assumption that graduation would mark the end of our relationship."

"I had no idea." Grace ran a hand along the side of his face, stopping to feel his high cheekbone, his sharp-angled jaw. "You seemed so cool, so distant, that night. You told me you'd already bought an open-ended plane ticket."

"A man has his pride, Grace."

"I see." She smiled, trailing her fingers down his nose, brushing them over his mouth. He caught her wrist with his hand and opened his mouth to suck gently on her fingertips. With his other hand, he reached for something under the counter. A quiet click and the room went dark. For a moment, Grace couldn't see a thing, but she felt his hands up the sides of her thighs, over her hips, around her waist. She squeezed her legs around him, pressed her hands into the lean muscles of his back.

"They say there's no going back, Grace."

"I've never believed that." And uttering the words, she suddenly knew that was true.

Heart of the West

*A brand-new Harlequin continuity series
begins in July 1999
with*

Husband for Hire
by
Susan Wiggs

*Beautician Twyla McCabe was Dear Abby
with a blow-dryer, listening to everyone else's
troubles. But now her well-meaning customers
have gone too far. No way was she attending
the Hell Creek High School Reunion with Rob
Carter, M.D. Who would believe a woman
who dyed hair for a living could be engaged
to such a hunk?*

Here's a preview!

CHAPTER ONE

"THIS ISN'T FOR the masquerade. This is for me."

"What's for you?"

"This."

Rob didn't move fast, but with a straightforward deliberation she found oddly thrilling. He gripped Twyla by the upper arms and pulled her to him, covering her mouth with his.

Dear God, a kiss. She couldn't remember the last time a man had kissed her. And what a kiss. It was everything a kiss should be—sweet, flavored with strawberries and wine and driven by an underlying passion that she felt surging up through him, creating an answering need in her. She rested her hands on his shoulders and let her mouth soften, open. He felt wonderful beneath her hands, his muscles firm, his skin warm, his mouth... She just wanted to drown in him, drown in the passion. If he was faking his ardor, he was damned good. When he stopped kissing her, she stepped back. Her disbelieving fingers went to her mouth, lightly touching her moist, swollen lips.

"That...wasn't in the notes," she objected weakly.

"I like to ad-lib every once in a while."

"I need to sit down." Walking backward, never taking her eyes off him, she groped behind her and found the Adirondack-style porch swing. *Get a grip,* she told herself. *It was only a kiss.*

"I think," he said mildly, "it's time you told me just why you were so reluctant to come back here for the reunion."

"And why I had to bring a fake fiancé as a shield?"

Very casually, he draped his arm along the back of the porch swing. "I'm all ears, Twyla. Why'd I have to practically hog-tie you to get you back here?"

HARLEQUIN®
SUPERROMANCE®

From July to September 1999—three special
Superromance® novels about people whose
New Millennium resolution is

By the Year 2000: CELEBRATE!

JULY 1999—*A Cop's Good Name* by Linda Markowiak
Joe Latham's only hope of saving his badge and his reputation is
to persuade lawyer Maggie Hannan to take his case. Only Maggie—
his ex-wife—knows him well enough to believe him.

AUGUST 1999—*Mr. Miracle* by Carolyn McSparren
Scotsman Jamey McLachlan's come to Tennessee to keep the
promise he made to his stepfather. But Victoria Jamerson stands
between him and his goal, and hurting Vic is the last thing he wants
to do.

SEPTEMBER 1999—*Talk to Me* by Jan Freed
To save her grandmother's business, Kara Taylor has to co-host a
TV show with her ex about the differing points of view between men
and women. A topic Kara and Travis know plenty about.

By the end of the year,
everyone will have something to celebrate!

HARLEQUIN®
Makes any time special ™

HARLEQUIN®
SUPERROMANCE®

Super Summer Reading Blitz!

With the purchase of any three (3) Harlequin Superromance®
books, you can send in for a readingear™ Book Bag, retail
value $9.99 *or* with the purchase of any six (6) Harlequin
Superromance® books you can receive a readingear™ Sweatshirt,
retail value $25.00. Act now, quantities are limited.

Send in for your special gift today!

On the official proof-of-purchase coupon below, fill in your
name, address and zip or postal code and send it, plus $3.20
U.S./$4.50 CAN. postage and handling (check or money
order—please do not send cash) to Harlequin Superromance®
Summer Reading Blitz, to: In the U.S.:3010 Walden Avenue,
P.O. Box 9071, Buffalo, N.Y. 14269-9071; in Canada: P.O. Box
609, Fort Erie, Ontario L2A 5X3. Please allow 4-6 weeks for
delivery. Quantities are limited. The Super Summer Reading
Blitz offer expires August 31, 1999.

Harlequin Superromance® Summer Reading Blitz!
OFFICIAL PROOF OF PURCHASE

❑ Included are three (3) Harlequin Superromance® proofs-of-purchase
Please send me a BOOK BAG   CSG3

❑ Included are six (6) Harlequin Superromance® proofs-of-purchase
Please send me a SWEATSHIRT (one size)   CSG5

Name: _____

Address: _____

City: _____

State/Prov.: _____ Zip/Postal Code: _____

Account Number: _____

HARLEQUIN®
Makes any time special ™   097 KHJ

HSRPOP99